ne.

Beth's expression   And
Mike felt the urge

"Hounded you, you mean?" He offered a crooked
smile.

To his astonishment, she returned a genuine one.
"Even that. You did it for Sicily. That was what was
really important. That you thought about her first. I
could tell you cared. That meant a lot to me."

He was reeling from the smile. It lit her face to real
beauty. He wondered what she'd look like when she
was truly happy.

He tuned back in to notice that awareness had
flared in her eyes.

"Why are you looking at me like that?" She was
almost whispering.

"Your smile..." He cleared his throat. "I was
wondering what you look like when you're happy."

Some bleak knowledge stole most expression from
her face. "I'm not very often. With Sicily, I've been
feeling my way." Even more softly, she finished, "I
want to be."

He held out his hand and surprised himself by a
naked truth he hadn't known until this minute. "I
want to be, too."

Dear Reader,

This book was an interesting challenge for me, because I've never written one that took place in such a short period of time. I had to ask myself: can a woman suffering serious emotional damage from childhood abuse learn to love in only one week? Can the hero, who has grieved for his dead son for eight long years, discover so quickly that a particular woman makes him ready to move on? What about the little girl, raised by a troubled, drug-addicted mother who died only a month ago? She's only ten—how much self-understanding can she arrive at so quickly?

My theory has always been that we change when under pressure—in this case, the more pressure the better. And boy, did I apply it! Beth Greenway has convinced herself that she doesn't feel very much...but her sister's death and the addition of Sicily to her life awakens memories, shame, guilt and regret—and the first trickle of hope. When Sicily vanishes from an innocent outing to the beach, Beth's facade cracks. The cracks widen when it becomes apparent that the police suspect her of killing this child, or at least of conspiring in her kidnapping. The relentless pressure put on her by Detective Mike Ryan—who is also, strangely, kinder to her than anyone ever has been—finally shatters Beth. As for Sicily, there's nothing like being a hostage, knowing she can only depend on herself, to make a frightened girl realize her own strength. And for Mike, the hope of saving Sicily may redeem him.

Answer: a whole lot can happen in one suspenseful, gut-wrenching week. In the end, I loved writing *Making Her Way Home,* and truly believe in the happiness these three troubled people find. I hope you believe, too!

Janice Kay Johnson

P.S. I enjoy hearing from readers! Please contact me c/o Harlequin Books, 225 Duncan Mill Road, Toronto, ON M3B 3K9, Canada.

Making Her Way Home

JANICE KAY JOHNSON

HARLEQUIN®

entertain, enrich, inspire™

Recycling programs
for this product may
not exist in your area.

ISBN-13: 978-0-373-60720-4

MAKING HER WAY HOME

ABOUT THE AUTHOR

The author of more than sixty books for children and adults, Janice Kay Johnson writes Harlequin Super romance novels about love and family—about the way generations connect and the power our earliest experiences have on us throughout life. Her 2007 novel *Snowbound* won a RITA® Award from Romance Writers of America for Best Contemporary Series Romance. A former librarian, Janice raised two daughters in a small rural town north of Seattle, Washington. She loves to read and is an active volunteer and board member for Purrfect Pals, a no-kill cat shelter.

Books by Janice Kay Johnson

HARLEQUIN SUPERROMANCE

HARLEQUIN ANTHOLOGY

SIGNATURE SELECT SAGA

*The Russell Twins
**A Brother's Word

Other titles by this author available in ebook format.

This one's for you, Sarah,
for all those mostly patient pats on the back I so need,
not to mention for the plotting ideas—the "something
weird" was the spark that allowed me to finish this book.
Love you! Mom

CHAPTER ONE

EVEN AS SHE AWAKENED SLOWLY, Beth Greenway felt the first pang of unease. The sun was warm on her face, which was strange since she never slept in the daytime. Whatever she was lying on wasn't very comfortable. Instead of immediately opening her eyes, she listened to distant voices—conversations, shrieks of delight, laughs.

Pebbles. That's what she seemed to be lying on. Puzzlement sharpened her brain and she opened her eyes to the sight of the sun and a glimpse of twisted gray driftwood.

She was at the beach. She and her niece, Sicily, had brought a picnic. Sicily had found some other kids to play with, and Beth read a paperback thriller until her eyes got so heavy she'd laid back and closed them.

That's why she felt uneasy—she hadn't meant to fall asleep. Sitting up, Beth quickly scanned the beach, searching for the ten-year-old. Sicily surely had the sense not to go far. The tide was on its way in, but there was still a wet, slick expanse of beach tide pools. A cluster of children crouched, gazing into one, but none of them had Sicily's bright blond hair.

The parents of the kids she'd been playing with had laid out their blanket over there...but the blanket and parents were gone.

Now she was on her feet, her head turning. Where on earth had Sicily gone? Beth snatched a glance at her watch and was reassured to see that she hadn't been asleep for more than half an hour. Inexcusable if her niece had been younger, but Sicily was, thank goodness, astonishingly self-sufficient. She'd had to be, with such an undependable mother.

Beth walked first north, then south on the beach, scanning each group, scrutinizing the beachgoers reading or strolling above the waterline. Her heart had begun to hammer. Was Sicily *trying* to scare her? Beth couldn't imagine. No, it was more logical to think it hadn't occurred to her niece that she needed to keep any adult in her life informed about her plans. It was new to her to have someone trying to establish rules.

She might have walked up the trail to the wooded land above. Hadn't they seen a sign for a nature trail? That made sense, Beth thought on a surge of what she wanted to be relief.

But she hesitated. If Sicily came back and found her gone...

Beth spotted a group of older teenagers listening to music and talking near where she'd been snoozing. She jogged up to them.

"Excuse me." Her breath came in choppy pants. "I can't find my ten-year-old niece. She's blonde, wearing red shorts and a white T-shirt. Have you seen her?" In unison, all five shook their heads. "Will you be here for a few minutes?" she begged. "That's my blanket right there. I'm going to check the nature trail to see if she went up there. If she comes looking for me, will you tell her I'll be back soon?"

"Sure," one of the girls said. "Do you need help looking for her?"

Surprised by the offer, she said, "As long as one of you stays here, I'd be really grateful if any of you are willing to look. Sicily is about this tall...." She held up her hand. "Skinny, long-legged. She was playing with some other kids and I guess I fell asleep."

Two of the girls stood up. "We'll look," the first one said. "There are lots of places to hide along here."

"Thank you." Beth began running, her searching gaze moving nonstop. She'd see Sicily any minute; she'd probably gone too far down the beach, or up the trail, or...maybe she'd needed to use the restroom the state park provided.

Beth went there first, pushing open the heavy

door on the women's side. "Sicily?" she called. "Are you here?"

Nobody was in the restroom. Beth raced to her car; her niece wasn't waiting at it.

Back to the nature trail, which according to the sign was half a mile long. Half a mile didn't take Beth long to cover if she jogged the entire loop. She asked the few people she passed if they'd seen a ten year old girl in red shorts, but no one had.

Oh, God, she thought, *please let her be there when I get back.* As she rushed back down the trail to the beach, Beth comforted herself by rehearsing how she'd scold Sicily. The moment she stepped onto the pebbly beach, she saw her blanket and the group of teenagers. There was no child with them.

She felt the first wash of real fear.

MIKE RYAN FROWNED AS HE DROVE, thinking about the interview he'd just conducted. The home owners had suffered a major loss. Mike had taken the case from the first responder, a patrol officer. Nobody in the detective's division would have gotten involved if this had been a garden variety break-in, with maybe a plasma TV, a laptop, a digital camera stolen. This one was bigger than that. A window into the family room at the back of the house had been broken and, yeah, TV, DVD player, Nintendo, camera and two iPods were reported stolen. More significantly, a locked metal outbuilding had been stripped of some heavy equipment the husband used in a landscaping business. The Komatsu dozer alone was insured for $37,000, never mind the attachments. There'd also been a commercial quality aerator, stump grinder, a couple of tillers, chain saws and more. Two flatbed trailers parked outside the building were gone, too. The loss added up to $200,000 easy.

Detectives in this rural Washington State county handled a mix of cases, from fraud and theft to rape, assault and murder. Mike had a dozen active cases already, and at least another dozen not-so-active ones that stayed in the back of his mind in hopes a break came.

He'd have to go back later in the day when neighbors were home to find out if anyone had seen or heard anything. Supposedly the home owners had been away for a weeklong visit to see their daughter in Ocean Shores. The house, a 3,500-square-foot faux Tudor with a three-car garage as well as the 2,000-square-foot metal outbuilding, sat on a five-acre wooded parcel. The buildings were visible neither from the road nor the neighbors' houses, which were also situated on five-acre parcels. It would be pure luck to find someone who happened to see either of the flatbed trailers being hauled away.

Mike was pretty damn sure he was being played, and he didn't like it. Right now, he was heading back into the station, where he would begin delving into the finances of J. N. Sullivan Landscaping Services. He had a suspicion he was going to find the business was in trouble. So much trouble, a nice insurance payoff would be an easy way for Mr. John Sullivan to take his retirement. Especially since he'd likely sold all that heavy equipment, and would thereby double his return once the insurance company paid out.

The radio crackled on and off as Mike drove, all routine inquiries and requests. "Possible missing child at Henrik Beach County Park." He was caught by the note of urgency in the dispatcher's voice. "Ten years old, last seen an hour or more ago. Park ranger search failed to turn up the child. Any nearby units please respond."

Oh, hell. If there was one thing that rubbed Mike raw, it was people who didn't keep a sharp eye on their kids in potentially dangerous situations. A park that combined a mile of Puget Sound waterfront, crumbling bluffs, a forest and a whole lot of strangers met that criteria. And by happenstance he was less than a mile from the park. In a county as sprawling as this one, it might take fifteen minutes to half an hour for a patrol response. He reached for his radio to gave his location and ETA.

Not ten minutes later, he was getting the story

from the park ranger, a short, wiry woman in her forties with weathered skin.

"Maybe we brought you in too quick, but I'd rather that than make the mistake of wasting time."

"That's our preference," he agreed. "Sounds like you've done the basic search."

She nodded. "We need help."

"All right. I'm going to put in a preliminary call to search-and-rescue, then let me talk to the aunt."

He knew the local head of the volunteer group and, when Vic Levine said he could have the first few searchers there within fifteen minutes, Mike hesitated. Standing by his car in the parking lot, his gaze moved slowly over the density of the old growth forest past the picnic ground. As county parks went, this was a big one, including a campground, as well as the picnic area, several trails and the beach. He didn't like to think about how many people were in the park at this moment, never mind the ones that had come and gone as the sun moved overhead and the girl's aunt failed to notice she was missing.

"Make the calls," he said. "Better safe than sorry."

"Good enough."

The ranger, who had introduced herself as Lynne Kerney, was waiting to lead Mike down to the beach. He followed, taking in the scrubby coastal foliage clinging to the bluff, the tumbles of driftwood, the tide that must be starting to come in. There were people all over the beach, most of them wandering or scrambling over the gray logs.

Ranger Kerney turned toward him. "Most every adult here is looking for Sicily."

There was one woman who wasn't searching. She stood beside a blanket maybe a hundred yards from where the trail they were on let out onto the gravelly beach. As he watched, she turned slowly in a circle, her arms wrapped herself as if she were cold. Or containing fear? But from this distance he didn't see any on her face.

He wasn't surprised when Lynne Kerney led him straight toward the woman. Anger began to burn inside him as the coals in his gut ignited. Her niece was missing and all she could do was stand there looking a little agitated, as if this were on the scale of discovering she had a run in her pantyhose or a button was off the blouse she'd intended to wear that day.

She was facing them long before they reached her. Her eyes fastened first on the ranger, then him, flickering from his face to the badge and gun he wore on his belt.

"You haven't found her?" She even sounded cool. No, that wasn't fair—she was worried, all right, but hadn't lost her composure. Mike couldn't imagine not being utterly terrified by this time.

"I'm afraid not," the ranger said. "Ms. Greenway,

this is Detective Ryan with the county sheriff's department. He's called in search-and-rescue."

"The first volunteers should be here in ten minutes or so," he said. "It's great so many people are already helping, but these folks are trained to search systematically. If your niece is in the park, we'll find her."

She swallowed, he did see that. A reaction of some sort. "If only I hadn't fallen asleep," she said softly.

If only were two of the ugliest words in the English language, especially when spoken by an adult who'd been negligent where a child was concerned. His slow burn was gathering force, ready to jump the fire line.

Not yet, he cautioned himself. People didn't all react the same to fear or grief or any other strong emotion. He knew that. This woman might be holding herself together by the thinnest of threads. If he severed it and she got hysterical, he might not get answers.

"Your name?" he asked.

"What? Oh. Beth Greenway. Elizabeth."

"And is your niece also a Greenway?"

"No. Her name is Sicily Marks."

He processed that. "Sicily. Like the Italian island?"

"Yes." She sounded impatient and he couldn't blame her.

Somebody shouted down the beach and they all turned to look. A question was yelled down the line. Did Sicily have a blue-and-white-striped towel?

Beth shook her head. "We only brought one towel. It's right here."

Mike glanced down at the towel, folded neatly and apparently unused. It was a sea foam-green and more of a bath sheet than a beach towel.

But this woman wasn't Sicily's mother. No surprise that she had to improvise for an outing.

The ranger hurried away to talk to the people excited by the abandoned towel. Mike looked at Ms. Greenway.

"All right," he said quietly. "Tell me what happened."

He knew the basics of what she had to say and didn't listen so much to the words as to her intonation, the way she paused over certain words and hurried over others. He hoped to see emotions and failed. She'd battened down the hatches with a ruthless hand. The only giveaway at all was the way she clutched herself, seemingly unaware that she was doing so.

"So then I talked to these teenagers." She turned her head, looking for them. "They're still here, helping search. They said they'd watch for her while I…"

As she spoke, he had the uncomfortable realization that anger wasn't the only reason his belly was churning.

He was attracted to her. Extremely, inappropriately attracted.

Beth Greenway wasn't a beautiful woman, exactly. She should have been too thin for his tastes, for one thing. The bones were startlingly prominent in her face, like a runway model. That was it exactly, he decided; her face was all cheekbones, eyes and lips. Those lips might be pouty and sultry in other circumstances, but were being held tightly together between sentences, as if she were thinning them deliberately.

Her hair was brown, but that was an inadequate description for a rich, deep color that was really made up of dozens of shades. Chin-length, it was straight and thick and expertly cut to curve behind her ears. Her eyes were brown, too, but lighter than her hair. Caramel, maybe, flecked with gold.

Fortunately, he was good at compartmentalizing. In the couple of minutes that passed while she talked, he'd assessed her appearance, decided his reaction to it was one hell of a stupid thing he could ignore and begun to question whether a single word coming out of her mouth was the truth.

"Will any of these folks looking for your niece be able to recognize her?" he asked.

She stared at him. Her eyes dilated at the instant

she understood what he was really asking. *Did any of these people ever actually* see *your niece?*

"I…I don't know." It was the first time she'd faltered. She rotated 360 degrees, her eyes so wide and fixed he wondered if she would even recognize a familiar face. "There was a family sitting near us. They had four kids." Her forehead creased briefly. "Or maybe a couple of the kids were friends. I don't know. But they were all close enough to Sicily's age, they latched right onto her. They were looking at tide pools when I—" her pause was infinitesimal "—fell asleep."

Rage came close to choking him. Instead of sleeping, Ellen had been busy chatting with her friend; that had been her excuse. She thought Nate was napping. Well, yes, the sliding door was open but she could have sworn the screen door was closed and latched. "It was only for a few minutes," she'd whispered. Then screamed, "That's all! A few minutes!"

A few minutes was all it took.

Beth Greenway had brought her ten-year-old niece to a crowded public beach and then settled down for a nap, contentedly believing the kid was completely safe because she was playing with some other children.

"Did you talk to the parents?" he asked.

She shook her head. "We smiled."

"You smiled."

"My niece was studying crabs in a tide pool with their children. There was no need for me to interview the parents for suitability."

Her voice and expression were marble cool. He kept waiting for her to shiver or something, but it wasn't happening.

"But these people are gone."

"Yes."

He could see the first people from search-and-rescue arriving in the parking lot. He excused himself from Beth Greenway and went to talk to them about where to start. Nobody suggested that the beach had been adequately searched; these men and women knew as well as he did how easy it would be for an adult who'd raped and murdered a child to pretend to examine the spot where the body had been stowed. No one wanted to believe yet that this was anything other than a case in which a kid had thoughtlessly wandered away. Maybe she had gone for a hike with someone, maybe gotten lost, maybe gone to sulk and hide from the aunt if the two of them were fighting.

"I need to ask the aunt some more questions," he said, and they proceeded to organize themselves.

When he returned, Beth had her back to him. Purposely, or was she truly engrossed in what the cluster of people way down the beach was doing? He looked to see if there was a flurry of activity, but there wasn't.

"Ms. Greenway."

Maybe she was hiding tears. But when she turned, her eyes were dry and curiously blank.

"Does your niece have a habit of wandering or hiding?"

"I don't know."

"What can you tell you me about her?" His voice had sharpened.

She blinked a couple of times. "Well…she's a good student."

"There's not much to read down here."

Her sharp chin was one of the features that kept her from true beauty. She lifted it now. "Was that meant to be sarcastic?"

"I apologize," he said expressionlessly. "Tell me whatever occurs to you."

"I think she does like science. That's why I checked out the nature trail right away."

"Can she swim?"

Both of them cast involuntary looks toward the choppy blue water of the Sound. Until now he'd been too preoccupied to notice the salty sea air and the faint scent of rot that was usual during a low tide.

"I don't know," she admitted. "Nobody swims here anyway, so the subject didn't come up. She didn't wear a bathing suit."

"Ms. Greenway—" civility was becoming harder

to maintain "—perhaps we should call Sicily's parents."

Those beautiful eyes met his. "She doesn't have any. I have custody."

Every instinct he had went on red alert. Did this kid even exist? This whole thing could be a hoax, an attention-grabber. Worse possibilities jumped to mind and if Sicily Marks didn't materialize pretty damn quickly, he was going to have to take those possibilities seriously.

"Her mother died a month ago." Ms. Greenway sounded stiff. "Sicily came to live with me then. We're still feeling our way."

He shoved his fingers through his hair and resisted the urge to give it a yank. Could this whole situation get any more unsettling?

"I take it you hadn't spent much time with your niece."

Was it possible the arms wrapping her had tightened? "My sister and I were estranged. I sent Sicily birthday cards and the like, but she tells me that Rachel—her mother—never gave them to her."

Mike digested the fact that this family was— or at least had been—majorly screwed up. Which meant the kid likely was, too. "Her father?" he asked.

"Hasn't been in the picture since Sicily was a toddler. She doesn't remember him."

Good. Great.

"Grandparents?"

"She has them," Ms. Greenway said tersely.

"Do they know her any better than you do?"

"I…don't think so."

She didn't think so. If she didn't know what kind of relationship her own parents had with her sister and niece, that meant *she* had no relationship to speak of with them, either. That poor kid's family was a mess.

He kept asking questions. Had she and Sicily quarreled today? No. Yesterday? No. Recently? No. In the month since her mother died, had the girl tried to run away or otherwise alarmed Ms. Greenway? No, nothing like that. Does she carry a cell phone?

She gave him a startled look. "She's ten years old! Of course not."

He'd have pursued the subject, except that even kids who did have a phone might not carry it to the beach.

Had Ms. Greenway noticed anyone else close by today? Seeming to pay attention to them? Maybe watching Sicily or pausing to talk to her?

No. Ms. Greenway was reading and only glancing up occasionally before she nodded off.

She was one hundred percent no help. The whole time he questioned her, she held on to that astonishing poise. Literally, since she never once uncrossed her arms. He kind of wished she would, since the tightness of her grip pushed her breasts up and created a distractingly deep cleavage above the white tank top that also revealed a fragile collarbone and long, slim arms. At least her legs weren't equally bared; she wore khaki pants that ended midcalf and the kind of sandals sturdy enough to be running shoes except somebody had decided to add cutouts for extra ventilation.

He let the silence spin out, thinking maybe that would shake her. As if to punctuate it, a seagull swooped low overhead and let out a strident cry. She jumped and gave a wild look around. Mike waited, but that was it.

Finally, he conceded defeat. "Ms. Greenway, is there anyone at all Sicily might go to or call if she got scared or separated from you?"

For the first time, he saw despair in her eyes. "I don't know," she whispered, and he knew she was ashamed to have to admit it.

Or, like that landscaper John Sullivan, she was playing him.

"You'll have to excuse me," he said abruptly. "I need to speak to some other people."

By this time, nearly two dozen members of the search-and-rescue organization had arrived and were spread out, combing the park for one little girl in red shorts. He spoke to a couple of the people in charge, then phoned another detective with whom he often worked. Eddie Ruliczkowski answered on the third ring and listened in silence to Mike's request.

"Yeah, hold on and I'll do a quick internet search." With his big, beefy fingers, Eddie had a heavy hand on a keyboard. The keys clattered and he grunted a couple of times before finally saying, "I'm finding an Elizabeth Greenway who owns some kind of event planning company."

"Event planning? You mean, like weddings?"

"No. Uh, looks like mostly auctions, big corporate shindigs, product launches, sports tournaments." He was clearly reading off a list. "Team building," he said with a snort. "Holiday parties."

"Huh. Anything personal about her?"

"Nothing. All I'm seeing are mentions of her in her professional capacity. She's a member of Rotary, some women-in-business group... Give me a minute."

Mike did. Aside from the basic stat that Ms. Greenway was thirty-two years old—only two years younger than Mike—Eddie came up with zip. Elizabeth Greenway had no record of trouble with the law, not so much as a parking ticket.

"Okay," Mike finally said. "If you have time, keep digging. This whole thing stinks."

Under any other circumstance, Eddie would have grumbled about having plenty of his own stuff to do. But he'd been around when Nate died.

He knew what Mike had gone through and how sensitive he'd be to any case with a child in peril.

Mike looked at his watch—he'd been at the park for an hour. Sicily Marks had now been missing for two hours. The odds that she'd been abducted were increasing by the minute, unless something else odd was going on.

Back to talk to Ms. Greenway, he decided grimly. It might not have been the father's decision not to be involved in his daughter's life. It was interesting, if true, that Ms. Greenway had acquired custody only a month ago. Somebody might not have been pleased, whether it was the child's father or the grandparents. Or were there other family members? He cursed himself for not asking and retraced his steps to the beach.

She stood exactly where he'd left her. He felt a pang of something strange when he saw her planted there, stiffer and less graceful than any of the madrona trees on the bluff above her. He wondered if she'd moved a muscle beyond those required to breathe.

When he reached her, he saw something else. There were goose bumps on her arms and she was quivering. No, shivering. In alarm, he laid one of his hands over hers, clasped the other on her upper arm, and found it icy. She jumped and swung to face him. "What…?"

"You're freezing," he said brusquely. This time

he wrapped his hands around both her upper arms and began rubbing. "Why didn't you say something?"

She looked at him with unshaken poise and said, "I'm perfectly..." *Fine*. That's what she meant to say, but it didn't come out because her teeth chattered.

"You're not." She was in shock and either hadn't recognized it or refused to acknowledge her own vulnerability. He urged her backward and said, "Sit."

"No! I..."

He all but picked her up and sat her butt down on the blanket, which he then gathered up and wrapped around her. Her teeth chattered again and she seemed to shrink. After a moment, she clutched the edges of the blanket and tucked in her chin, turtlelike. Squatting on his haunches next to her, all he could see was her hair, which had swung forward to veil her face.

"Better?" He was trying for gentle, but his voice came out gruff.

Her head bobbed, and after a minute she said, "Thank you."

"I'm afraid I have more questions."

She didn't so much as sigh. She was the toughest read of anyone he'd ever met. After a moment she lifted her head. "You think somebody took her," she said steadily.

Or that she was never here at all, but he wasn't going to say that.

"I don't think anything yet. I'm leaving the search to the experts and preparing for the possibility we won't find her here."

A shudder wracked her. The cold again, or a ghost had walked over her grave.

"Dear God."

"Sicily's father. Is there any chance he wanted custody?"

"No. He walked out on Rachel and Sicily and never so much as paid child support. I thought... I don't know what I thought, but after Rachel died I tried to find him and failed. He might even be dead."

"What's his name?" Mike produced the small notebook he always carried in a hip pocket and flipped past the pages of notes he'd made earlier at the Sullivan place.

"Chad Marks. I don't know his middle name. I...never met him."

"Were they divorced?"

"I don't know." Her three favorite words in the world. This time she sounded uncertain, though. "I'm not sure if Rachel ever bothered. She kept the last name. It's on her death certificate."

"Okay. What about your parents?"

"Their names are Laurence and Rowena Greenway. They live in Seattle." He sensed a reserve so deep he doubted she could swim up through it.

He nodded. "Do you have other siblings? Step or biological?"

"No. There's no one else."

"Aunts? Uncles?"

"My father has a brother, but he lives in Dallas. I don't know him well. I doubt Sicily has ever met him. My mother had a brother, too, but he was killed in a small plane crash when I was a child."

"Was your sister involved with anyone recently?"

"I think," she said carefully, "men came and went. My impression from Sicily is that none of them stayed long."

"How did your sister die?"

"It was…an accident."

His knees were beginning to protest his squatting position, but he didn't move. He was looking right into those caramel eyes, watching for every deeper swirl, however subtle. "What kind?"

"They think she fell from the ferry."

"From the ferry? Wait. I remember that," he said slowly. It had dominated local news recently. He thought it had been the Kingston-to-Edmonds run. The ferry had arrived and no driver showed up to claim one of the cars, which of course created a godawful tangle in trying to unload in an orderly way. Apparently this happened regularly, but usually the missing driver had fallen asleep on one of the bench seats on the passenger deck. This time, workers scoured the ferry from end to end and the woman never turned up.

"Her body washed ashore, didn't it?"

"Yes. She had some barbiturates in her system."

"Did she have a drug problem?"

Her lips compressed before she said, "Since she was a teenager. Alcohol and downers. I understand from Sicily that Rachel mostly managed to hold a job, but I suspect Sicily had been handling many of the practicalities of their life for some time. She admitted she was used to being left alone for two or three days at a time."

He stared at her in exasperation. "Why didn't you tell me that sooner?"

She blinked. "What does it matter?"

"You don't think that increases the likelihood that she didn't hesitate to take off without consulting you?"

"No." Ms. Greenway bit the word off. "No, I don't. She's not like that. I did think about it when I couldn't find her, because she does do things without asking, but not like this. She's too sensible. Sicily is everything Rachel wasn't. She looks ten, but inside she's more like a thirty-year-old who has been on her own for years. She's not impulsive. Today I was pleasantly surprised that she was willing to join the other kids. I thought of it as her playing with them, but she doesn't. I don't think she knows *how* to play."

He digested her burst of speech. Her voice had risen toward the end, a hint of passion or even outrage infusing it. For a minute there, she'd almost seemed like a real person. Some pink showed in her cheeks. He'd have liked her the better for it, if he'd totally believed in it.

"Okay. Do you have a phone with you?"

"Yes." Her head turned. "In my bag."

"Does Sicily know the number?"

"Of course she does."

"She'd call it instead of your landline?"

"I don't have a landline. This is the only way to reach me outside of work."

"And you'd have heard it ring."

"I… Oh, God. Not while I was hunting for her." She dropped the blanket and scrabbled in her purple tote, retrieving a cell phone. After pushing a button, she exhaled. "Nobody has called."

"Make sure you keep it close now."

Her look said, *Do you think I'm stupid?*

The answer was no. He knew she wasn't stupid. She was something else, but he didn't know what. Unfeeling? Nuts enough to have made up this entire story? Cold-blooded enough to have killed the kid she didn't want dumped on her and come to the beach with the intention of claiming the girl had disappeared? He didn't want to believe that, but couldn't be sure. There was something off about this woman.

What he couldn't understand was why pity wanted to take the place of his suspicion.

Frowning, he rose to his feet, looking down at her. She gazed up at him, still fighting to hold on to her composure, but unless he was imagining things some cracks were appearing. Through them, he could see anguish.

Maybe pity wasn't so unreasonable. If Beth Greenway *wasn't* truly unfeeling, if she wasn't crazy or cold-blooded, then she was damaged in some other way. She had to be. He'd seen people under stress act in a lot of different ways, but never like this, as though nothing in the world scared her more than showing what she felt.

He grunted, turned around and walked away from her. Who was he kidding? The chances were really good that she had something to do with her niece's disappearance. Sure she knew how to put up a front. That's what people with something to hide did.

CHAPTER TWO

THE DAY WAS INTERMINABLE. BETH began to doubt her ability to hold in all the terrible emotions moving inside her, but she had to. Every time she felt herself slipping, she dug her fingernails into her flesh wherever she could reach and concentrated on the pain. When she hurt, she could empty herself. She hadn't had to do it in a long time.

I will not feel.

But she did. Today, most of all, most horrifyingly, she felt helpless. Being always and entirely in control was as basic to her as breathing. She planned everything. Everything.

Except she hadn't foreseen the consequences of her sister's death. She might have if she hadn't been so certain Rachel hated her.

Rachel *had* hated her. Of course she had. In the end, though, she hated their parents more. Beth should have realized that.

From the moment Sicily came home with her, Beth had battled panic. There was a reason she'd never shared her life with anyone else. And a child…she knew nothing about children. She couldn't even bear messes at home. She knew she was obsessive, but that's how she survived. How was she supposed to juggle another person's needs with her already full schedule and her need for order?

The irony was that in the past week she had begun to relax. Her niece was quiet, organized and trying very hard to fit in. Too hard. Beth could see that, and it made her feel guilty because a kid should be confident she could belong without changing herself. But she could also tell that Sicily was skilled at going unnoticed, which meant she'd worked at it. That caused Beth to feel a rare flash of fury—what kind of men did Rachel keep around, that her daughter had to learn to be invisible? Or had Rachel herself been abusive?

But that, of course, led to more guilt, because Beth could have tried harder to have a relationship with Sicily—Rachel might have given in— and she hadn't.

Still, even with all the turmoil, they were working out a routine and she was finding her ten-year-old niece unexpectedly easy to live with.

Now this.

Swept by a maelstrom of terror and guilt and that overwhelming sense of herself as small and useless and unable to do anything at all to impact the outcome, she drove her fingernails into the inner flesh of her upper arms.

I will not feel.
It didn't help at all.

Her initial gratitude to that cop—Detective Mike
Ryan—slowly changed to resentment and eventually anger and something even more bitter over
the course of the afternoon. It was like food left
out, spoiling until it would have sickened anyone
who took a bite. She kept thinking there wasn't
a single thing left he could ask her, that he'd go
away and leave her alone, but he never went for
long. The crunch of footsteps on the pebbles would
herald his return. Sometimes she refused to look
up until he was right in front of her. Other times
she couldn't help but turn her head to watch him
stride toward her. It was hope, she tried to tell herself, that made her look at him. He was going to
say they'd found Sicily—she'd taken one of the
nature trails and sprained her ankle, or gotten lost
exploring in the woods, or... Beth couldn't think
of any other explanations that were innocent, that
meant Sicily would be returned to her now, today,
safe and sound.

Those small, irresistible spurts of hope might
have been part of why she couldn't help but look
at the detective, but they were only part. He stirred
something in her. Something dangerous.

It wasn't that he was a gorgeous man. He had
a rough-cut face and hair not quite light-colored
enough to be called blond. No talent scout would

have grabbed him to be a *GQ* model. He did have nice broad shoulders and an athletic build and the walk of a man able to get where he wanted to go with speed and no deviation from the path. With that body, he probably would have worn beautifully cut suits well—if he didn't shed the suit coat, roll up the shirtsleeves, tug loose the tie, scuff the shoes and get the whole ensemble wrinkled.

When he'd hunkered down next to her, Beth had found herself staring at the powerful muscles in his thighs outlined by the fabric of his slacks. He likely ran, or something like that, to keep in shape. People in law enforcement were supposed to stay fit, weren't they? She doubted he did anything like lift weights to increase muscle definition—his haircut looked barbershop instead of salon and his slacks and rumpled shirt did not resemble the ones worn by the businessmen she often dealt with through work. If Detective Ryan cared about his appearance, it didn't show.

What he was, was pure male. Dominant male. No question he was in charge from the moment he strode onto the beach. Beth wondered if his superiors ever tried to give him orders.

His eyes were the one part of him she'd call beautiful. They were that rare crystalline blue, untouched by hints of gray or green. It had to be the color that made his every look feel like a scalpel cut. He turned those eyes on her, and she was terrified that he was seeing all the way inside her to the little girl huddled behind the suitcases in the under-the-staircase closet.

She wanted him to go away and never look at her again. After he found Sicily.

She also wanted to stare at him and drink in whatever quality it was that made him seem so strong.

The sun sank behind Whidbey Island. Beth watched it go down as the shadow of dusk crossed the Sound and finally reached her beach. One moment, she could see everything clearly—rocks and dried gray driftwood logs, the peeling red bark of madronas, the weave of the blanket she clutched in tighter and tighter hands. And then, from one blink to the next, the clarity became muffled. Her surroundings were purplish and dim.

She recognized the particular crunch of Detective Ryan's footsteps.

He crouched beside her, so close she had to look at his face.

"We're calling off the search for the night."

"No!" Her voice came out thin and high.

"We'll resume it tomorrow, although..." His voice was a deep rumble, "I'll be frank, Ms. Greenway. We've covered the park pretty thoroughly. I don't believe your niece is here."

"Then where...?" she whispered.

"I don't know."

She hated hearing her own words cast back at her. She couldn't tell on that impassive face whether he'd chosen them deliberately as a slam at her.

He'd kept her updated as the afternoon had waned. Small boats had trawled offshore. They couldn't be sure Sicily hadn't gone in the water, but the beach had been crowded enough today he thought someone would have noticed.

Not a single trace of Sicily's presence had been found. Beth kept telling him that Sicily hadn't carried anything to drop. She'd worn exactly three items of clothing: panties, red twill shorts and a plain white crew-neck T-shirt. On her feet were a pair of thick-soled flip-flops that Beth had bought her when she first came to stay and it became obvious how inadequate her wardrobe was.

That was it. No towel, no iPod—really? Did people buy cell phones and iPods for ten-year-olds? No sweatshirt tied around her waist, no jewelry of any kind, no cheap camera. Nothing.

They wanted a photo of her, but Beth didn't have one in her wallet. Rachel had never sent her not-so-beloved sister school photos, even assuming Rachel had wanted or paid for them in the first place. She'd been touched when Sicily offered her a couple of pictures not that long ago.

"I have pictures at home," she told Detective Ryan rather desperately, "but they aren't recent ones." Even she knew they wouldn't be useful, given how quickly children changed.

"Would her grandparents have something better?"

"I don't know," she'd had to say, and hid her wince at the brief expression of disbelief—or was it contempt?—that flashed on the detective's face before he hid it.

During one of the many stretches where she had nothing to do but wait, she'd tried to think of some other way to say *I don't know*.

I'm not aware. Pretentious.

You'd have to ask someone else. He would want to know who, a question to which, of course, she'd have no answer. Or she'd have to say, again, *I don't know*.

Not a clue. Inappropriately flippant.

So were her thoughts. But she couldn't control them, however hard she tried.

"You need to go home," he told her, with some gentleness this time.

"No," she said again. "No, I can't!"

Fingernails. This time she knew she'd drawn blood. *I don't feel. I don't.*

"I'll drive you," he said, but already she was shaking her head.

"No, I can drive myself. There's no need."

"Then I'll follow you."

Staring at his face, she realized he wasn't offer-

ing her an option. He intended to see her home.
The grim set of his mouth told her more. He'd want
to come in. No, not want; he *would* come in. He
still wasn't done with her.

And that was when she let herself know what
she'd blocked out all day: he doubted everything
she'd said. He thought *she* might have something
to do with Sicily's disappearance.

Nausea rose so swiftly she couldn't do anything but clap her hand to her mouth and swivel
sideways. She retched onto the beach, nothing but
bile so acidic it burned her throat and mouth. She
couldn't seem to stop heaving, as though her body
was determined to make her give up everything
she had.

Not until she finally sagged, spent, did she realize the detective had laid a big hand on her back
and was rubbing it in soothing circles. He was
murmuring something; she couldn't make out
words. It was more like a croon.

She had a sudden flash of remembering Maria,
the housekeeper who'd left—or been fired—when
Beth was five or six. A plump bosom, consoling
arms, the songs she sang, all in Spanish. In Beth's
life, no one but Maria had ever given her comfort—and that had been so long ago, Beth had almost forgotten what it felt like.

It was the strangest feeling. She marveled at
why he would worry about her distress despite

the fact that he clearly suspected her of something horrible. It didn't make sense.

Beth took long, slow breaths: in through her nose, out through her mouth. Her stomach, entirely empty, gradually became quiescent. She focused enough to realize the detective was holding out a can of soda. He must have taken it from her small cooler, unopened since she and Sicily had arrived. Beth seized it gratefully and after rinsing her mouth, took a long drink.

"Ready?" he asked, rising to his feet.

No, she wasn't ready to leave without Sicily. To drive home to her empty house. The thought sent a shudder through her, but she nodded and let go of the blanket, stuffed her book into her bag and got up. To her surprise, Detective Ryan grabbed the blanket, shook it out and folded it with quick, effective movements. He picked up her small cooler, too, obviously prepared to carry it.

They walked in silence the short length of beach and up the trail. She was suddenly aware that they were virtually alone. The searchers had already been called off. She stopped at the top for one last look at the beach. The tide had long since come in and was turning to go out again. The light was so murky, she could barely make out the spot where she'd spread her blanket, or see the heaps of driftwood as anything but angular shadows. Again, she shuddered.

The parking lot had emptied, too. Toward the campground she could see flickers of firelight.

"You looked there?" she asked.

"Yes. And talked to all the campers. We asked permission to look in their tents and trailers. Everyone let us without argument."

She nodded dully and unlocked her car. "You don't have to follow me."

"Yes, I do."

Without a word she got in, started the engine and after letting it warm up for barely a minute, backed out of the slot and drove away. He'd catch up to her, she had no doubt. He knew where she lived anyway.

The lights of a bigger vehicle appeared almost immediately in her rearview mirror. All she could tell was that it was an SUV, big and dark.

The drive took nearly forty-five minutes. She lived in Edmonds, an attractive town built on land sloping down to Puget Sound. There was a ferry terminal there. Once upon a time, she'd enjoyed her view from the dining nook of the water and the arriving and departing green-and-white ferries. Now, every time she saw one, she imagined her sister standing at the railing on the car deck, looking at the churning water and choosing to climb over and cast herself into it.

That was what Beth thought had happened. She didn't believe Rachel had fallen accidentally. The barbiturate level in her bloodstream wasn't that high, for one thing. And it wasn't as if you *could* fall over the substantial railing. Only at the open front and back of the car deck would it be possible to stumble and tip in, and even then Rachel would have had to step over the chain the ferry workers always fastened in lieu of a railing. And there were usually ferry workers hanging around the front and back of the boat.

No, in her heart she believed her sister had committed suicide. Beth wasn't sure why she was so certain, given that she didn't really know Rachel anymore.

Sicily had, only once, asked, "Do you think Mom really fell in by accident?"

Beth had had to swallow a lump in her throat. Now she cringed at the memory of what she'd said. "I don't know."

I really don't know, she thought. *I didn't know my own sister. My niece.* She hadn't wanted to know them. She didn't even want to know herself, not well enough to recognize the sometimes turbulent undercurrents of emotion she was determined to ignore.

She used the automatic garage-door opener and drove into her garage. She pushed the button again so that the door rolled down behind her, cutting off the SUV that had pulled into the driveway, leaving her momentarily alone.

Not for long. She wondered whether he would go away at all tonight. He'd have to, wouldn't he? Probably he had a wife and kids waiting at home for him.

Please. Please leave me alone.

THE HOUSE WASN'T WHAT MIKE HAD expected. As cool as Ms. Beth Greenway was, he'd expected her to live in a stylish town house or condo with white carpet and ultramodern furnishings.

Her home was an older rambler, dating from the 1950s or 60s, at a guess. With night having fallen, as he approached the front door he couldn't even see what color the clapboard siding was painted or how the yard was landscaped.

She didn't so much as say, "Come in" when she opened the front door to him. Instead, she'd stepped back wordlessly, letting him past.

The interior surprised him. An eclectic collection of richly colored rugs were scattered on hardwood floors. Some of the rugs looked like antiques, the wear obvious; others appeared hand-hooked. He knew because his mother had experimented with the craft before moving on to tatting or God knows what. Her hobbies came and went like Seattle rainfall.

Ms. Greenway had bought or inherited antique furniture. Nice stuff, not real elaborate, not pretentious. Not heavy and dark—they were warm woods finished with sheen. The colors of the walls, upholstered furniture and blinds were all warm, too. Buttery-yellow, peach, touches of deep red and rust.

The house, Mike thought, was a startling contrast to the brittle, unfeeling—or emotionally repressed—woman who owned it. He could speculate all night on the psychology behind her choice to create this haven.

Ms. Greenway asked if he would like coffee.

What he'd really like was a meal. Breakfast was a long-ago memory, since he'd skipped both lunch and dinner. Just as, he realized, she had. What's more, she'd emptied the meager contents of her stomach.

"Sure," he said. "Ms. Greenway, you need to have a bite to eat. Why don't we go in the kitchen and talk while you're heating some soup. Something that'll go down easy."

She looked perplexed. "I'm not hungry."

"You're in shock," he said gently. "Your body needs fuel."

She gazed at him with the expression of someone translating laboriously from a foreign language. Sounding out each word, pondering it for meaning. At last her teeth closed on her lower lip and she nodded.

He ignored a jolt of lust and followed her through the living room into a kitchen that was open to a dining room. Again, he was struck by the hominess of cabinets painted a soft cream, walls a pale shade caught between peach and rust—maybe the color of clay pots that had aged outside. A glossy red ceramic bowl held fruit on the counter. A copper teakettle was on the stove. In the middle of the table, a cream-colored pitcher was filled with tulips, mostly striped in interesting patterns. A few petals had fallen onto the shining wood surface of the table.

Ms. Greenway had stopped in the middle of the kitchen and was standing there as if she had no memory of her original intentions. After a minute he went to her, gripped her shoulders to turn her around and steered her to one of the chairs around the table. When he pushed, she sat, staring up at him in bewilderment.

"You're in no shape to be doing anything," he said, more brusquely than he'd intended. He was mad at himself for letting her drive. She'd been a danger to everyone else on the road. "Stay put. I can heat some soup if you have any."

Of course she tried to pop right back up. Her knees must not have been any too steady, because she fell back when he applied a little pressure. This time she stayed, not so much obediently, he suspected, as because she'd forgotten why she wanted to be on her feet.

He found cans of Campbell's soup as well as

some boxed macaroni and cheese and the like. The usual kid-friendly foods. He chose tomato, and added milk to make it cream of tomato. The milk was two percent, not skim; maybe because she thought her niece needed it? After a minute he decided to feed himself, too. He assembled and grilled two cheese sandwiches with sliced tomatoes, the way his mom had made them, then brought plates and bowls to the table. Instead of making coffee, he poured them both glasses of milk.

Ms. Greenway stared at what he'd put in front of her as if she didn't know what to do with it.

"You need to eat," he told her again, and watched as she finally lifted a spoonful of soup to her mouth. "Good."

He ate hungrily and went back to start coffee in the machine she had on the counter. She was eating way more slowly, but sticking to it with a sort of mechanical efficiency.

It bothered Mike that he couldn't get a more certain read on her now than when he first set eyes on her. Initially he'd tagged her as a cold bitch. Beautiful, but unlikable. Fully capable of disposing of a kid she didn't want and lying to cover up her crime. But he'd come to believe her shock was genuine. Unless she was an Oscar-worthy actress, it almost had to be.

But there *were* people who lied that well. He'd met a few. He couldn't be sure about her.

And the one didn't preclude the other. She could have killed the kid. Perhaps in a burst of rage or only irritation—planned the cover-up, and now was suffering a physical reaction to what she'd done. Or she could be frightened, after discovering that everyone didn't totally buy into her story.

He wished he wasn't attracted to her. That made him second-guess everything he did and said. Was he being nice because that was a good way to lower her guard, or because she was getting to him? Should he have gotten aggressive, in her face, hours ago?

Mike poured their coffee, put one of the mugs in front of her and took a sip of his own. Then he said, "I'd like to look at Sicily's bedroom, but first I need to see any photos you have of her."

Ms. Greenway carefully set down what remained of her sandwich. Her expression was momentarily stricken. She gave a stiff nod and stood. Mike let her go, managing only a few more swallows of coffee before she returned with a framed five-by-seven photograph.

"This is the most recent," she said. "It was her fourth-grade school picture."

So, over a year old. Kids changed a whole lot in a year.

He took it, both wanting to see her face and reluctant because now she'd become real to him. An individual.

There she was, a solemn-faced little girl who had apparently refused to smile when the photographer said, "Cheese!"

Sicily had a thin face and blond hair with straight bangs across her forehead, the rest equally bluntly cut above her shoulders. Her eyes were, he thought, hazel. She had her aunt's cheekbones, which made her almost homely now, before she'd grown into them. No one would call her pretty. Her grave expression was unsettling, probably only because of what he knew about her family, but he couldn't say she looked sad or turned inward. More as if she were trying to penetrate the photographer's secrets. This was a child who tried hard to see beneath the surface.

After a moment he nodded. "May I borrow this?"

"Yes, of course."

"Okay. Her room?"

She didn't ask why he wanted to see it, which meant she'd guessed that he was suspicious.

"This way," she said, voice polite but remote.

He was able to glance in rooms to each side as he followed her down the short hallway. The house was a three-bedroom two-bath, although none of the rooms were large. The first seemed to be a home office. Across the hall from it was a bathroom, tiled in white up to waist level and wallpapered above that. Beyond it had to be her bedroom and through it a doorway leading into a second bath. Next to the home office was Sicily's room.

Ms. Greenway stood aside and let him go in. He was worried more than relieved to see signs of a young girl's occupancy. He'd have been pissed if this whole thing was a hoax and Sicily Marks didn't exist at all, but at least he wouldn't have had to worry about her being dead in a shallow grave, either.

He wondered what this room had been used for before Sicily came to stay. Maybe nothing. The walls were white. The only furniture was a twin bed and a dresser. No curtains to soften the white blinds. No artwork. Only one throw rug, right beside the bed, and it was one of those hooked ones that might have been moved from elsewhere in the house. One of the sliding closet doors stood open, letting him see a few pairs of kid-size shoes in a neat row and exactly one dress hanging on a hanger beside a pink denim jacket. He crossed the room and opened each drawer on the dresser in turn. The contents were startlingly skimpy.

"She didn't come with much." The words were soft. Ashamed? "Mostly she'd outgrown what she did have."

Sicily Marks still didn't have much, he couldn't help thinking.

"I didn't use this room." Ms. Greenway still hovered in the doorway. She was looking around. "We're going to paint or wallpaper or something, but she hasn't decided yet…." She didn't finish.

That was believable, he supposed. "She into pink and purple? All that girly stuff?"

"I'm…not sure." At least she hadn't said *I don't know.* "She seems to like red. But she did pick out a pink jacket. And some pink flats."

Flats? His gaze fell to the shoes and he saw a pair of pink leather slip-ons.

"I think—" and she sounded sad "—Sicily hasn't ever been able to buy new or really pick out what she liked. The whole idea that she *can* is taking her some getting used to. I wanted to buy her a whole new wardrobe in one outing, but she had to think so long about every single thing we bought, we haven't gotten that far."

She was talking about her niece in the present tense, which was good. People sometimes slipped up that way, when they were talking about someone they knew was dead.

Yeah, but he'd already concluded Beth Greenway could be one hell of a liar.

"Does she have a school bag?" he asked. "A binder where she might have written down her thoughts? Or does she keep a diary?"

"A diary?" She sounded slightly uncertain. "Not as far as I know. I'm sure she didn't bring anything like that. Everything she owned was in one small suitcase that had lost a wheel. Her book bag is probably in my office. She usually does her homework there or at the dining-room table. We're going to get her a desk for in here eventually…." Again her voice trailed off. She backed into the hall and turned toward the office.

Sicily was in fifth grade, she told him. Flipping through the girl's binder, he learned that she was organized, had careful handwriting with generous loops but no flourishes, and was getting top-notch grades. *Excellent!* the teacher had scrawled on returned assignments. *99%. 100%. Fine work*.

Behind him, Ms. Greenway said, "She's been in eight schools so far. Rachel kept moving. Mostly around here, but she went to L.A. for a little while, then San Francisco. Somehow Sicily managed to do well in school everywhere she went."

He caught the note of sadness in her voice. Something else, too. Guilt? Or was it grief, because she knew damn well Sicily wasn't going to have a chance to do well in school ever again?

What he didn't find was anything personal. No diary, no notes that might have been passed to or from another girl. Nothing helpful.

"Does she have friends?" he asked.

"I…" Ms. Greenway stopped and he saw that she'd closed her eyes. "I don't think so. She says she has other kids to sit with for lunch, and another girl asked her to partner in badminton during gym class, but as far as I know no one has invited her over to play or anything like that."

"You said she didn't know how to play."

"No." Brown eyes that were both bleak and dazed met his. "She's determined to help me. She wants to clean house and cook dinner. I feel like… like…"

"She's trying to make you want to keep her?"

"Maybe." She heaved a sigh. "Mostly, I think that's what she's used to doing. Taking care of her mom."

He nodded. Mike had seen plenty of that kind of role reversal in families with a parent who was mentally ill, a drug addict or a drunk. Their kids grew up too fast. They learned quick that if there was going to be food on the table, they had to put it there. They also learned excellent cover-up skills; most kids were afraid of losing whatever family they did have. It was up to them to make sure school counselors, neighbors and social workers didn't notice how dysfunctional their home situation really was.

He wondered what Sicily Marks had made of this house.

"All right," he said abruptly. "I'll need your parents' phone number."

She looked almost numb. With a nod, she turned and walked away down the hall. Turned out she had to get her smart phone, which she'd had on the table right beside her as she ate, so she could look up her own parents' phone number.

He remembered already having jotted down their names. Laurence and Rowena Greenway. After adding the phone number, he remarked, "Your father's name is familiar."

"He's in the financial news regularly," she said with an astonishing lack of expression. "He was a big contributor to Governor Conley's campaign."

"Your parents have money, and your sister and her kid lived without?"

"I doubt they ever offered help, or that she would have taken it if they had."

"Did they help you get started in your business?"

"No." Flat. Final.

"Put you through college?"

She hesitated. "They did do that." Then her eyes met his. "My relationship with them is hardly the point, is it?"

"Not if this turns out to be a stranger abduction." Her flinch made him feel brutal. "More kids are snatched by members of their own families than by strangers, Ms. Greenway. I need to keep that in mind."

Her lashes fluttered a couple of times. "I see," she said, ducking her head.

He needed to talk to Sicily's grandparents, start

a search for her father. Find out more about her mother's death. Part of him wanted nothing so much as to get away from this woman. But seeing how utterly alone she looked, he frowned.

"Is there someone you can call to be with you tonight?"

Her chin lifted. "That's not necessary."

"You shouldn't be alone."

"I'm always..." She stopped. He couldn't help noticing that her hands were fisted so tight her knuckles showed white. "I'm comfortable by myself, Detective. Please don't concern yourself."

He'd been dismissed. Mike gave a brusque nod, said, "I'll call in the morning, Ms. Greenway," and left.

CHAPTER THREE

SICILY GROANED. *OH,* HER HEAD hurt so bad. Instinctively, she lifted a hand up, but her elbow banged something and she cried out.

Once the pain subsided a little, she tried to think. It was dark so she must be in bed. First she thought she was at home—well, at the apartment Mom had rented in the Rainier Valley, which was kind of a pit and they hadn't been here that long... Except then she remembered Mom was dead. Images flickered through her mind: the police coming to the door, the tense hour waiting for the aunt she didn't know to come for her. The funeral and the night she spent on Aunt Beth's couch before the twin bed was delivered the next day. A new bed! Only it didn't even have a headboard, so what had she banged her elbow *on?*

Something hard pressed into her hip, too. And her shoulder, and even her thigh. Sharp edges and weird bumps.

She heard herself panting. She was suddenly scared. Really scared. Her instinct was to huddle and be really, really quiet, except she'd already made sounds. Still, she tried to stifle her breathing and listened hard. After a minute she realized she was hearing traffic. Not like the freeway, these were city streets. And someone a long ways away yelled, and then another voice answered. There was a siren even farther away. It sounded… like what she'd have heard from practically any apartment she and Mom had lived in. Regular city sounds. Aunt Beth's was different. Especially late at night, it was quiet. Once in a while she'd hear a car, some neighbor coming home, but hardly ever sirens or loud voices or stuff like that.

Finally, timidly, she stretched out her hand and felt around her. If only it weren't so *dark*. First she found a wadded something that was soft, like clothes, but when she brought it to her nose it stunk like gas or oil. There was a crumpled bag that smelled like French fries. All the surfaces were hard and angular except for…whatever was under her hip. She felt her way along it, remembering the story a teacher had told about the three blind men groping an elephant. Beth got the point, but she'd been able to tell that most of her classmates didn't.

A tire. She was lying on a car tire. Why was there a tire under her?

A weird sensation swelled in her chest. It felt hot and scary and she finally recognized that it was fear. She lifted her hands above her, knowing what she'd find.

She was inside the trunk of a car. A car that wasn't running, that was parked somewhere in the city. And it had to be night, because there'd have to be cracks, wouldn't there? And she *could* see light, now that she was concentrating, but only a little, leaking around or through taillights.

Now her breath came in whimpering little shudders. *Mommy, Mommy. Aunt Beth. Please somebody come and get me.*

What if I scream?

She was curled into a tiny, terrified ball now, containing that scream behind chattering teeth. Because, really, she'd maybe rather not find out who'd unlock the trunk and lift the lid.

MIKE TOOK A CHANCE THAT HE'D catch the grandparents at home and drove straight to Seattle, checking his computer on the way for Laurence Greenway's address. Somehow he wasn't surprised to find the Greenways lived in Magnolia, one of the wealthiest neighborhoods in the city. When he got there, he found the enormous brick home was a waterfront property.

An eight-foot brick wall fronted the property and iron gates kept out the hoi polloi. He rang a buzzer and when a voice inquired who he was, he said into the speaker, "Police. Detective Mike Ryan."

After a pause, the gates slowly swung open. He followed the circular drive and parked beside the front porch.

He recognized the man who opened the door to him. He'd seen Greenway on the news or in photos in the *Seattle Times,* he realized.

Beth Greenway's father was handsome in the way wealthy men often were. His slacks and polo shirt were casual but obviously expensive. At maybe five foot ten, he was lean and fit for sixty years old. He undoubtedly belonged to a club, played racquetball, probably had a personal trainer. His hair had been allowed to go white but had a silver gleam to it that didn't strike Mike as natural. He had the tan of a man who spent time on his sailboat.

He stood in the open doorway and said, "May I see your identification, Detective?"

Mike flipped open his badge and handed it over.

"Aren't you out of your jurisdiction?"

"Yes, I am." Mike met his gaze stolidly. "May I come in, Mr. Greenway? I'd like to speak to you and your wife."

"What is this about?"

"Your granddaughter, Sicily."

After a moment he nodded. "Very well." Shutting the door behind Mike, he led him to an elegantly appointed living room, where the ten o'clock news was playing on a flat-screen television that would be hidden within a gilt-trimmed armoire during the day.

The woman who'd been watching it turned her head, saw him and rose gracefully. He knew she was fifty-eight, but she sure as hell didn't look it. His first reaction was to her looks; Rowena Greenway was an astonishingly beautiful woman. She'd gifted her daughter with those magnificent cheekbones and gold-flecked eyes. He saw money here, too. Her hair was still dark, short and beautifully cut. She could have been in her thirties, which made him suspect a facelift.

"Laurence?"

Greenway introduced Mike and said, "He says he wants to talk to us about Sicily."

Her eyebrows rose. After a moment, she said, "Please have a seat, Detective."

He chose a wingback chair that was bloody uncomfortable. The Greenways sat on the sofa facing him, the middle cushion between them. He found himself irritated by the flicker of the television, which neither of them reached to turn off. The sound wasn't loud, but he still had to raise his voice slightly.

"First, let me ask when you last spoke to your granddaughter."

They glanced at each other. "I believe it was at the funeral," Laurence said. "Are you aware Sicily's mother died recently? It was a terrible tragedy."

His sad tone sounded staged; there was nothing really personal in it. He might have been speaking about the daughter of a colleague of his. Neither he nor his wife looked exactly devastated.

"I was aware of that. My condolences."

"Thank you," Rowena murmured.

"Did you know that your daughter Rachel intended for her sister to raise Sicily in the event she herself was unable to?"

"No, we did not," Rowena said crisply. "I'm sure it goes without saying that we would have welcomed our only grandchild into our home."

Funny how sure he was that she hadn't cared one way or another. Mike couldn't remember meeting a chillier pair of people. Certainly explained Beth's ice-princess mode.

Laurence made a sharp gesture with one hand. "We've been more than patient. Why the questions?"

"Beth took Sicily to the beach today. Just before midday, your granddaughter disappeared. Search-and-rescue volunteers turned up no sign of her at the park. We must now consider the possibility that she was abducted."

After a pause, during which both looked startled, Laurence snorted. "I suppose we can expect a ransom call then."

Mike raised his eyebrows.

"Well, why else would anyone want her?"

"Unfortunately, men who abduct young girls are most often sexual predators."

"Do you have any reason to suspect such a thing, or are you merely trying to alarm us?"

Mike schooled his expression with an effort. No wonder both daughters had apparently been estranged from their parents. "I wouldn't think I'd have to alarm you," he said mildly. "The fact that Sicily has been missing for eleven hours now seems to speak for itself."

"Dear God. Poor Sicily," Rowena murmured. Then her eyes widened. "Surely you didn't think *we'd* taken her?" She reached out a hand to her husband, who took it without moving any closer to her. "You do understand that we'd have had our attorney file for custody if we felt our daughter Elizabeth wasn't doing an adequate job of caring for Sicily."

"I hoped you'd answer some questions."

"Like?"

"Do you know whether Sicily can swim?"

He expected an "*I don't know*" or some equivalent, so it came as a surprise when Rowena said, "I'm sure she can. We were somewhat estranged from Rachel, but she did call home from time to time. I recall her mentioning swim lessons. They were in Los Angeles at the time. She said that Sicily loved the water."

He nodded. "How would you describe your granddaughter? Is she likely to take off with someone on impulse, for example?"

"Heavens, no! She's quiet and rather *ordinary.* Oh-so practical. But I suppose she'd have had to be," she continued, nostrils flaring in disdain, "with the mother she had."

Mike stared at her. She gazed coolly back.

Her husband let go of her hand and reached for the remote control and turned up the sound on the TV. "Excuse me," he said. "I need to see this."

Mike swiveled. A segment had come on about the governor's stance on a proposal to expand funding for higher education. He realized incredulously that Laurence had been watching with one eye this entire time for items of interest to him.

Did either of them give a damn that their granddaughter was missing? Did *anyone* actually love Sicily Marks? he wondered.

He asked more questions. Laurence tore his attention from the television long enough to express disgust for Sicily's father.

"Thank God, he's been out of the picture for years. Although Rachel found plenty of substitutes. She had a gift for picking losers."

"I understand that she may have had a drug problem herself."

"We'd have paid for rehab if she had ever been serious about licking it." Laurence's cell phone rang; he glanced at the number and silenced it. "I'm afraid I don't know Rachel's habits. As I said, we saw very little of her or Sicily."

"Would you describe yourself as estranged from your other daughter, as well?"

His face closed. "She chooses to keep to herself," he said, voice clipped. "But at least she hasn't made a mess of her life like her sister did." His phone rang again; once again he didn't answer it. "What do you suggest we do to help, Detective?" He was clearly becoming impatient. "It would seem Elizabeth has no intention of calling on us. The least she could have done was let us know what was happening. This is our granddaughter."

He found himself compelled to defend Beth Greenway. "I doubt she let herself believe Sicily wouldn't turn up. It's a good-size park, and the search continued until dusk."

He explained that it would resume at first light, that the girl's disappearance would be widely publicized. He asked for the most recent pictures they had of their granddaughter. Rowena produced the same fourth-grade school photo Beth had. The sight of the little girl's face gave him another pang. He wished she'd have at least smiled.

He very much hoped he would have the chance to see her smile.

BETH HAD WANTED DESPERATELY TO be alone, but almost from the minute the detective left, she wished he hadn't. At least he'd distracted her. And—oh, it was an illusion of caring, not the real thing, but he'd mostly been kind.

Now all she could think about was Sicily and what could possibly have happened to her. Beth simply couldn't imagine her as foolish enough to go off with someone she didn't know. Even a family with children. She might have gotten bored, yes, and decided to hike one of the short nature trails—although Beth wasn't even sure about that. Gone up to the restroom. She wouldn't necessarily have woken Beth to tell her where she was going. She was used to making her own decisions. But she didn't do dumb things.

The park had been so busy, if someone had grabbed her and she'd screamed, plenty of people would have heard. So that didn't seem likely, either. And the idea of her wading into the water and going swimming was ridiculous. The beach was so rocky she couldn't have gone barefoot, and she'd never have discarded her brand-new flip-flops, which had so pleased her. And think how cold the water was! Besides, people would have seen her. There'd been plenty of other adults around.

None of it made sense.

The part that made Beth most uneasy was the

disappearance of the kids Sicily had been with when Beth fell asleep. The kids *and* their parents. It seemed so coincidental that they'd decide to leave within the same half hour when Sicily vanished.

Beth had seen from his expression that Detective Ryan doubted the family had ever existed. She'd heard him talking to some of the search-and-rescue volunteers.

"No one here remembers seeing the kid at all."

But some of the people *had* to have seen Sicily. Beth knew they had! If only she could remember the faces of anyone who'd been near when she and Sicily spread the blanket and she began to read. But the truth was, she hadn't really looked. Even at the parents of those other kids. She hadn't wanted to make eye contact and maybe be forced to chat.

She could be charming at work; it was a job skill. But she liked to keep her distance the rest of the time. Sometimes, toward the end of a day at work, she thought if she had to make smiling conversation for one more minute, she wouldn't be able to bear it. She frequently longed to be by herself.

Like I am now. Only now—*please God, are you listening?*—she didn't want to be by herself. She desperately wanted to hear Sicily in the kitchen saying hopefully, "I could make cookies. Do you like chocolate chip, Aunt Beth? Because I make really good ones."

And she would argue at first, saying, "I don't eat desserts very often. If you're hungry, we have ice cream," but then she'd see the anxiety mixed with the eagerness in her niece's golden-green eyes. She would realize that baking those cookies would make Sicily happy, because she'd feel as if she was contributing something. So then Beth would say, "You know, I haven't baked in ages. Do you mind if I help?" And they'd mix the dough and make a mess and the heavenly smell of cookies baking would fill the kitchen. They might even giggle, and at some point Beth would discover in amazement that she was having fun.

When did I last have fun?

Never? There must have been times, but if so they were lost in the more painful memories.

I could drive back to the park. The impulse was powerful. She saw herself walking slowly, calling, "Honey? I'm here," as if Sicily were only hiding. Which she wouldn't be. But…what if she'd fallen and hurt herself, been knocked out, and was now regaining consciousness in the dark? What if she had a broken leg and couldn't get up to walk?

The idea of continuing to do nothing but sit here was unendurable. Beth heard a thin, anguished sound and realized she'd made it. She was horrified; she knew better than to make any noise at all! No matter how much she hurt, she knew how to be silent.

She made herself draw slow, deep breaths. Look around, ground herself. This was home. *Her* home. No one was hurting her; that was long in her past. Her hurt now was for her niece, who had to be scared and bewildered somewhere.

She'd have her cell phone if she went back to the park, so Sicily could call her if she were able. Detective Ryan could reach her, too, in case he had news.

A part of her knew this was ridiculous, but she rushed to her room and changed clothes, into jeans and a sweatshirt warm enough for the evening, plus thick socks and athletic shoes. She caught a glimpse of herself in the mirror and looked quickly away from that pale, haunted face.

She carried a flashlight in her glove compartment, but she had a better one here in the house, big, sealed in rubber, with a bright beam. Beth grabbed that, and a zip-up sweatshirt she'd bought Sicily, because if she was out there she'd be cold.

Then Beth left the house.

SICILY WOKE WITH A START TO A scraping sound. By the time the trunk lifted, she realized what she'd heard was key in the lock. She cringed toward the back of the trunk, then thought, *No! I should have jumped out. Really fast, and run.*

Too late. A man bent over her, too quick for her to really see him. He flung a blanket over Sicily. Even as she started to fight, he bundled her in rough, scratchy wool so tight it was like the Egyptian mummies. She could hardly move at all except to buck and kick and she couldn't get enough air to scream.

Nothing she did made any difference. He was way bigger than her, and he carried her in his arms, not over his shoulder, where she might have been able to squirm her face or arms free. He didn't walk very far. Doors opened and closed. She thought maybe they went down some steps, which she couldn't figure out until she understood. *Basement.* Once he banged her head against a hard surface, maybe a door frame. More steps and then abruptly she was dumped onto what felt like a mattress.

As she fought her way free of the blanket, the door slammed shut and she heard the distinct slide of a lock. Sicily found herself in complete darkness. No light came in any window, and for a minute she heard nothing at all. And then...was that a *television?*

WHETHER DRIVEN BY UNEASINESS or only a gut feeling, Mike went straight back to Edmonds. He'd wanted to assess the grandparents, but he had the bad feeling he'd made a mistake. He should have parked down the street and kept an eye on Beth Greenway's house.

He pulled up in front to find the porch light on and one light somewhere inside, but the house was darker than when he'd left. If she'd gone to bed, why had she left lights on at all? He had trouble imagining her brushing her teeth, changing into a nightgown and settling comfortably into bed. Maybe with the aid of a sleeping pill—but would she be willing to knock herself out so that she might not hear her phone ring?

Yes. If she already knew where Sicily was. If her anxiety was only for herself.

He went to the porch and rang the bell, hearing the deep tolls inside. There was no stir of activity. He rang again. Swearing, Mike circled the garage and found a side window. Of course it was dark inside, but he stood patiently waiting until his eyes gradually adjusted enough for him to see that the small space was empty. Goddamn. Where had she gone?

He went back to his Tahoe and sat with the door open so the overhead light was on. He snatched his cell phone from his belt, then had to flip open the notebook he carried to find her number.

She answered on the third ring, her voice quick and eager. "Yes?"

"Where the hell are you?" he growled.

"Detective Ryan? Did you find anything out?"

"No. What I want to know is why you aren't home."

The silence was long enough he began to wonder if the call had been dropped, or she'd ended it. But finally she said, "You came back to see if I was there."

He could have lied and told her he'd come back to check up on her because he was worried about her. He didn't. "Yes."

"I'm not."

"I figured that out."

"How?"

"Your car isn't in the garage."

Another pool of silence fell, but he didn't make the mistake this time of thinking she wasn't there. This time he could *feel* her, all of that tension stretched quivering and tight beneath the surface.

"I'm at the park."

"What?"

"I couldn't do nothing but sit there. I'd have gone crazy. Knowing that no one was looking for her…" Beth's voice cracked.

"It's pitch-dark!"

"I brought a flashlight," she said defensively.

"How long have you been there?"

"I left not that long after you did."

He slammed his door and turned the key in the ignition with a jerk. The engine had barely roared to life before he gunned away from the curb. "You thought you'd find her in the dark when twenty trained search-and-rescue personnel couldn't find her in daylight."

"No." She said it so softly he strained to hear. "But I had to try. I didn't today, you know, not once…after everyone else started looking. All I did was sit there and wait. I can't do that anymore."

Pity joined the anger and frustration crowding him. He could imagine all too easily how she felt. If she were sincere and this wasn't all an act for his benefit. If she were actually at the park at all.

"Where are you right now?" he asked.

"Um…on the beach. I keep thinking she could have fallen and been knocked out. And now it's dark. If she woke up and it was completely dark…"

Something in her voice told him she wasn't entirely talking about the missing child. "Darkness can be comforting," he said. "It can hide you." He didn't even know why he said that.

"Yes." She sounded calmer. "I know that. You're right."

"Are you ready to come home?"

"No. I feel better being here."

He growled an obscenity under his breath, but she must have heard because she said stiffly, "It's my choice. The park isn't closed. I can answer the phone here, as well as at home. I can't sleep anyway."

"She's not there, Ms. Greenway."

"You don't know that."

"I think we both know that."

"No! No, we don't. And if I want to keep looking for her, that's my business. If you need to talk to me in the morning, you know where to find me." She ended the call.

He reached the freeway and got on. Traffic was sparse at this time of night, so he'd make good time. Once he'd maneuvered into the inside lane and was pushing the speed limit, he hit redial on his phone. She didn't answer.

THE NIGHT WAS SO QUIET, SHE heard the powerful engine when a vehicle pulled into the parking lot up above. Beth knew who it was. For a moment, guilt squeezed her throat, but it subsided when she remembered that he was here not out of concern for her, but because he thought…what? That she was taking dinner to Sicily, wherever she'd stowed her? Was visiting the grave? Who knew? He'd already have seen her car, which confirmed that she was here. That didn't mean she had to go to meet him. He'd never find her if she didn't want him to.

Which would be childish and completely ridiculous. She should reassure him and send him on his way. Maybe even give up and go home, if that would allow him to go home, too.

His voice roared from up above, "Ms. Greenway? Beth?"

"Down here," she called, but felt the night swallow up her too-small voice. She tried again, cupping her hands. "Down here."

It took her some scrambling to get back to the beach proper. She'd had this image of Sicily having fallen down the bluff, bouncing off a driftwood log, ending up wedged behind it and hidden by some of the shrubby growth that had taken root in the red soil of the bluff. The whole time, she knew her search was futile. Of course, others had looked in the same places today. Probably over and over.

The sweep of a powerful beam of light and the crunch of beach pebbles heralded his arrival. "Beth?"

"Right here." Suddenly exhausted, she wasn't paying enough attention and her foot skidded on the last log as she scrambled over it. She teetered and fell, landing painfully on her hands and knees. Exactly, of course, at the moment the beam of light found her.

"Damn it," he said, and reached her while she was still blinking back tears of pain. As angry as he sounded, his hands were gentle when he picked her up and set her down on the log. "You've hurt yourself."

Determined to regain her dignity, Beth said,

"Nothing permanent. I slipped, that's all." Blinded by his light, she couldn't make out his face at all. Her own flashlight had fallen and gone out. She lifted an arm to protect her eyes. "Do you mind?"

The detective sighed and turned the light away from her. He found and picked up her flashlight, fiddled with it for a moment until it came back on and then switched it off before handing it to her.

She hurt, and was mad at herself. She couldn't think of anything she wanted to say.

He sat down next to her and turned off his own flashlight. They sat quietly for a minute, the soft shush of small waves the only sound. It wasn't really totally dark, either, not the way it might be on a cloudy night. The moon was only a quarter full, but the stars were bright. Beth found that to be comforting.

When I hid, I would have liked to be able to have seen the moon and stars.

"You shouldn't have come," she said. "I'm all right."

"You shouldn't be here alone. Why didn't you call someone if you were determined to come?"

She almost said, "Who?" But that sounded— and was—pathetic. And she did have friends, of a sort. It hadn't occurred to her to call any of them. They weren't those kinds of friends. If Rachel were still alive, if this were Beth's daughter missing... *No,* she thought sadly, *I wouldn't have called Rachel, either.* She'd failed her sister too devastatingly to expect her to feel any obligation.

"I met your parents."

She was already tense; now she went rigid.

He waited for her to say something. When she didn't, he continued, "I was a little surprised when your mother said she hadn't seen Sicily since your sister's funeral."

Beth shrugged, guessing he'd feel the movement even though they weren't touching.

"Why is that?" he asked.

"I told you we don't have a good relationship."

"But she's their granddaughter." His tone sharpened. "Or is it not them? Did you refuse to let them spend time with Sicily?"

"The issue hasn't arisen."

"But if it did?" he persisted.

"I suppose I'd let them see her," she said slowly, reluctantly. "But not stay with them."

"Why?"

She turned toward him and exclaimed, "What does this have to do with anything? You don't have to know everything about us!"

"Yeah, I do. I never know what's going to turn out to matter."

"You don't seriously think they stole her," she said incredulously.

"Not now that I've met them, no, I don't." He

sounded thoughtful. "Clearly that never crossed your mind."

"Of course it didn't."

"As your mother pointed out, if they'd wanted Sicily they could have contested for custody."

"No." She had never in her life been so tired. She was afraid she sounded it. "They wouldn't have won."

Of course, he asked, "Why not?"

Some things she didn't have to tell him. "Why would they? Rachel named me as guardian. I'm an upstanding citizen, a business and home owner." She'd managed to inject a note of indignation. "I'm the logical age to raise a child. I live in one of the best school districts in the state. What grounds could they have used to persuade a court they'd do better than I can?"

Beth ached from holding herself so rigid. She hoped he wouldn't notice that she'd been evasive.

"All good points." He still sounded reflective. His mind was working, poking and prodding at her words, suspecting…something.

Turn this back to him, she thought. "Why are you here? Surely you don't work around the clock."

"Actually, I sometimes do when a case first breaks. With a homicide or a kidnapping, it's best not to let people's memories fade."

She swallowed. "You really think…"

To her astonishment, his big hand found hers and engulfed it rather gently. "I do think."

Fear swooped over her like a bald eagle descending on a tiny, cowering field mouse, so swift and black she couldn't have done anything to save her life. The fear was even greater than her terrible sense of guilt.

"Nothing to say?" Detective Ryan's hand was still gentle, but his voice had turned cold. "If you know something…"

She wrenched her hand free and stood up. "I don't know anything," she said, and turned to march down the beach toward the trailhead.

He fell into step beside her. He turned on his flashlight to light the way up the trail. Even so, she stumbled a couple of times. Before they reached the parking lot, he had a firm hand under her elbow to steady her. He steered her to the passenger side of his SUV. She tried to pull away.

"No," he said, "You're in no shape to drive. I'm taking you home. I'll pick you up in the morning and bring you back to the park."

"There's no reason…"

"There's every reason." Now he sounded impatient, and she clamped her mouth shut. It was true that her head was swimming and her knees wanted to buckle. She felt ashamed of how desperately she wanted to curl up in her own bed and close her eyes.

Beth didn't last that long. They hadn't been on their way five minutes when she listed sideways in the big bucket seat, thinking, *It won't hurt anything if I rest my head against the door frame.*

The next thing she knew, he was shaking her awake.

CHAPTER FOUR

KNEES TO HER CHEST, SICILY LAY curled on her side.
The mattress was on the floor of the small, mostly
bare room, and she clutched the too-thin comforter
around her. Positioned so that she was looking at
the door, scared and miserable, she waited. There
wasn't anything else she could do.

Practically the minute *he*—whoever *he* was—
had left her alone, she'd leaped to her feet, wanting desperately to throw herself at the door and
hammer at it. She was bewildered and terrified
and her head hurt and she wanted Aunt Beth.

Thinking about Aunt Beth was what had
stopped her. She was *so* different from Mom. Aunt
Beth was always dignified and careful. She was
super organized and thoughtful. You could tell
she wouldn't do impulsive or dumb things. If she
were here, she'd stay cool.

I can, too. Even if my head does hurt.

Sicily had already figured out that she was more
like Aunt Beth than Mom. That comforted her a
little. After all the stuff Mom had told her about
Grandma, Sicily had always hated the idea that

she might be anything like *her*. But it was okay
to be like Aunt Beth.

So instead of sobbing or screaming or anything
useless like that, she inched carefully off the mattress and explored, shuffling her feet forward and
holding her hands out in front of her. She'd never
been anywhere that was utterly black. That was
one of the scariest parts of all.

She hadn't encountered anything until her hands
flattened on a wall. It was just a regular wall,
she thought at first, until she felt downward and
came to a shelf that was really rough, and discovered that the bottom half of the wall was cold and
rough, too. Concrete. Okay, that made sense, if she
was in a basement. She and Mom had lived in a
basement apartment in Portland for a year. It was
dank and mold kept growing in the shower and
it had only little tiny windows high on the wall.
Sicily had hated it.

She groped her way around the room, hoping
she didn't touch anything really gross, like a big
spider or a cockroach. She *hated* cockroaches.
She reached a corner and discovered that *this*
wall didn't have the concrete part. So it must be
an inside wall. Partway along it, she came to the
door. It was cold to the touch and felt different
from the way her bedroom doors had always felt.
That was because it was metal, she realized, and
fear stabbed at her. Why would somebody put this

kind of door on a bedroom unless it was to keep someone prisoner? She stood there for a minute, breathing hard, trying to picture her aunt's face, always calm, no matter what.

Aunt Beth would be looking for her. Of course she would be. Even though Sicily wasn't sure she'd actually wanted a kid.

But that doesn't matter. She'll still look. Because...because I saw the look on her face at the funeral when she put her arm around me, stared hard at Grandma and said, "Sicily will be living with me." Just like that. No question. As if saying, "Don't argue with me, because there's no point."

Reassured, Sicily calmed her breathing and wrapped her hand around the knob. It turned, but nothing else happened. So there must be a deadbolt lock, like Aunt Beth had on her front door—except doors usually locked from the *inside*. But Sicily hadn't expected to be able to just walk out. After a moment, she slid her hand along the wall. The light switch was always right next to the door, right?

But it wasn't. It turned out to be in a weird place, on the opposite side of the door from where it should have been. If you came into the room, the switch would be *behind* the door, which so totally didn't make sense. But then, she thought, her fear peeking out of hiding again, someone must have added this door later. Maybe really recently.

Maybe for *her*.

She hesitated, afraid of what she might see, then flicked the switch.

For a minute the bright light blinded her and she squeezed her eyes shut. Then, heart pounding, she opened them. Oh, no! There wasn't even a window. She had really, really wanted a window, even if it was one of the kind that was in a well in the ground and you couldn't see out of it but a slice of sky. It still might have given her a chance somehow to break the glass and get out, or attract someone's—anyone's—attention. But this was like being in a concrete box.

Well, not quite. She'd been right; on two sides, rough concrete reached halfway up the wall. There was a closet on one of the regular walls, but instead of a regular sliding door it had a curtain rod but no curtain, and she could see that it was totally empty. So was the rest of the room except for the mattress and…oh, wow, a bucket. Now her eyes widened. He didn't think she was going to pee in *that,* did he? But why else would it be there?

She might have to puke in it pretty soon.

Sicily shivered, wondering if *he* could see light under the door. But maybe he didn't care, even if he could. It wasn't like anyone *else* would see that a light was on. And anyway, maybe that heavy door fit so tight there wasn't any kind of crack around it. She hadn't been able to see light from the other room. And she could still just barely hear voices and laughter that she was sure were coming from a television.

Sicily wrapped her arms around herself. It was kind of cold in here. She remembered how that other basement apartment had been cold all the time, too. It hadn't had a furnace or even baseboard heaters. Mom and she had to use plug-in space heaters, and Mom always said they should never leave them on when they went out or at night when they were asleep, because they could cause fires. So they'd each had a huge heap of blankets and comforters on their beds, and Sicily had gotten used to pulling covers over her head at night. When Mom got drunk or stoned, she would forget to turn off the heaters, but Sicily never did. She would always sneak into Mom's room after she passed out, even if there was a man with her, and hurriedly yank the plug from the wall.

Sicily looked around. This room didn't have any heating vents or a baseboard heater, either. She was lucky it wasn't winter.

Lucky. Right.

The bed did have a fitted sheet on it, one scrawny pillow and an old comforter with stuffing seeping out of the places where fabric had worn through.

Eventually she went back to the bed and sat down on it. She felt sick, but also hungry. She and Aunt Beth had never eaten the lunch they'd brought to the beach. And it was dark when that man carried Sicily into the house, so she'd missed dinner, too. She wondered what time it was. And if he would feed her.

Mostly, shivering, she wondered what he wanted. What seemed like hours later, she was still wondering.

BETH DID SLEEP AFTER DETECTIVE Ryan left her, even though she hadn't thought she could. But she woke only after a few hours had passed, and lay frozen in her bed. All she could think about was Sicily. Where was she? What could have happened? And in only half an hour?

Oh, God, Rachel, you shouldn't have trusted me. Why did you? she all but begged, but there wasn't any answer. And she knew, anyway— Rachel's friends weren't the kind of people you trusted with your ten-year-old daughter, and her worst nightmare would have been for Sicily to live with her grandparents. Rachel hadn't actually trusted Beth at all. It was only that there wasn't anyone else.

This wasn't what Rachel would have feared, though, if her last thoughts when she went over the ferry railing had been of her child.

But then Beth felt a burst of anger. Wasn't abandonment as bad as abuse? How could Rachel have done that? Sicily *needed* her mother.

Lying in bed shuddering, Beth almost hated her sister now. But she couldn't, because Rachel's problems were *her* fault.

I could have rescued her, but I was selfish.

In the end, that's what it came down to, didn't it? No matter how apprehensive Beth was about suddenly having a child depending on her, there'd never been any real choice.

Ever since Beth had left home, she'd been torn by guilt. She couldn't live under the burden of more. Maybe the person Sicily really needed was her mother, but she couldn't have her. What she had was Beth.

And look how quickly she'd failed her.

If only I hadn't fallen asleep.

As exhausted as she was, she struggled against it now. It was wrong that she was cozy in her own bed when Sicily was…wherever she was. Her sin was sleep. Closing her eyes and succumbing to it now felt like another betrayal.

She should have hidden and not let the detective find her at the park. She'd *meant* to stay, even though her rational side knew how fragile the hope was that Sicily was actually there and alive. Beth didn't want to think he was right, that Sicily had been kidnapped or even murdered, but the terror pulsing in her agreed. Someone had taken Sicily.

As unrelenting as a sheepdog snapping at her heels, her mind spun through all the reasons someone might have wanted Sicily. Over and over and over.

THE SOUND OF THE ALARM JOLTED Beth awake. She was shocked to realize she'd slept after all.

She took a hurried shower and then, queasy and not at all hungry, still made herself sit down with coffee and a toasted bagel slathered with peanut butter. The detective was right. She did have to eat if she was going to stay strong enough to help find Sicily.

She was trying not to think about him. He was ally and enemy both. No, that wasn't right—*he's Sicily's ally, and my enemy,* she realized. She hated him and feared him and needed him all at the same time. It wasn't a comfortable feeling.

At exactly 7:30 a.m., her doorbell rang. As promised, he was here to pick her up.

She'd half hoped he would look different to her this morning. Less dominant, less sexy, less appealing. Or maybe his eyes would have softened and she'd realize that his hostility and suspicion had all been in her head.

But there he stood on her doorstep, exactly the same. Instead of yesterday's slacks and wrinkled white shirt, he wore jeans, running shoes and a heavy sweater over a T-shirt. The sweater made his shoulders look even broader.

His face had not softened. His eyes, sharp and clear, assessed her, but she couldn't read any emotion in them at all.

"You're ready?"

"Yes." She let herself out and locked the front door, dropping the keys in the tote bag that already held her wallet, phone and a bottle of water.

Once they were in his SUV and backing out, he said, "I hope you got some sleep."

"A little." She hesitated. "It's my fault you didn't get much. I'm sorry."

"I don't need much."

She nodded even though he wasn't looking. After a minute she said, "You haven't heard anything?" even though of course he'd have told her if he had.

"No."

After that she looked out the side window, clenching the seat belt in one hand where it crossed her chest, and didn't say a word. Neither did Detective Ryan. The entire drive passed in silence.

There were already other vehicles in the picnic area parking lot.

"Good, they've gotten started," he said, and she realized he meant the volunteers who'd spent yesterday searching.

"Where can they look that they didn't already yesterday?"

He shot her a glance she couldn't read. "Some of the park is old growth forest with no trails. There's also wooded acreage, pasture and beach outside the park boundary."

"Why didn't you issue an Amber Alert yesterday?"

His stare was cold. "Because the reasonable first assumption was that your niece was lost. Lost kids are a regular occurrence. The word will be out now, for what good it does this long after she went missing."

The moment he braked in the parking slot, she unbuckled her seat belt and got out. He did the same, circling to her and nodding toward her car.

"You know, nothing's to be gained by you staying. We can call you if we find anything at all."

"You really think I'll go home?" she said incredulously. "I'm here to look for Sicily."

"I'll have to pair you with someone."

Staring at that rock-hard face, she kept herself from recoiling with an effort of will. *I think you know where her body is.* That's what he was really saying. He thought she would claim to have already searched someplace so nobody else would. Beth wanted to be angry but instead felt momentarily dizzy.

He frowned and reached out a hand to her,

which made her wonder whether she'd gone completely pale or her eyes had done a whirligig like a Saturday-morning cartoon character. She stepped back so that his hand dropped without touching her.

"I don't want to talk to you anymore."

"You don't have any choice."

She turned and walked away, toward the sound of voices. She knew he was following, but she couldn't do anything about that.

The woman who had been organizing the volunteers yesterday had a clipboard in her hand and seemed to be directing the cluster of people around her. Mike introduced her as Phyllis Chang. She nodded brusquely and went back to what she was doing.

"I'd like to help," Beth said, hating how small her voice was.

Phyllis's glance went right past her to Mike. She could feel the silent consultation taking place. It made her ashamed and angry. Her stomach churned and her chest felt unbearably tight.

After a minute, the woman said, "Ms. Greenway, my volunteers are trained. I understand that you want to be involved, but they're used to working together." Satisfied that she'd dismissed Beth, she looked around her. "Margie, Chuck, you know where you're going. Garcia, Fay, I've circled in red

the area I want you to search." She handed over a
photocopied map with red marker lines.

So much rage filled Beth, she shook with it.
"I can help," she said loudly. "This is my niece."

Two other women had just arrived. Everyone
looked at her, their expressions startled and pity-
ing. Did they blame her for Sicily's disappearance?
Of course they did, she realized, even if they didn't
know that the detective suspected her of something much worse than carelessness. They were
people who were regularly called out to search for
missing children. They probably got so they despised the adults who should have been guarding
those children. There was nothing kind or sym-
pathetic on those faces. She felt suddenly as if she
were standing too close to a fire. The condemna-
tion singed her as surely as the heat would have.
She backed away, one step, two, three—and then
she came up hard against something solid.

The minute the hands gripped her upper arms,
she knew who they belonged to, and wrenched
herself away. "Don't touch me."

His eyes narrowed. "You walked into me."

Beth spun away and started walking. After
a minute she broke into a run. She'd search on
her own. They couldn't stop her. She had to do
something. She thought she might go insane if she
didn't. Yesterday had been torment. She couldn't
do it again, sit there and wait and wait and wait.

"Ms. Greenway! Beth!"

She ran regularly for exercise. Mostly on a treadmill, but not always. She was fast. Her bag bumped against her belly as she tore past the concrete-block restrooms and across the paved road toward the thick woods that lay beyond. His feet slapped the pavement behind her. Something like terror joined the rage that impelled her forward. As his running footsteps neared, she put on a spurt of speed and crashed through shrubbery.

"Goddamn it, *stop!*" he roared.

Beth risked a look over her shoulder. He was close, so close.... Her shoulder slammed into a tree trunk and she staggered, trying to keep her balance. But she failed and went down hard, even harder than she had last night when she fell off the log.

Pain and humiliation washed over her, making the anger and shame even more volatile. She twisted her body so that she was on her rump and then scrambled backward, away from him, even though her palms burned and both wrists and her shoulder hurt enough to bring tears to her eyes.

Mike Ryan had come to a stop a few feet from her. He was gasping for breath and she was glad, *glad*, that she'd at least winded him. She'd expected to see anger on his face, but saw something else instead, although she didn't know what it was.

"I'm not going to hurt you." He sounded as if he

were speaking to an injured wild animal. "Why did you run?"

Breathing hard, too, she crab-walked a few more feet away from him. He didn't move, only held up his hands as if to say *I won't touch you.* "Are you afraid of me?"

Yes. The vehemence of her immediate reaction rattled her. *Yes!* But she shook her head, because she wasn't, not the way he meant.

"I know this is hard for you."

She shook her head again, inching farther away. He didn't know. He couldn't possibly.

"I do." He squatted, so he was at her level if a good ten feet distant. "I...lost someone important to me. A child."

"And did everyone think it was your fault?" Her voice came out harsh and dry.

Lines seemed to deepen on his face. "No."

"Then you don't know."

He only looked at her. "Is that the worst part for you?"

Her arms were trembling, supporting her weight. No. No, that wasn't the worst part. Of course it wasn't. The worst was the wondering and the fear, followed by the guilt.

She sat up and bent forward, the pain so awful she didn't feel the stab in her shoulder or wrists. "No," she whispered. Behind the curtain of her hair, she said, "I suppose you think I'm crazy."

And maybe she was. She'd become a stranger to herself. She never showed what she was feeling. She'd had to learn to manufacture the responses people expected to see because they didn't come naturally. And now look at her!

"No," he said, in that deep, slow voice that reminded her of the way his hand had moved on her back while she retched. Comforting. "I think you're scared. I think you haven't had enough sleep, or enough to eat, and I've been pushing you."

She swallowed and stared down at her knees. Dark earth and leaves clung to them.

"We'll look together. We can be partners."

Bitterness gave her the strength to lift her head. "You mean, you can watch me. *I* won't be any help at all, because you'll need to look everywhere I have."

"I don't think you stashed her body out here." He gestured, taking in the forest around them.

"Where do you think I put her, then? Managed to push her over the railing of the ferry without anyone seeing? Maybe I pushed my sister, too. Did you ever think of that?" Beth didn't even know what she was doing or why. Only that she was so angry still. Anger was the cork preventing an even darker emotion from escaping. The terrible fear.

"Two sets of eyes are better than one."

She snorted, knowing when she was being

placated. But, really, what were her choices? Go home? She wondered, suddenly, whether she'd have been followed if she had. Maybe he'd wanted her to go so he could find out where she headed.

"All right," she said wearily. "I'm sorry. I'm being irrational. I know I am. I'll go...go sit at one of the picnic tables, if that's what you want."

"No." He sounded kind now, as he had off and on yesterday. "I want you to help me look. There's no reason we can't take a sector."

"Shouldn't you be doing something else?"

"I'm waiting for phone calls. I can take them anywhere."

"Phone calls?"

"We've put out a plea for anyone who was here at the beach yesterday and remembers seeing Sicily to call."

"But nobody's going to call who had anything to do with her disappearance."

"Somebody might have seen her get into a car."

Beth nodded.

He rose with that same ease she'd noted yesterday and came toward her, holding out his hand. She scrambled to her feet without taking it. She didn't like his touch. It was too...something.

Her shoulder hurt badly, but she didn't let it show on her face. "I'm sorry," she said again. "I'll do whatever you want me to."

He walked her back to the picnic area where

the woman with the clipboard was sending another pair off on their assignment. She watched
Beth and Detective Ryan approach, her look both
searching and—Beth thought—disgusted. But she
didn't say anything to Beth, only conferred with
him and eventually he steered her along the road
leading out of the park.

It turned out that they'd been allotted a stretch
of land just outside the park, thick with alders and
vine maples, a few Douglas firs and vast blackberry thickets. They walked slowly, searching the
ground for hollows, getting on hands and knees
to peer into the blackberries or wriggle under a
deadfall. Every thick growth of salal or salmon-
berry had to be investigated. Where shade had
grown deep enough, big clumps of sword ferns
could have hidden a lot more than one little girl.

Within a couple of hours, they were sweaty,
dirty and had scratches on their arms and faces.
He had to stop a couple of times to answer his
phone. Once he turned and looked at her as he
was talking, and the weight of his gaze made her
skin prickle even though she couldn't tell what he
was thinking.

But then she heard him say, "You don't remember her wearing red?" Pause. "You don't know
who she arrived with?" A few "uh-huhs" later, he
said, "Thank you for calling. We may be in touch."

When he ended the call, he said, "You're sure

her shorts were red. They couldn't have been pink?"

"No!"

"Did Sicily carry anything down to the beach?"

She frowned. "Anything?"

"The cooler? The blanket? You had a tote bag, too, and…what else?"

She tried to remember. "Nothing. My book was in my bag." Had Sicily carried anything? "I don't think so," Beth said slowly. "She started to reach for the cooler, but I thought it would be too heavy for her. And I already had the blanket draped over my shoulder."

"Once you got down there, did she help you spread the blanket?"

What was the *point* of these questions? Then she remembered the little bit she'd overheard of his phone conversation. She stiffened. "Those people didn't realize Sicily was with me."

"Assuming we were talking about Sicily at all, and not some other kid."

"If it was her, why wouldn't they remember she wore red shorts?"

"Do you remember what the other kids were wearing?" he asked, the voice of reason.

She opened her mouth, then had to close it. Dear God. "No," she whispered. "I didn't pay that much attention."

"Probably they didn't, either."

"So...were they the family I told you about?"

"I can't be sure. They were settled in the vicinity of you, they had four kids with them, they know another girl hung around with their crowd for a little while, and they left shortly before anyone started looking for Sicily."

"But...where was she when they left?"

"They thought she was rejoining her parents a little farther down the beach."

"So it wasn't her at all."

He studied her, his blue eyes cool and analytical. "Doesn't sound like it."

"You haven't found *anyone*..."

"Who saw her for sure? No."

Despair rose in her. "Then why are you even looking?"

"Sicily Marks is somewhere." He swept her with one more, hard look. "We'll find her."

SWEATY, BLEEDING AND frustrated, Mike took a break to eat the lunch the nearest Grange Hall ladies had brought for the volunteers. While he ate, he kept his distance from Beth Greenway. He wished he could keep his distance from her permanently. She was the most confusing damn woman he'd ever met.

What had happened today? Ms. Freezer Burn had either begun a major meltdown or she'd faked it. Truthfully, she'd scared the crap out of him

when she took off like that. That last sight of her
face, bleached pale with her eyes huge and dark
with humiliation and pain, was all he could think
about as he chased her. Mostly he'd been pissed;
she had to know he'd have no choice but to go after
her, and that there were more important things
he should be doing. And then, man, when he'd
seen her terror, when she'd scrabbled away like
she thought he was going to rape or beat her…
That had gotten to him.

She'd been subdued ever since. Embarrassed,
maybe, or she'd used up her limited emotional
content for the day, or she was satisfied that she'd
deflected his suspicion into pity? Who the hell
knew?

Fact: he would swear that last night and this
morning he had seen real anguish on her face, un-
like yesterday when he hadn't been so sure.

Fact: not a single person they'd yet found who
was at the beach yesterday had seen a skinny,
blonde, ten-year-old girl with Beth Greenway.
A few men admitted to having noticed the aunt.
No one had seen Sicily, unless she was the girl
the Bradshaws remembered, albeit they thought
vaguely she'd been wearing pink shorts and that
she'd headed in the wrong direction when they
packed up and left.

Fact: Sicily Marks's mother had died, by accident or suicide, barely over a month ago. Dad was

a no-show. The grandparents were cold fish. Aunt Beth was either another cold fish or…something else. Pack one box of the kid's possessions, take it to Goodwill or the Salvation Army, and Sicily's impact on Beth Greenway's home would be erased. And *that* alarmed Mike. Kid gone, stuff gone, problem solved.

Fact: he didn't want to believe Beth had anything to do with her niece's disappearance.

Fact: he felt wrenching pity and compassion every time he looked at her. When he wasn't feeling fury that a bunch of strangers cared more about what had happened to Sicily than anyone else seemed to. Except, maybe—and that was a big maybe—her aunt. And, yeah, he felt resentment, too, that Beth Greenway could awaken so many confusing emotions in him.

Fact: his *job* demanded that he look hard at everyone closely related to the missing girl. And Beth was closest of all.

SICILY HAD COME UP WITH A PLAN. The man had to open the door eventually, right? Unless he was going to starve her to death, which might work because she was *really* hungry. Or let her die of thirst, which was possible, too, because she was even thirstier than she was hungry.

But thinking logically—and Sicily was almost always logical—neither possibility was likely.

Why would the guy take the risk someone might see him carrying her in here if he meant to just ignore her until she was dead? He could have hit her over the head and buried her in the woods where no one would ever find her. And he *had* put a mattress in here, and bedding, and even the bucket, which she had finally had to hurriedly use.

Anyway, what she *thought* was that pretty soon he'd open the door and at least shove a bottle of water and maybe some food in. Or else he'd come in here to do something she didn't want to think about. Something like she'd seen guys do to Mom, except Mom seemed to want to do it, too. But Sicily knew about rape, and that men sometimes abducted little girls because they wanted to do *that* to them instead of with a grown woman.

Either way—when she heard the lock make that sliding sound, she'd dash over and flatten herself next to the door. The absolute *instant* it opened, she'd fling herself out. She'd decided she would go low. That would be a mistake if the man was bent over to push a tray in, but probably he would have food or a bottle of water in his hands. And she was really skinny and she'd catch him by surprise and wriggle past his legs. If he got his hands on her, she'd struggle like anything. She could kick and bite and scream, and all it would take was a loosened grip and she'd run like anything. She could knock furniture in his way. *Anything* to get to the outer door ahead of him and have the couple seconds she'd need to unlock it and fling it open and run up the few stairs she knew were there and then she'd be outside where she'd have a chance.

It was the best plan she could come up with.

Only she couldn't help herself, she fell asleep. And she didn't hear the door opening. The first thing she knew, a man was in the room staring at her. She had the creepy feeling he might have been staring for a long time. He had a Burger King bag in his hand and a giant drink from Burger King, too, with a straw already in it. And he said, "You're probably hungry, kid. So here you go."

He set both on the floor and backed out while she was sitting up.

"Wait!" she cried. "I want to know…"

The door closed, the lock scraped and she was alone again.

CHAPTER FIVE

AT TWO O'CLOCK, MIKE GOT THE call he'd been waiting for all day. In grim silence, he listened to his partner and then asked, "What about Thursday?"

Sometime during that call, Beth had turned to look at him, caught either by his expression or his tone of voice the few times he spoke. She went completely still, and her eyes dilated.

To Rulickzkowski, he said, "I need her cell phone records."

"I'll get on it."

When Mike snapped his phone shut and hooked it on his belt, she only waited.

"Tell me about Sicily's last couple of days."

"Last couple…? You mean, before…?"

"That's what I mean. Thursday. Friday."

Her face changed. "You know she didn't go to school Friday. How?"

"You didn't think I'd find out?"

"It didn't occur to me it mattered," she said stiffly, then corrected herself. "It doesn't matter. She wasn't really sick."

What a piece of work. "Yeah, then what was she?" He made his voice soft, dangerous.

"She was upset Thursday. She got a C on a math test."

"You told me how smart she is."

"Sicily *is* smart. And she's always gotten straight As. But I told you how often Rachel moved and Sicily had to change schools. There was no consistency. And all of a sudden she's in a school district where a really high percentage of the students excel. She's behind, and for the first time ever she's surrounded by students who are ahead of her. Friday morning she told me she had a stomachache. I think maybe she did, but that it was because of stress, so I let her stay home, okay?"

"By herself? All day?"

"No. I left her for a couple of hours while I went into work. But I didn't have an important event this weekend and so I went home at eleven. I worked from there the rest of the day, okay?"

They could check on her computer to see how much time she'd actually spent on it.

"And Sicily?"

"By early afternoon, she said she felt better. We spent an hour working on the math—" she made a face "—for what good I did her."

"What do you mean?"

"She's in an accelerated class. They're already doing algebra. I didn't like algebra when I took it, and I don't remember much. *She* seemed to figure out a concept she'd been missing, though, so she was happy."

"Did anyone else see Sicily on Friday? Or from the time she left school on Thursday?"

She was shaking and holding herself in by force of will. Mike had seen corpses with more color in their faces. Her very dignity made him feel like a son of a bitch, but all he was doing was his job. And somehow he had no trouble predicting what she was going to say.

"I don't know." She closed her eyes momentarily. Then, so quietly he could barely hear her, she said, "No. Probably not. Unless one of the neighbors saw us driving away Saturday morning. Sicily didn't leave the house Friday."

Goddamn. This thing only got uglier.

"You called the school."

"My partner did. It took most of the day to track down Sicily's teacher to confirm her attendance records."

"So now she knows…" She broke off.

"Sicily's disappearance is plastered across the newspapers today. Did you think we were keeping it secret?"

"No. It doesn't matter." Those wounded dark eyes met his. "What are you going to do now?"

Deploy officers to question her neighbors. Find out when someone *had* last seen the girl. It would

be very, very good for Beth Greenway if someone
had happened to be looking out the window to see
Sicily and Beth in the car backing out of the garage, the girl chattering and smiling.

Mike wasn't putting any money on the odds of
that happening.

"You and I are going to keep looking," he said,
and walked toward the next clump of sword ferns.
It was a minute before he heard her footsteps behind him.

The afternoon had been as worthless and frus-
trating as the morning. If Mike was tired at the
end of it, Beth had to be ready to collapse. After
the earlier exchange, they'd barely spoken. His
phone rang on and off, but she didn't ask any questions about those calls and he didn't offer any information.

What really frustrated him was how aware of
her he remained. He didn't have to turn his head
to know exactly where she was at every moment.
When he did look at her, his gut clenched. She
was dirty and sweaty, and all he could think was
how beautiful she was. His gaze would catch
on the graceful line of her neck when she lifted
damp, tangled hair from it to cool herself momentarily. The swell of her breasts beneath the T-shirt.
The length of her legs or the way a narrow waist
flowed into a great ass. Never mind those amaz-

ing cheekbones or mouth that was a little pouty when she relaxed it.

Lucky he didn't think with his dick. Where she was concerned, it and his head were in opposite corners of the rink. Right now, she was his best suspect in Sicily's disappearance. The fact that Mike Ryan, the man, didn't believe she'd hurt anyone didn't count.

At about five, he talked to Phyllis Chang, keeping this conversation private by walking a distance away from Beth, who was exploring the edges of a particularly dense blackberry thicket. He saw her stop at what looked like a small tunnel leading into it and drop to her knees. By the time he reached her, she lay on her belly and was apparently trying to squirm into the hole, which wasn't big enough for her. He was pretty sure she was swearing under her breath as thorns hooked her hair, shirt and skin.

"That was made by wildlife," he told her. "Probably raccoons. The canes aren't disturbed around it. There's no way Sicily could be in there."

Beth's head dropped onto her forearm. After a minute she wriggled backward, giving him one of those uncomfortable jabs of lust as she half rose to her knees and her hips waggled back and forth a couple of times as she retreated.

Then she sat up, face flushed. "I told you Sicily's skinny. I think she could have gotten in there." Her voice was a little husky, maybe from disuse, given that the muttered profanities he'd heard were the first words from her in close to two hours.

"If she was running from someone, maybe," he agreed. "But she disappeared a day and a half ago. Why wouldn't she have come out by now?"

Beth looked both mutinous and defeated.

"It's almost five-thirty." He hesitated, knowing she wouldn't like what he was going to say. "We're suspending the search."

Her head lifted. "What? But it'll be daylight for another three hours!"

"We're not taking a break until tomorrow. We're calling it off for good, until we have some clue where to look."

Hot red color rose to her cheeks as if he'd slapped them. "You said you'd find her! You swore!"

Once again, he squatted to bring himself to her level. One of his knees creaked. This had been a hell of a couple of days. "Ms. Greenway, we've had between twenty and thirty volunteers scouring this park and the surrounding land. You and I have worked our way from the road to the bluff." He gestured and she turned her head. A stand of vine maples and a couple of scraggly red-barked madronas were all that separated them from the drop-off to the beach.

"We can keep going."

"She's not here." He tried to make his voice

gentle, in case she was genuine, but implacable because she had to face facts.

Fact: not a single person they'd yet found who was at the beach yesterday had seen a skinny, blonde, ten-year-old girl with Beth Greenway. As of this moment, there was no confirmation that *anyone* had seen Sicily Marks since she left school Thursday afternoon.

"You're exhausted," he said. "How much sleep did you get last night? Four or five hours? You can't keep on this way."

"I can," she said stubbornly. "I'll keep looking."

"No."

"You can't make me leave."

"Yeah, if you force the issue, I can. County search-and-rescue and the sheriff's department had permission to search on this land. Once we call it quits, you're trespassing."

She stared at him as if caught between shock and hate. Then, without a word, she stood up, walked around him and started back the way they'd come.

He followed. "I'm not giving up, Ms. Greenway."

She didn't stop or look back. "What would you call this, Detective Ryan?"

"Changing tactics."

"To what?" Her tone was curiously flat. This was the woman he'd first encountered, so locked down that no real emotion seeped into her voice. "Digging up my backyard?"

"If necessary."

There was a hitch between one step and the next; her shoulders stiffened. That was all. She kept walking, looking neither to the right or left.

A few birds chittered in trees. Farther away, gulls let out harsh cries. He heard a rustle in the blackberries, saw a squirrel dash up the trunk of a fir. He and Beth didn't talk.

They reached the blacktop road and were passed by several cars. He recognized volunteers and raised his hand to them. Marching along the verge, Beth didn't even glance toward the passing vehicles or their drivers.

"They gave a hell of a lot of time," he remarked mildly.

"Not a one of them would meet my eyes."

He frowned, only now realizing that it was true. Yeah, he'd noticed how dismissive Phyllis was this morning, but thought he was the one to trigger Beth's emotional breakdown. But maybe it hadn't been only him.

If she'd been a different woman, if circumstances were different, he might have lied and said something like, "I think you're imagining things. They were preoccupied, that's all. Thinking about Sicily, not you." But he didn't.

"They maybe get angry if they've been at this

long," he finally said. "Mostly they're looking for adults who are in trouble because they didn't take common-sense precautions or who've done something stupid, or kids who got lost because no adult was paying attention."

"I would give anything not to have fallen asleep." She turned a flushed face to him. "Is that what you want to hear me say?" A long scratch marred one of her cheeks. Dried blood was beaded along it. "But she's ten years old. Not five, not six or seven. I don't know that much about children, but you can't tell me most parents of a ten-year-old wouldn't have felt comfortable lying back on a blanket in the sun and closing their eyes." Her voice had begun to rise. "If you're right and she's not here somewhere, hurt or… If she's not there, then someone abducted her right in the middle of a crowded park. Have you even tried to find out who or why? Or have you already made up your mind she was never here at all?" One last glare, and she stalked away.

"I'm pursuing all possibilities," he said to her back, and wondered if he was being entirely honest.

SICILY HATED THAT THE COLA made her have to pee again, but she'd been so thirsty. She'd worried, staring at the cheeseburger and French fries, whether maybe they were drugged or poisoned, but in the end she was so hungry, she had to take a chance. First she took the pickles out and scraped as much of the ketchup as possible off the bun, like she always did unless she was the one doing the ordering, in which case she asked for her cheeseburgers plain.

That was one thing she liked about Aunt Beth. Even though they ate fast food all the time, Mom had always—*always*—rolled her eyes when Sicily explained to the person taking orders that no, she didn't want anything except hamburger and cheese and lettuce. Aunt Beth had only nodded and, the one other time they stopped for burgers, ordered Sicily's just the way she liked it.

Sicily was so hungry now, she hardly even noticed the ketchup that had soaked into the bun. The French fries were so good, she almost moaned.

Only after she'd eaten did she sit and think about the man. She wished he hadn't surprised her when she was asleep. Even if she hadn't had the chance to put her plan into action, she should have been as observant as possible. What if she never saw his face again and later the police wanted her to describe him? When she was way younger, she'd been big into Nancy Drew. Now she read young adult books, a lot of which were paranormal, but Nancy had been kidnapped and held prisoner lots of times. *She* could always tell every detail later.

But Sicily realized that when she closed her

eyes, she could see him. He had a goatee that was lots darker than the long streaky blond hair that had fallen forward and hidden part of his face from her. But his nose was straight, and his eyes were kind of a gray-green and bloodshot, like Mom's eyes were a lot. He was tall and super thin and the hands that had held the pop and the Burger King bag were shaking. So...he was probably using drugs. Not the kind of stuff Mom liked. He was so skinny and wired, Sicily thought he could be a crackhead. There were always some around the places she and Mom had lived. Even Mom had avoided them, because she said they were desperate and they'd steal from anybody.

But...why would one want to steal me? she asked herself miserably.

When she cried, she tried really hard to be quiet, so he wouldn't hear her.

BETH DROVE HOME BECAUSE SHE didn't know what else she could do. She felt like a wind-up toy whose workings were slowing down. Things that should be automatic required conscious thought. Her eyes were dry and burning because she had to remind herself to blink. Every movement was stiff and jerky. She struggled to concentrate when she was on the road.

Now it's time to put your foot on the brake. The light turned green. Go.

Even though the truck ahead of her on the freeway was going below the speed limit, it seemed to take too much effort to check the rearview mirrors and change lanes, so she stayed where she was, slowing when the truck did, speeding up when it did. It was like giving herself up to the current in a river, letting it carry her. City traffic required more effort than she thought she could bear, but at last she was safely in her garage. As the door rolled down behind her, she sagged forward and rested her forehead on the steering wheel.

She didn't fool herself that she'd gotten away from *him*. A couple of hours later, he showed up. Beth hardly looked at him as she let him into the house, but even so she felt his imposing presence. She went to an easy chair in the living room and sat down. He settled on the sofa and placed his notebook and pen down on the coffee table. Elbows on his knees, he looked at her.

"Did you get anything to eat?"

"Yes." Soup—she hadn't been sure she could swallow anything more substantial.

He nodded. "All right. Tell me about your search for Sicily's father."

That surprised Beth for some reason, enough that she met his eyes and was startled anew by how blue they were. "What do you mean?"

"You said you looked for him. How? Did you

look in the phone book? On the internet? Did you have a starting place?"

"I hired a private investigator."

"Who?"

She told him and he nodded again, as if he recognized the name.

"Would you give me access to whatever information he gave you?"

"He didn't find him."

"But knowing where he looked could save me time."

"Oh." Her thoughts were wading knee-deep in sludge. "Okay. Um…give me a minute and I can find his report."

It took her longer than a minute, because she hadn't put it in the file she'd started with a label that said Sicily. She had intended for it to hold vaccine records, report cards, that kind of thing. Instead, the report was in Miscellaneous.

Detective Ryan read it, head bent. She found herself fixated on the hand holding the single sheet of paper. She'd noticed his hands before. They were big, the fingers blunt-tipped, nails cut short. The tendons stood out. A few hairs, darker than those on his head, curled on the backs of his fingers. He had enough scratches on his hands and forearms to make it look as if he'd lost the battle with an enraged raccoon. Her hands looked as bad. The scratches on her face and arms and even legs, made when a long thorn had snagged her through her pants, had stung when she'd showered.

"He's a musician." Detective Ryan looked up. *Mike.* She was trying not to think of him by his first name, because she didn't want to kid herself that he was anything to her but a cop.

"Well, he was. I don't know about now. He was a lead guitarist for a Seattle heavy metal group that got far enough to open for some bigger bands. I... went to see them play once."

"Then you did know him."

She shook her head. "I was curious, that's all. I never even told Rachel I was there. We talked on the phone once in a while in those days, and she kept on about Chad, so I wanted to see him. That's all."

"Was he good?"

"I don't know. I'm probably not a very good judge. I hated the music."

He grinned, a flash of white teeth, and she felt a bittersweet pang in her chest. Oh, dear Lord, what a smile did to that hard face!

"What kind of music do you listen to?"

She wondered if he was trying to relax her, soften her up so that he could take her unaware when he slipped in a stiletto of a question. But she said, "Jazz. Folk. Some classical. I have a weakness for Broadway show tunes."

"Phantom?"

"I've seen it four times."

He laughed again. "You're a romantic, then."

"No." Being romantic implied some faith in human relationships. She had none. "I like the music, that's all."

He quirked an eyebrow, but his eyes were so sharp she knew he was trying to see more than she liked.

After a minute, he asked, "Do you have any idea how long it's been since your sister has had any contact with this—" he glanced down at the P.I.'s report although Beth doubted he'd forgotten the name "—Chad Marks?"

"Not really. Sicily doesn't remember him at all. I'm pretty sure he and Rachel had broken up by the time Sicily turned two. I think Rachel tried to get child support from him and that's when he more or less disappeared. The band had broken up. Rachel kept watching for him to crop up with a new band, because it made her mad that he wouldn't pay anything. Supposedly he had wanted kids, too."

"All right," Mike—no, Detective Ryan—said. "We'll try to find him. We have resources the P.I. didn't, but if he's no longer in the state it may be tough."

He asked questions about Rachel: her friends, who had come to the funeral, if Sicily had talked about any of those friends or men her mother had been seeing. Beth had to keep shaking her head or saying, "I don't know," which set her stomach to churning because it reminded her of that first day, when she'd been so humiliated by how little she knew about her own niece.

She was unprepared when he held her gaze and said, "What was the problem between you and your sister?"

Her throat closed. It was a minute before she said, "It's ancient history. It has absolutely nothing to do with Sicily."

"You don't get along with your parents, you didn't have anything to do with your sister, *she* didn't get along with your parents or you, either. Right now, I want to know everything about Sicily's life. Family's real basic to a kid. Why does nobody in her family speak to anyone else?"

With difficulty, Beth answered, "My parents shouldn't have had children. My father was a virtual stranger to both Rachel and me. My mother..." *Breathe.* She thought about her mother as seldom as possible. "You met her."

"I did."

"Did you ask *her* why we're estranged?"

"No, but I will."

She nodded and sat with her back straight and her hands folded on her lap.

He contemplated her. "You're a tough nut to crack, Ms. Greenway."

"I have nothing to do with Sicily's disappearance. I would do anything to get her back. Please don't waste time trying to figure me out."

"But you know I have to."

He asked more questions. Was it a surprise that Rachel asked her to take custody of Sicily? Yes. When had she taken Sicily home? As soon as the police called; her phone number had been in Rachel's address book. Was Sicily surprised that an aunt she didn't know had come to take her home? No.

"Her mother had told Sicily that if anything ever happened, she would go live with me."

How long had Rachel been back in the Seattle area? Two years. Where had she and Sicily lived? Beth knew only the address of the apartment where she'd picked Sicily up; she didn't remember the exact number but told him close enough.

"Tell me about her drug use."

Beth shared as much as she knew, which was very little.

It went on and on. He kept working his way back to her parents, but now she was prepared.

They, or at least her mother, had seemed miffed that Rachel had named Beth guardian of Sicily rather than them.

"Given the estrangement, why are you so sure they won't contest for custody?"

"They don't want her."

She wondered if that were entirely true. The very idea that her mother might *want* to have a vulnerable girl in her care once again sent shivers of horror through Beth. For herself, she had never been brave. But she would do anything to keep Sicily away from them.

Safe.

She shuddered, and the detective's eyes sharpened.

Too late.

He wanted to know more about school— whether Sicily had gone home with any kids, mentioned any parents or other adults. No, no, no. Had Beth taken Sicily to work with her? No.

He asked questions until she had gone numb. She felt like she had on the freeway last night, as if she were being pulled along in the slipstream of something—some*one*—more powerful than her. As if the will to change lanes, to pull to the shoulder and say, "No more," was beyond her.

And then he said, "Would you permit a search of your home?"

Her stomach cramped. She hadn't felt a pain so intense since she was a child, living in a state of constant fear. She couldn't stop herself from hunching forward slightly. "Yes."

"I'll leave you alone now, then. Did you intend to go to work tomorrow?"

She looked at him incredulously. "You're kidding."

"I want to be sure you're here in the morning."

"No. I don't plan to go to work. I'll be here."

She didn't stand. Couldn't. After a moment he nodded, rose to his feet and let himself out. Beth curled forward, hoping to ease the pain. She'd looked at the clock a minute ago. It was after nine. Sicily had disappeared almost thirty-four hours ago.

THE MAN BROUGHT HER A cheeseburger and French fries again. Once again, his arrival surprised her. "Stay where you are," he said sharply when she started to stand.

She sank back down. "Can I use the bathroom?"

"That's what the bucket's for."

This time she thought he looked kind of familiar. She didn't think she'd met him, but maybe she had a long time ago. Mom had lots of friends. Sicily might have seen him back when they used to live here in Seattle.

"Can't I *please* use the bathroom?" she begged.

He hesitated, then said, "All right. It doesn't have a window, so don't think you can get away. Then you gotta do something for me."

Sicily nodded meekly even though the last thing he'd said scared her a lot. This time when she stood up he only backed away, leaving the door standing open.

"That way," he told her, jerking his head.

It was a basement apartment, just like she'd thought. She entered the living room, with a small window that allowed only a glint of lights that must be in another building or the house up above them. It was nighttime, she could see that much. Some strange music was coming from outside... well, probably upstairs. Sort of tinkling, but without much melody.

There was a TV, a futon with a really grungy cover and an upholstered chair that looked like a cat had been tearing at it. They were gross; Sicily wouldn't have wanted to sit on either. Trash was heaped everywhere, mostly from fast food, but also dirty dishes and some magazines with naked women on them. It took her a second to tear her fascinated gaze from the cover of one that lay open on the floor. What was the woman doing...?

The tiny kitchen was really disgusting. Sicily wondered if he'd let her out of the bedroom if she offered to clean, but *ew*. She bet he didn't have any rubber gloves and she wasn't touching anything without them.

The outside door was at the end of a small hall. Kitchen and bathroom were on one side, a second bedroom on the other. Pretending she was Nancy Drew, Sicily paid careful attention. If it was night now, she'd been here a whole twenty-four hours. Aunt Beth might be looking for her, but that didn't mean she'd find her.

It's up to me. Somehow, I have to escape.

She turned her head enough to see into the bedroom, with dirty clothes all over the floor and filthy sheets on the bed.

"There's the bathroom," he said, in a voice that told her not to take one more step toward the outside door. Which was big and also had a dead bolt.

Sicily braced herself and went into the bathroom. She shut the door and gazed in dismay at the toilet. The seat was up and he obviously missed *a lot*. Plus the toilet bowl and sink both were scummy with brown rings. The shower was really little, like one of those in an RV, and of course it was scuzzy and the curtain was cracked.

She hesitated, then grabbed a wad of toilet paper and used it to let the seat down. There was a bar of soap beside the sink, so she wet the toilet paper and got it soapy, then scrubbed the seat and finally dried it before she sat down. This was better than using the bucket, and anyway now she knew the layout of the apartment. She could go even faster when she did make her break.

He knocked on the door. "What are you doing in there?"

"What do you think I'm doing?" she yelled back. She wiped and flushed, washed her hands and then tried to turn the fan on, but it was broken. She let herself out of the bathroom and immediately started toward her bedroom. Which was clean. And she was so hungry, she didn't mind eating the same thing again. She tried to think about that, and not what he'd said. *Then you gotta do something for me.* He wouldn't have brought her food if... She couldn't finish the thought.

"All right, kid, hold on a minute."

He went out and closed the door, but she didn't hear the lock. She didn't have time to even think about dashing for it, though, because he came back with something in his hand. It looked kind of like a smart phone, but not quite.

"I'm going to record you. You're going to say what I tell you to say and nothing else. All right?"

Her voice shook a little when she said, "All right."

CHAPTER SIX

HE TEETERED ON THE EDGE OF THE kidney-shaped swimming pool, frantically searching the water, which a part of him knew ought to be clear and sparkling blue. It wasn't. The pool was deep: so deep, he couldn't see the bottom. So deep, he couldn't tell how far down he was looking. Finally, desperate, he dove in, swimming down, down, down, his eyes open and his head turning.

It seemed like forever before he saw anything. Despairing, he knew he'd have to go back up for a breath, and then... Oh, God. *There*. The shape was dark, unmoving, hanging in the water like submerged garbage. But he could see—God!—pale hair floating around the head. His lungs screamed for air, but his hands closed on the small child and he kicked hard to drive them upward. Light began to penetrate the water and he could almost see the face. He didn't have to—it was Nate, of course it was Nate.

I'm too late. I should have been here.

His entire body was in agony now. Bubbles trailed behind him as he released his last remaining air. With a final kick, he burst through the surface and dragged in a breath, then another. He lifted the child, turning him onto his back, and saw the still, white face.

It was Sicily's dead face, not his son's. Not Nate's.

Mike couldn't fall back asleep after waking from the nightmare. He hadn't had it in a long time. Months. And now there was a new twist, though he supposed it shouldn't be a surprise.

Hell, he'd wanted to get up early anyway, he thought wearily, sitting on the edge of the bed with his head hanging. A couple of Edmonds P.D. officers had knocked on doors in Beth's neighborhood yesterday, but as usual hadn't found anyone home at a few houses. Mike hoped to catch people before they left for work this morning.

At 5:00 a.m., it was still dark as he heated frozen waffles in his toaster and sipped coffee. The sky was beginning to lighten when he backed out of his garage. Drizzle on the windshield told him the weekend's nice weather had passed. Disgruntled, he thought about going back for a rain slicker, but it wasn't coming down that hard. The prospect of getting wet didn't make the morning sound any worse than it already was.

He hated knowing exactly what the expression on Beth's face would be as she let them in. They'd been lucky she'd agreed to the search. Lucky she

hadn't yet lawyered up. As heavily as he was leaning on her, she likely would soon. It was a point
in her favor that she hadn't yet, that she was being
more than cooperative.

He parked in front of her house, and avoided
looking toward the light in the front window. He
wondered if she'd slept any better than he had last
night. Was she having nightmares, too?

Shoulders hunched against the rain, he walked
four doors down to the first of three homes where
no one had answered the door yesterday. The sky
was fully light now, and the drizzle had picked up,
chilling him. It was—he glanced at his watch—
six-thirty in the morning now. There were lights
on in about half the houses on the block.

Still no answer at the first place.

At the second house a balding man answered
the door. The collar of his shirt was turned up
and an unknotted tie hung loose. He looked irritated. "Yeah?"

Mike showed his badge and explained who he
was and what he wanted.

"Which house?"

"The green one across the street and two doors
down. Number 6134."

He looked. "Don't know the people there."

"Have you seen anyone coming or going recently?"

"I wouldn't have paid attention if I had," he said brusquely.

Mike showed him Sicily's school photo. "You're certain you haven't seen this child?"

"If a kid lives there, I've never seen her."

Mike thanked him, turned the collar of his thin jacket up and crossed the street to the last house. Someone was home here, too, unless a light was on a timer.

But no one came to the door; he didn't hear the faintest stir inside. So maybe the home owner was away and the light was indeed on a timer.

So—one down, two still to go. He'd keep an eye on the two places, try them both later. But any hope of calling off the search was dead in the water.

Walking back toward Beth's house, he pulled out his cell phone and called in to find out whether he'd gotten the warrant to place a tracking device on her car.

HAVING YOUR HOUSE SEARCHED WAS unspeakably awful. Degrading.

When Beth answered the door and stared stonily at Mike, he nodded and said, "Morning."

She simply stood back to let him in, as she'd done too many times already. This time was different; she came close to hating him. What hope was there that he'd find Sicily when he was focused so intensely on her?

"I'm heading out," she said abruptly, reaching for her purse. "Call me when you're done."

"I need to ask you to stay, Ms. Greenway."

She went still and her fingers flexed into a fist. "Ask, or order?"

"At this point, it's a request." Expressionless as his voice was, there was no mistaking the message. He expected soon to have grounds to compel her to answer his questions and open any part of her life that he chose. It was a warning, a threat. *Cooperate or else.*

"Why do I need to be here?" She turned to face him, chin high. "So you can achieve maximum humiliation?"

"You know that's not what I want." The pity—if that's what it was—in his eyes enraged her.

That rage gave her the backbone to say, "Then what possible purpose will be served by making me sit here while strangers paw through my closets and my underwear drawer and dig up my new flower bed? Answer me that."

"We might have questions for you. The process might go easier and faster with your cooperation."

Oh, God. She didn't know if she could bear any of this.

The doorbell rang.

Burning with that hate, Beth walked away,

going straight through the house to the back patio. She left the French door open and stood outside beneath the cover of the green-striped awning. She clasped her arms as tightly as she could against the cold and stared at the gray drizzle. She needed the cold, to cool fury and mortification that radiated from her belly and chest, which seemed to have become a furnace with the thermostat cranked lethally high.

There were voices, footsteps. More voices. She refused to look. She assumed there was something like a CSI van in her driveway now. Perhaps a couple of them. Other police cars. How the neighbors would stare. Beth wondered how long it would take for someone to tip off a reporter, for a news truck or two to roll up to the curb. What a nice addition to tonight's TV news: footage of her house being searched. *Search for missing child suspended, aunt now under suspicion.* She could hear it as a lead-in to the six o'clock news.

He came out to ask if she'd mind if they backed her car out of the garage. How courteous.

"You know where my purse is," she said tonelessly, not looking at him. "The keys are in the outside pocket."

"Beth…"

She dug her fingernails into the flesh of her arms. *I will not feel.*

It didn't work any more than it had Saturday at

the beach. She felt frighteningly like she had Sunday, when she'd come so near to imploding. She wanted to hit him, scratch him, *hurt* him. Beth had never known a feeling could be so corrosive. *Oh, Sicily.*

It had been forty-five hours since Sicily had disappeared off the face of the earth.

Eventually, when she didn't answer, he went away.

"Here's your food, kid."

Sicily looked without enthusiasm at the Burger King bag he tossed toward her. She used to *like* cheeseburgers and French fries. Now she didn't know if she'd ever want them again.

"Don't you ever eat anything different?" she asked.

"You complaining, kid?" He sounded offended.

Um…yeah?

"Usually I have cereal for breakfast," she muttered, thinking maybe it hadn't been such a good idea to say anything.

He grunted. "I guess I could get you an egg sandwich tomorrow morning."

Okay, that was good. He planned to keep feeding her. Of course, he might keep feeding her even if he'd cut off her little finger to mail to her grandparents. Sicily hoped he didn't see her shiver. She didn't like the way he kept leaning there in the doorway, watching her.

"Why are you doing this?" she blurted out.

"They owe me."

"They?" she asked cautiously.

"They're filthy rich, you know. Did they ever share any of that money with you and your mommy?"

She didn't like the way he said *mommy*. It was creepy.

He knew Mom. He must have. And...hated her?

She almost said, "I should remember you, shouldn't I," but stopped herself in time. She was already freaked by the way he looked at her sometimes. She couldn't figure it out. It was as though he was supercurious about her and maybe bothered because he didn't want to be. Or something. It was a good sign that he wanted to hang out talking to her, wasn't it? It might mean he'd become lots less careful. She was waiting for her moment.

"No," she admitted. "Mom didn't like them. I barely even met them."

He snorted. "All your mother had to do was be nice to them and they'd have bought you pretty dresses and shit. Anything you wanted. Anything *she* asked for."

A huge, really awful thought came to Sicily. This man could be her father. That could be why he stared at her the way he did. He hadn't seen her since she was, like, a baby. That could explain why he was sort of curious.

She squinted at him, trying to match him up to her remembrance of the too-tiny figures in the photograph of her dad's band. She couldn't. But... he did look familiar. People had actual memories from when they were really little, didn't they? Could she remember him from when she was two? Or maybe she'd seen him after that. Mom said he'd walked out on them, but she didn't say she'd never seen him again. He might have come by sometimes for a while. Or...maybe Mom had had pictures around. They could've gotten left behind during one of their moves. Sometimes when they were evicted they couldn't get all their stuff.

Oh...yuck! was all she could think.

"Mom really hated them," she told him, although that wasn't quite right. Mom talked like they'd been horrible to her, but sometimes she called home and sounded...sort of soft and pleading. And then she'd cry after she'd hung up. Hearing her voice like that had always made Sicily feel hollow inside. She'd known for a long time that her mother wasn't very strong. That *she* had to be strong for them both. But she didn't understand even a little bit why, if they'd treated Mom as badly as she said they did, she'd *want* to talk to them. Sicily wondered if Aunt Beth called home, too. If she had since Sicily came to live with her, it was when she wasn't around.

"Then you'd think she'd have gotten off on taking them for everything she could get," the guy said. *Oh, please, not my father.*

When Sicily didn't say anything, he shrugged and left. The lock scraped, and she was alone again. Her stomach growled, so she opened the bag and looked inside.

"Oh, wow." The room was so empty, her voice sort of echoed. "A cheeseburger."

MIKE STOOD AT THE KITCHEN window looking out at the back of that goddamn stubborn woman's head. She was playing the martyr, which pissed him off big-time. Her message wasn't subtle: he'd forced her to stay, but he couldn't force her not to suffer. She had to be freezing out there in jeans and a thin cashmere sweater that clung to her slim body and had a V neck that bared her pale throat and chest. At one point, in a fit of frustration he'd snatched a coat from her closet and carried it out, thrusting it into her arms as he snarled, "Put this on."

She didn't acknowledge his existence with even a flicker of her eyes. When he checked five minutes later, the coat lay over the back of a chair.

He was painfully reminded of the day Sicily went missing, Beth standing like a marble statue while the search went on around her. He knew damn well this would end the same way, too, with Beth so cold her bones would rattle. But what the hell was he supposed to do? Pick her up and haul her ass inside? In her eyes, he'd already stripped her of her dignity. Why not rip away any last shreds?

But he couldn't do it. All he could do was hide his turmoil, be the professional he was and keep an eye on the techs working her house, looking in every nook and cranny, checking out her computer, using black lights and luminol in a few places where they were likely to find blood splatters. The shower drain showed a hint of blood. He had to go out to ask her about it.

"I cut my leg shaving this morning." She bent down and lifted the leg of her jeans to show a wince-worthy two-inch raw gouge on her shin. "I was…distracted." Her voice was flat but not dull as it had been Saturday at the park. He took a closer look at her unemotional, marble pale face, which gave no clues. Something was going on inside her, but he didn't know what. He returned to the bathroom.

"Yeah, that'd be about the right amount of blood," conceded the tech. She took a scraping anyway.

They'd borrowed a cadaver-sniffing dog that arrived with its handler about eleven. When Mike let them out in the backyard, he saw the first emotion on Beth's face in hours. He felt like a monster.

She swiveled on her heel and went in the house. Voices came from the bedroom wing. Someone was in the kitchen, banging cupboard doors. Her eyes got wild and her head turned, as if she sought a bolt hole. Following her, Mike was slashed by regret. *I'm doing this to her. I'm hunting her as relentlessly as a foxhound.* Body still stiff, eyes frantic, she got as far as the middle of the living room and stopped, apparently having realized she had nowhere to escape to. Standing in the doorway to the kitchen where he could see her, Mike wanted to slam his fist into a wall. He didn't think he'd ever felt like a bigger son of a bitch.

He was breaking her.

It's my job.

He'd done it before, he'd do it again. He hadn't had any choice this morning. Until they found some proof that Sicily Marks had lived beyond three-thirty Thursday afternoon when she stepped off the school bus at the corner, they had to take seriously the possibility that her aunt had killed her or was otherwise involved in her disappearance.

He was doing what he had to do.

But this time, he believed he was hounding an innocent woman. Worse yet, a woman so vulnerable he dreaded finding out who or what had wounded her deep enough to leave those unseen scars.

She stood where she was, as if afraid of being cornered. He saw how hard she was breathing. Whatever had been sustaining her earlier wasn't working anymore. Now, he suspected pride alone held her in place. She stared at the wall, refusing to look at a single person invading her house.

Including him.

Half an hour later, the dog handler brought his now wet and muddy lab through the side gate, shook his head at Mike and opened the door to his van so the dog could leap in. "Nothing." The computer geek let him know that on Friday Beth had been on her computer most of the day, off and on, the way she'd said.

"Nothing," echoed the head of the crime scene crew in a low voice that wouldn't be overheard by the reporters hovering avidly on the sidewalk, crowding as close as they could, cameras and microphones bristling. "If anything happened to that girl here, it didn't involve blood."

"Thanks," he said then watched as they departed, ignoring shouted questions. "No statement," he said, and went back inside the house.

She was right where he'd left her. Arms clasping herself as if for comfort or to hold in…what? *Déjà vu*, he thought.

"We're done," he said, as gently as he could.

"Then get out of my house." Her voice had the texture of broken glass. It didn't sound like her. She turned to face him, her eyes glittering with rage. "Don't come back without a warrant."

"You know we had to do this."

"You've likely destroyed my reputation and with it my business. All so the police could look like they weren't sitting on their hands. If Sicily is found alive…" She fought for control. "I don't know what she and I will do. That's what you accomplished today."

He felt like he'd taken a fist to the gut. Right this minute, it didn't help to tell himself he'd had no choice but to take this step. "I'm sorry that's how you see it." He sounded wooden.

"Please go."

He nodded wordlessly just as his phone rang. He glanced down, not recognizing the number although it was a Seattle prefix.

"Ryan."

"Detective Ryan, this is Sergeant Chen. Seattle P.D. We talked."

"Sure, I remember," he said hoarsely. "You've got something?"

"A possible address for Chad Marks. A house in the University District. We plan to move right away."

"Tell me the address. I can be there in twenty minutes." If he drove like a sixteen-year-old out for his first solo with dad's car. Chen agreed to hang back until Mike got there.

He'd paused on Beth's doorstep, and realized the door was open behind him. He hesitated, then turned. "We may have located Marks."

Fear and hope flared in her eyes. She nodded.

"I'll see you are kept informed."

Her thank-you was stiff. He still hadn't moved when she closed the door. Mike had the sick feeling he might not see her again unless it was on the Channel 5 news. But he knew better. She might think she was done with him, but whether she liked it or not he was still primary. He'd be back, and she'd by God let him in whether she detested him or not.

MIKE WONDERED WHY, GIVEN THE price of real estate in Seattle, anyone would let what had once been a decent house end up in this condition.

Most of the other houses on the street shadowed by the Ship Canal Bridge were shabby. They were probably all rented to students. Lawns were patchy and yellowing, porches sagged, paint peeled. But this one looked as if it had been transported from a slum: several windows were boarded over, moss was eating the roof and broken beer bottles made the front walk perilous. A faded, torn U.S. flag served as a curtain in the only upstairs window that was intact. A rusting hulk rested on cinder blocks in the tiny backyard off the alley.

Mike, Chen and a detective named Jarrel Wright were walking up to the front door. Two more Seattle P.D. officers had all possible exits covered.

Glass crunched under their feet. All three stepped gingerly up rotting front steps. Movement inside sounded like rats scuttling for holes. Mike's hand slid to the butt of his gun.

The doorbell hung two inches out from the wall, one wire severed. Chen hammered on the door.

Silence.

They glanced at each other. The sergeant called, "Police! Open the door."

After another delay, and a couple of thumps and bangs, the door cracked open a few inches and a face appeared. Mike wasn't sure he'd ever seen so much metal on any face—eyebrows, nose, lip, ears. Damn, it would weigh you down, he couldn't help thinking with the part of his brain that wasn't warily watching for the wrong kind of movement.

"Police." Chen held up identification. "May we come in."

"Cops? What the…? We didn't do anything."

"We need to talk to you and anyone else residing in this house." Chen was a mild-looking guy, but he didn't sound mild.

Reluctantly, the pierced dude opened the door

another foot. He was well on his way to covering the rest of his body with tattoos.

"Yeah, okay," he muttered. Backing up, he yelled over his shoulder, "Cops here! They want to talk to us."

More rustles and thumps and some creative obscenities had Mike almost as nervous as the possibility of crashing through the squeaky, uneven floor. This place needed to be condemned and razed.

The living room was flophouse décor—a couple of filthy sofas with stuffing poking out, a mattress with bedding Mike wouldn't have touched with latex gloves on, a half-decent flat-screen TV resting on plastic crates, more plastic crates filled with empty booze bottles and—good God—was that one *filled with* used condoms? Seven people gathered: four guys, three women, all skinny, seedy, shifty-eyed. Tattooed and pierced. One had a swastika tattooed on his neck. Mike found himself hoping like hell one of these men wasn't Sicily's father. He searched their faces and couldn't tell, even though he had seen a driver's license photo.

A couple of them didn't seem to mind giving their names. The remainder were reluctant but finally mumbled them. Jarrel Wright had his eye on one man. Mike suspected he'd be making an arrest on their way out. The guy was edging away, trying to get toward the back of the group. His hands stayed at his sides, though. Lucky for him.

Chen explained that they needed to speak to Chad Marks. All but the guy who was trying to ease himself out of sight stared blankly.

"Who's that?" one of the women finally said.

"I know him." It was the heavy metal dude. "He lived here when I first came. Like, four years ago? Man, he hasn't been around in a long time. He played an awesome guitar. He had some band that almost made it, I remember that."

"This him?" Chen showed the photo.

"Yeah! That's the man."

Mike kept his stance beside Chen, but out of the corner of his eye watched a slow-motion chase. Wright, easing to block the exit from the room, wanted this guy real bad. The guy wanted to be gone. No violence had yet erupted, though.

Chen and the residents participating in the conversation established that no one knew where Chad Marks had moved. Heavy Metal thought the house had been getting too crowded. "I think maybe he was putting together another band."

"Would you mind if we walked through the house?"

The whites of their eyes showed. "We're not interested in drugs," Chen told them.

For the first time, the group noticed that one

of their number was trying to fade away and that the Seattle detective was in not-so-subtle pursuit.

"Hey, man, what's going on?" a skinny kid who didn't look over sixteen asked, and the target broke and ran.

Five strides down the hall, Wright had him with his face to a wall and cuffed. The racket brought another Seattle officer through the back door, weapon in hand. He holstered it, smiled and said, "Well, well. Jiggs. What a nice coincidence."

He departed with the prisoner, and Wright, Chen and Mike did a walk-through. They ignored the drug paraphernalia and the sickening odor. There was nothing to suggest Sicily Marks had ever been held here. Hell, there didn't seem to be a door sturdy enough to hold a hostage, slight as she was. The basement had only cobwebs, broken furniture, a washing machine and a few wooden clothespins hanging dispiritedly from a line strung from one side of the dank space to another. Mike wondered if the washer worked or anyone ever made use of it.

That was it. They walked out. Chen thanked the other officers for their time, and got a big grin from Wright, who said, "I'm happy with my bonus."

Chen grunted, "Well, that was a bust," and they parted ways.

Mike sat in his car for a few minutes, more discouraged by the dead end than he usually let himself be. He didn't like thinking about how long Sicily had been missing. So far the focus, inevitably, had been on the Greenways and Sicily's father. The scariest possibility was that none of them had anything to do with her disappearance. Stranger abductions were a nightmare, the chances of a happy ending remote.

So where to go from here? he asked himself.

Intensify the pleas for public assistance. Calls were still coming in from people who claimed to have been at Henrik Beach County Park on Saturday. He wanted to hear from every single person who'd been there. He knew damn well the beach and picnic area had been crowded.

Plaster Sicily's photo everywhere. The process had started, but if he had his way her face would become familiar to every resident of four counties.

Return to Beth's neighborhood to call on the two neighbors who hadn't yet been home. He supposed he should talk to the grandparents again, but didn't see that serving a lot of purpose unless they received a ransom demand. He intended to visit Rachel Marks's last known residence and talk to neighbors there. Who was the last boyfriend? Roommates? Anyone who'd been especially interested in her kid?

He reached to turn the key in the ignition, then exhaled with a huff and instead opened his cell phone. It would be interesting to see if Beth answered or let his call go to voice mail.

One ring and she answered, having snatched it up. "Hello?" Mike heard anxiety in her voice. Of course she'd been sitting there counting the minutes, praying.

"Detective Ryan," he said. "We didn't learn anything useful. Marks did once live in this house, but moved out years ago. Nobody knows where he went." He closed his eyes. "I'm sorry, Beth."

There was a moment of silence. "Thank you for calling," she said very formally, and was gone.

He swore out loud, thumped his head a couple of times against the headrest and tried hard not to picture Beth Greenway alone in the house that probably felt polluted to her now, no longer the refuge it had been.

BETH DREW EVERY SINGLE WINDOW blind, then went to huddle in her home office. Earlier, the doorbell had rung several times. The reporters knew she was in here and didn't want to give up. She'd called to warn her staff that they would be inundated with phone calls. Tracy, her assistant, said, "That won't be anything new."

"I've left you to deal with it. I'm so sorry."

"Don't be silly. This is not your priority."

They discussed a couple of upcoming events, but Beth couldn't focus and Tracy could obviously tell.

"Nothing is at a critical point," she said firmly. "We'll keep things going, don't worry."

Don't worry. Right. Under other circumstances, it would have been funny. As it was, if she'd laughed she was afraid of what sound might emerge. Something horrible, angry, hurt and so terrified she might not be able to put herself back together again.

Finally, she went through the motions of making a lunch and pretending to eat it, then cleaning up afterward.

She began to wish she hadn't said those things to him. Not because she hadn't meant every word; Tracy hadn't said anything about cancellations, but Beth suspected she wouldn't have even if they'd been getting them. And she knew—hoped—she could salvage her reputation anyway. The best thing she could do right now was issue a statement saying yes, the police had searched her home at her invitation. She fully understood that they had to look at family members when a child disappeared and she wanted to help them eliminate her as a possibility so they could focus on finding Sicily. She urged the public to blah, blah, blah.

That's what she should do. Instead, she sat at her

desk, colder than she'd ever been, and wished Detective Mike Ryan could tell her more about what was going on. Her rage still simmered, but she also remembered his occasional kindnesses—that hand gently rubbing her back, the low-voiced croon, the fact that he *had* kept her informed every step of the way even as he let her know she was a suspect. He'd included her in the search yesterday because he knew she needed to be doing something even though she'd likely been more of a nuisance than a help. Maybe he'd driven up to the park the night before to find her because he thought she was…who knew? Moving Sicily's body? But… some instinct said that wasn't all of it, that he'd been worried about her, too. She remembered the meal he'd cooked for her, the way he coaxed her to eat. The blanket he'd wrapped around her when he saw her shivering.

She squeezed her eyes shut, but tears seeped out nonetheless.

CHAPTER SEVEN

MIKE SPENT HOURS chasing down Rachel Marks's friends, who were mainly male, as well as roommates, neighbors. The more time he spent with people who'd known her, the sorrier he felt for her poor kid.

Her last apartment building wasn't terrible. The neighbors hadn't liked the looks of the people who came and went, though.

"Seemed like there was always a different man living there," one of them told him, shaking her head. "I couldn't help worrying about the little girl, but she always seemed cheerful. To think that after losing her mother, this happened to her."

Nobody knew the last boyfriend's name. He'd only been around a couple of weeks, but did stay on in the apartment until the end of the month, the super said. "Place was paid up. It was only a week. I asked if he wanted to rent it but he didn't. Got someone else in there right away."

When asked about the boyfriend, one of Rachel's women friends crinkled her forehead. "Yeah, she said stuff about him, but I don't really

remember what. I know he didn't work or anything. She said if he didn't get a job she'd have
to kick him out, that she wasn't going to support
him."

Finally, in the late afternoon Mike drove to Edmonds. He had a wary eye out as he approached
Beth's house, but the press had apparently de-
camped. He wondered how long they'd stayed,
like hounds baying under a treed coon. The image
made him wince.

There was no light on in one neighbor's house
and nobody came to the door, either. At the other
place, he finally got lucky, if you could call it that.
The young couple who lived there had been away
for two weeks on a second honeymoon in San
Francisco. They hadn't lived here that long and
didn't remember seeing a girl at that house at all.

"Actually," the woman said apologetically, "I
don't have any idea who lives there. We have
a yard service, so we're not outside much. You
know."

He knew. He thanked them and walked to his
Tahoe, parked at the curb in front of Beth's. He had
no idea if she knew he was there or not; she had
her house sealed up air tight. The bloodsuckers
had left for now, but she had to have been under
siege for a while.

A part of him wanted to go knock on her door,

but he didn't have any real excuse and could imagine the reception he'd get.

No, ma'am, I don't have a warrant.

He gave a grunt that was half laugh, although his sense of humor seemed to be in cold storage. Speaking of which, *he* was cold and damp and hungry. Sick of fast food, he tried to think of what might be available at home, but suspected there wasn't anything very promising, since he couldn't remember the last time he'd been grocery shopping.

Mike unlocked the car door with his remote and was walking toward the driver's side when his cell rang.

His lieutenant said, "The kid's grandparents are going to make a televised plea for her return. Turn on the local news."

Mike swore and hustled to Beth's door, where he leaned on the bell. She opened it far enough for him to see a chain and one eye studying him suspiciously.

"What are you doing here?"

"Beth, the local news is coming on. I was informed that your parents are being interviewed. Can I come in and watch?"

The door closed. He waited in suspense, but then the chain rattled and the door swung open. He locked it behind him and turned to see her pointing the remote at the television.

A canned sitcom came on rather than local news, and Mike glanced at his watch. "I'm early. News won't be on for ten—no, twelve—more minutes."

She muted the set. "You're here only to watch the interview with me?"

"I was questioning a couple more of your neighbors," he admitted, suspecting that wouldn't thrill her.

Her expression wasn't friendly, but she didn't radiate hostility like she had this morning. After a moment, she grudgingly asked if he'd like coffee.

"I would love coffee," he said fervently. He took the liberty of trailing her to the kitchen and watching her take down a mug for him and pour. "You had dinner?" he heard himself ask.

She gave him a scathing look. Mike guessed that suggesting he put together soup and sandwiches again was a no-go. He should count his blessings; she'd let him in the door without that warrant.

They returned to the living room in silence and both stared at the muted action on the screen. Mike felt as if he were trying to step softly, knowing something as tiny as the crunch of a twig could bring a hail of bullets. Truthfully, he wasn't quite sure why she *had* let him in the door. He inhaled his coffee before taking a swallow. She used the good stuff.

"Is it true what they say? That police stations always have the world's worst coffee?"

Startled, he turned his head and saw she wasn't looking at him. Still, however stiffly, she was talking. "Yeah." He gave a short laugh. "It's pretty bad."

After a minute, she said, "Where is Sicily?"

Oh, hell. "I don't know."

Words burst from her. "Somebody, somewhere, had to see her! Nobody could sling her over a shoulder and carry her up to the car park without someone noticing."

"We'll renew our appeals to the public, Beth. But I think it's unlikely she was snatched on the beach. She might have gone up to the parking lot on her own. Maybe for an innocent reason. One of the kids she was hanging around with suggested she walk them up." Seeing her objection forming, he said, "Yeah, you'd think the parents would have noticed, but what if some other people were leaving around the same time so there was a crowd going up the trail?"

"Then why haven't *they* called?"

"Could be they don't pay any attention to the news. Or they were visitors from out of the area. We get a lot of Canadians, you know. Or they thought all the kids were from the same family."

Head bent now, she nodded.

"Would Sicily have gone up to the restroom alone?"

Beth squeezed her eyes shut for a moment. "Yes. If she saw I'd fallen asleep, I don't think she'd have thought twice about heading up there alone. She wouldn't have wanted to wake me up, and it wasn't that far."

He hesitated only briefly. "And then there's the possibility she was lured."

She sucked in a breath. "She's too old to go with someone because they offered her candy or…" She obviously couldn't think of another possibility.

"But what if it was someone she knew? A former boyfriend of her mother's? A friend? A teacher from school?" He was relentless and she stared back at him in horror. "A man who said he was her father."

"No." She finally balked at that. "She wouldn't have gone with him without waking me."

He felt exultant. She was talking to him. Really talking. To keep her going as much as out of any need to know, he asked, "Would she recognize him from pictures?"

"I don't think so," Beth said, but sounded uncertain. "Sicily didn't remember her mom ever having pictures, although surely she did at some point. Rachel called Chad 'that scum.' Maybe she got mad and burned them. Sicily told me she'd looked online because she wanted to know what he looked like. She thought since he was a rock star there might be one, but even though she found a few reviews of the band the only photo wasn't great and she couldn't tell who was who."

Keeping an eye on the TV, Mike saw that turn-of-the-hour commercials had come on.

"I looked up the old one from the DMV," he told Beth, "but his license expired five years ago."

"So he left the state."

Mike shook his head. "Not right away. Four years ago he was cited in Pierce County for a moving violation and not having a license. He didn't appear in court, didn't pay the fines. Unfortunately, there's a pretty good-size substrata out there who don't bother with driver's licenses or insurance."

"And the address on his last license?"

"Rental records show he was evicted not long after your sister left him."

Her eyes searched his. "You think it might be him, don't you?"

He didn't want to say, *No, I think some sicko grabbed your niece. I think there's a good chance she's been raped and maybe killed. Probably killed. Or will be.*

"The vast majority of child abductions are familial."

"But why, when he's never even tried to see her?"

"Do we know that for a fact? What if your sister was angry because he hadn't paid child support and refused to allow him visitation? Would she have told you or your parents?"

Beth sagged. "No."

"Or Sicily?"

"She didn't spare Sicily most of the ugliness in her life, but I suppose in that instance… Maybe."

"We'll find him." His attention sharpened. "Turn the sound on. Here we go."

They'd missed a few words of lead-in, from the looks of it the usual banter. Already the camera was closing in on the woman anchor's face, which was solemn. "Police are saying only that they are pursuing all leads in the disappearance of ten-year-old Sicily Marks." She summed up the events of Saturday, seguing into a mention of the morning search of the "Edmonds home of Sicily's aunt, Elizabeth Greenway, with whom she lived." Video ran showing law enforcement vehicles in front of her house, people with Police emblazoned on their backs going in and out. Mike slid a glance sideways to see Beth watching, body rigid.

Back to the studio, thank God. The anchor said, "Today, King Five reporter Emily Lyons spoke to Sicily's grandparents." The scene shifted to the Greenways' living room. This time, Rowena and Laurence sat side by side, holding hands. He was leaning protectively toward his wife.

The pretty blonde reporter said, "The police are being closemouthed about the direction their investigation has taken. Sources say the search of the park has been suspended. Have they told you whether they now believe Sicily was abducted? Have they yet identified a person of interest?"

Rowena pressed her fingers to her mouth as if to stifle a sob. Her husband let go of her hand to put an arm around her and momentarily lay his cheek against her hair. Then he straightened to glare at the camera.

"The police have not seen fit to share their suspicions with us. Like everyone else, we learned from the ten o'clock news last night that the search for our beloved granddaughter had been called off. We weren't given the courtesy of a phone call. We had no idea our daughter Beth had become a suspect. Frankly, I'm outraged that we've been kept in the dark. I have to question the competency of this investigation."

Mike couldn't suppress a growl. Beside him, Beth stood stiff, staring at the TV.

"Have they interviewed you at all?"

"Yes, a Detective Ryan spoke with us once, on Saturday evening. We answered his questions as best we could about Sicily's personality, her likes and dislikes, her recent history. The interview was quite short. That is, to date, the *only* contact we've had with the police supposedly searching for our granddaughter."

"It's our understanding that her mother died quite recently."

"Yes." Again, his gaze went directly to the camera lens. His expression was grim, and yet suggested great suffering that was nobly suppressed. "The death of our daughter Rachel only a month ago was a terrible tragedy. You may know that she fell overboard—or was thrown overboard—from a Washington State ferry. Her body washed ashore two days later. Her death was very difficult for our entire family, and Sicily most of all, of course. An only child, she went temporarily to live with our older daughter, Elizabeth. As you know, she was with Elizabeth when she disappeared." The pause was brief, but long enough to allow his implication to sink in, even for dim-witted viewers. "We simply can't imagine what Rachel's death could have to do with Sicily's more recent disappearance."

The reporter gazed with practiced sympathy at the grief-stricken grandparents. "Mrs. Greenway, this must be a very difficult time for you."

Rowena's face contorted, but with an obvious effort she regained her poise. "We're heartsick." She lifted her chin and, like her husband, looked straight into the camera. "We're pleading for anyone who saw anything at all to call into the hotline. This is her picture." With shaking hand, she lifted that fourth-grade school photo, beautifully framed though it sure as hell hadn't been on display in the Greenways' living room when Mike visited. The camera closed in on it. Her voice tremulous, tears apparently close, she said, "Please, please, if you have Sicily, we're begging you. Bring her home to us."

Below the close-up of Sicily's face ran the phone number that had already been widely publicized.

Back in the studio, the anchor exclaimed, "How terrifying! Every parent's worst nightmare."

"Every grandparent's," agreed the man.

The remote control thudded to the rug at Beth's feet. With an inarticulate scream, she snatched something from the coffee table and threw it at the television. A glass vase, Mike realized, as it smashed into the wall, barely missing the set. Still screaming, she had another object in her hand within seconds, a bronze rabbit. This missile connected with its target and the flat-screen TV seemed to explode, bouncing backward and then crashing forward onto the floor. She already had something else in her hand and flung it. Mike grabbed it out of midair, dropped it and turned to capture the wild woman in his arms.

She fought viciously, an inhuman keening sound tearing from her throat. Shocked, he held on, containing her. He didn't try to talk to her, only to keep her from hurting herself or him. It had to be a full minute before her desperate writhing slowed and the scream became a series of dry, hiccupping sobs.

What in the hell had just happened? He loosened his arms enough to see her face, expecting tears, but instead he found her eyes squeezed shut. She trembled.

"Beth," he said. "Beth, what's going on here? Look at me. Talk to me."

Still shivering, she tried to curl in on herself. Had she gone into shock? In a panic, he wondered if he should get the paramedics out here. Unless she was faking this. But he didn't believe that. He'd seen a burst of rage so primal it had raised the hair on his arms.

Operating on instinct, he lifted her and laid her on the sofa. A fluffy red throw blanket was neatly folded on the back of a rocking chair. He grabbed it and spread it over Beth, tucking it around her for maximum warmth.

Sitting beside her, he said, "Beth. Honey, talk to me. If I get your coffee, will you take a drink? Damn it, talk to me! Help me out here."

He was reaching for his phone when she gave a longer shudder and then a sigh.

"That's it," he murmured. Through the soft comfort of the throw, he kneaded her shoulders and arms. "Come back. Tell me what's happening."

She blinked. Once, then several times. Another quake that was almost a sob.

"Come on, honey. That's it. You scared me. Don't do this."

Beth's head turned slightly and her eyes fastened on his. Her look was dazed, bewildered, anguished. With no conscious volition on his part, his hand lifted to stroke her hair back from her face and cup her cheek. He kept talking, probably all nonsense, but maybe the sound of his voice gave her something to hang on to. His heart thudded in his chest as if he'd run ten city blocks to take down a suspect. No, this was worse than that.

"See if you can sit up." He gently eased her up, then grabbed his mug. The coffee he hadn't finished had cooled, but was still warm enough to do her some good.

He sat close to her again, cradled her hands in his larger ones and lifted the cup to her mouth. She sipped, then took a longer swallow. Her skin was fine-textured, her lashes thick and dark. He inhaled her scent, so subtle it took him a minute to decide it might be honeysuckle. His mother had let a honeysuckle vine get away from her and become a monster, devouring twenty-five feet of fence in her backyard. The scent when it was in bloom could be as elusive as Beth's, but at night it was sweeter than anything he'd ever smelled.

Her hands were steadier. He withdrew his but

watched as she drank more of the coffee. At last she sighed, bit her lip and looked at him. "I'm sorry."

"You have nothing to be sorry for," he said roughly.

Her voice shook as she looked at the carcass of her television lying on the floor. "I've never done anything like that before."

"You came close yesterday at the park."

Those lashes swept down again, veiling her eyes. "I guess I did." She took a ragged breath. "It's not like me. I never..." She stopped, pressed her lips together.

"You don't like to show any emotion, do you?"

Her eyes flashed briefly to his face. "No."

He sat there thinking about the televised interview and the moment when she'd shattered. Maybe when she saw her niece's face...but he didn't think so. Beth had handed him the same photo with little discernible emotion. It might only be the accumulation of too much terror that had sent her over the edge. But his instincts said no again.

"They were acting for all they were worth," he mused, watching her closely.

Only by the smallest jerk did Beth Greenway betray any reaction. But after a moment she said, "Yes."

"Why? Why bother?"

She frowned. "How did you know they were faking it?"

"I met them," Mike said flatly. "They didn't give a damn. I'm trying to talk to them about their missing granddaughter, and your father was keeping his eye on the ten o'clock news over my shoulder. Your mother said the right things, but as if we were talking about a stranger."

"Sicily *is* a stranger to them."

"You defending them?"

"No." She straightened. "No."

"You didn't answer my question. Why are they bothering now?"

"Appearances are important to them. My father is not only a successful businessman, he's a powerful political figure in this state. He doesn't want to run for office himself." Her bitterness could have etched glass. "God forbid he have to try to win the approval of 'the dim-wits that make up the masses.' I'm quoting him. He's…a kingmaker, I suppose you could say. I've heard him say the state house is his. Some of the congressmen owe him. Our current governor consults my father before he blows his nose. For once, Dad has to think like a politician. If he comes across badly now, some people will distance themselves from him."

"Your mother?"

"Oh, she loves the money, the respect, the status. Having dinner at the governor's mansion." She laughed and it was the least happy sound he'd ever heard—it rang with the cracked earth and shimmering, heat-distorted air of a high summer day in Death Valley. "I hate her."

Digesting the matter-of-fact statement, he removed the coffee cup from a hand that had acquired a new tremor. "What did she do to you, Beth?"

Her burning gaze found his. "Does it matter?"

"It matters."

Maybe not to Sicily; he couldn't say yet. But to him, yes, it did. One whole hell of a lot. He couldn't say yet why that was so, either.

Beth drew her knees up under the blanket. Curling protectively in on herself. "It doesn't have anything to do with Sicily. It really doesn't."

She was begging him. *Please don't make me say this.* Maybe he was wrong, but he thought this was a secret that had to come out. What had that elegant, poised, cold woman done to her daughter that was so terrible?

Then it came to him. To her daughters. Plural. Rachel, too, maintained only minimal contact with her parents. Rachel, child of wealthy, educated parents, had left home at seventeen, gotten pregnant and married her rocker boyfriend. Rachel had very possibly committed suicide.

"They abused you." No, she'd said "I hate *her*." Not *them*. More slowly, he said, "She abused you."

Beth sat still as marble, staring straight ahead. At her ruined television set? He didn't think so. He didn't think she was seeing anything here and now. It was a long time before she whispered, "Yes."

"Tell me."

Like any good cop, he'd learned to wall off emotions. He'd never have survived if he'd let himself grieve for every victim, hurt for every survivor, feel sadness or rage even when the emotions were called for. He'd already felt more this time than usual, in part because anything involving a lost or dead child was his Achilles' heel. But now, a need to protect uncoiled inside him, so powerful it hardly left room to breathe. It was every bit as huge and terrible as his nightmares, and as useless. He couldn't protect this woman from whatever she'd suffered a decade or more ago.

But maybe he could do something else for her. Maybe he could give her justice. And maybe, he thought, looking at her dry-eyed anguish, she still needed saving.

"Tell me," he said again in a hard voice.

Her gaze swung toward him. If he'd been breathing, he quit now, when he saw her expression.

"Why?"

Instead of answering, he asked a question. "Have you ever told anyone?" Maybe she'd been in therapy; maybe she didn't need him.

"Yes." She bent her head so he couldn't see her face anymore. "My father."

"And he didn't do anything. Didn't believe you."

"Or didn't care. I don't know."

The need to wrap her in his arms was tearing at him, but he fought it. He was on the job. He had an obligation to stay professional. And maybe the fact that he was the police detective investigating her niece's disappearance was the only reason she was talking to him. Maybe it was why she was admitting to something that had been eating at her for so long it had done incalculable damage.

"What? What did she do?" He sounded harsh. Couldn't help himself.

Beth looked down at her knees. Her hair had swung forward to veil her face. She was rocking slightly now. "She...hurt me. All the time."

So prosaic. So gut-wrenching. Mike didn't want to hear the rest, but he needed to. "How?" he asked, and this time he kept his voice low and as gentle as he could.

HE WAS PLAYING GOOD COP/BAD cop. Beth thought semihysterically, but he had no foil, so he was taking both roles. Demanding one second, coaxing the next.

It was the coaxing that got to her.

Or maybe he only happened to be here when she unraveled. She struggled desperately to regain the control she'd learned as a little girl. How could it have failed her now, when it was so basic to her personality that she'd had to teach herself to *fake* emotions?

But she knew. Oh, she knew. In one short month, Sicily had bared Beth's shame. In a weird way, she'd also given her hope. Not at first; at first there'd been only shame. Sicily was a living, breathing reminder that she'd sacrificed her sister to save herself. The first week had been nearly unbearable. Somehow, she had to meet this child's needs while she herself…

Began to unravel. *Yes,* she thought, clutching her knees, *I started falling apart then, one weak thread at a time.*

Mike Ryan was waiting for her. She sneaked a sidelong peek to see that his steady cop's gaze remained implacable, however kind he'd sounded. Why had she even let him in the door when she'd sworn she wouldn't?

He's interrogating me.

The awful thing was, she didn't know if she wanted to resist. She had hated and feared her mother so long, she'd learned to contain the emotions. They never went away—sometimes they were all she was sure she felt. They stayed like a hot little ball in her belly. A coal that refused to go ash-gray and die. But she had never, never felt a burst of rage and hate so all-consuming, she thought she'd have attacked her mother if she'd been here. She'd have flung herself at her, screaming and clawing. She imagined her hands around her neck, squeezing, squeezing, squeezing.

The hate raised her gorge, choking her. This wasn't anything like what she'd felt this morning, when she'd decided she hated Mike Ryan. She shouldn't have used that word, even to herself. She'd only been angry and humiliated, nothing like this. Nothing.

"Tell me."

"When my mother was mad about something, or woke up in a bad mood or got mildly irritated, she hurt me." Without making a conscious decision to tell him anything, Beth heard herself talking.

"She hit you."

"Carefully," she explained. "I never once had a bruise on my face. And sometimes…she did other things. She burned me, but not my hands."

He jerked. Beth continued to study the weave of the throw where it draped over her knees.

"It was always so…deliberate." Now that she'd started, she couldn't seem to stop. Telling someone threw her back in time. Old scars ached. The scenes were so vivid in her mind, it was as if she were there, rather than sitting on her couch. No, that wasn't true; she was telling this hard-faced cop her most terrible truth. She stole a single glance, to be sure that he believed her. His eyes seethed with rage as great as anything she'd ever felt.

Comforted, Beth ducked her head again and continued in that small, dry voice. "She broke bones. I can't even tell you how many times I had broken bones. Sometimes only ribs, because they don't show, you know. Then she wouldn't have to take me to the doctor. For broken arms or collarbones, if it was too obvious we had to go to the emergency room. Different ones every time, of course. I have scars, too. Some burns, and a few cuts, and there was the time she accidentally dropped a bottle of expensive wine and since I was standing there, right in front of her, she grabbed the biggest piece of the bottle and… and slashed me."

"Show me."

The voice was so dark and resonant, she vibrated with it like a tuning fork. After a moment, she dropped the throw and lifted the hem of her sweater. She half turned from him, knowing what he'd see though she hardly ever looked at her body in the mirror. These were the worst scars. She'd spun that day in the kitchen and tried to run. The broken glass had raked her side and back instead of her belly. She'd fallen to her knees screaming but there was no one home to hear. Her mother had had to call 911 that time, there was so much blood. She'd been prepared with a distraught story about dropping the bottle, her daughter slipping in the spilled wine and falling.

Mike was swearing. His fingers touched the scars so lightly she barely felt them. She didn't have much sensation there. But then he found one of the burn scars, and then another. She felt his breath, expelled along with furious words, against her nape. At last, his hands, astonishingly gentle, he pulled down her sweater and placed the red throw back around her, as if he were tucking in a child for the night.

But fury burned on his face. "Your father had to know."

"He didn't want to. He convinced himself I was clumsy, stupid, who knows. I was so afraid of her—" Beth's voice broke, but with long practice she steadied it "—and I suppose… Well, it was all I knew. I never even tried to tell anyone else. Isn't that pathetic? We had this housekeeper I loved when I was little, Maria, and later I wondered if she knew. She was suddenly gone when I was five or six, maybe." Had she said something? Had she been fired because she'd noticed too much? Later housekeepers had come and gone; Beth hadn't grown attached to any of them.

She continued, "I learned as I got older to recognize the look in my mother's eyes and I'd hide. I had several places she never found. It's a big house, you know. I'd stay in them for hours, until I heard Dad come home, or the housekeeper arrive, or I knew I could slip out and catch the school bus. I lived for the moment I could leave home. I promised myself I would never come back, and I didn't. While I was in college I got summer jobs in eastern Washington, I always had someone who'd invited me home for Thanksgiving or Christmas, or I pretended they had. My parents both came to my graduation, so proud, because I was *summa cum laude,* you see. They basked in my achievement."

A sound broke from his throat.

"Rachel never forgave me for leaving her behind."

"How much younger was she...? It was four years, wasn't it?"

"Yes. She was only fourteen when I left."

"You were a kid yourself." Astonishingly, he sounded as if he meant it. Was he trying to absolve her?

I will never absolve myself.

"I told myself it hadn't been quite as bad for her. I protected her when I could." Once again she let herself meet his eyes. She desperately wanted him to believe that she'd done this small bit for her sister. "I showed her all the places to hide. Sometimes we hid together. I would hold her and whisper stories to her. Until she got older, of course."

He made another sound, inarticulate but adequate.

"But if I'd had the courage to tell someone, maybe Rachel never would have been hurt. Maybe she'd have gone to college, and met a man who loved her. She might not have become a drug addict or killed herself."

"You think she killed herself."

She plucked at the soft fibers of the throw. "I suppose I do."

He was silent for a long time. When he finally spoke, he surprised her. "What would you have done if Rachel hadn't named you as Sicily's guardian?"

"I would have gone to court and asked for custody." At that moment she remembered she was an adult now, and anger buried the childlike vulnerability. "When I was a senior in college, I compiled my medical records. It wasn't easy, but I got the X-rays, too. I had ones taken of my torso that show that I'd suffered multiple rib fractures. I can prove a history of abuse. At the time, I didn't even know why I was going through all the trouble, because once I was eighteen they couldn't make me come home again. But I felt safer, knowing I had something to hold over them. I wished I'd thought of it sooner, because I could have gotten Child Protective Services to take Rachel away. I always thought, I don't know why, that my word wouldn't be enough."

"Your scars would have been enough," he said, in that deep, grim voice.

She didn't quite believe that. Or maybe she couldn't let herself, because then she'd know she *hadn't* been powerless to help Rachel escape, as she'd often told herself she was.

"When I got the call that Rachel had disappeared and somebody had to come get Sicily, I knew that I had the weapon I needed to do for her what I hadn't been able to do for Rachel."

"You told me your parents would never get custody," he said, sounding thoughtful. "That's how you knew. You'd threaten to expose them."

"Yes."

"Beth…"

Something in his tone made her look at him.

"Where do you keep those medical records?"

Her eyes widened. "Here, at home."

"Will you let me see them?"

CHAPTER EIGHT

THAT WAS A SURPRISE. SHE'D have expected him to say, "Get them." Not ask. Not look at her with as much kindness as anger.

For a moment, panic climbed in her. She'd showed him her scarred flesh, hadn't she? So why did the idea of opening that huge manila envelope for him seem worse? As if she were going to completely strip herself for him?

But she'd come this far, and finally she nodded. She set the blanket aside and went to her bedroom. The bulging packet of records stayed flat in the bottom drawer of her dresser, where she otherwise kept out-of-season clothes.

She removed the down vest, the heavy sweaters, and took the envelope out. She turned to see him standing in the bedroom doorway.

He didn't look embarrassed. "I wanted to see where you kept them. We searched your house. They should have been noted."

Beth flushed with anger. "Why? You were searching for information about Sicily."

"I wouldn't necessarily have looked at these, beyond checking that they *were* your records and not hers. But their existence should have been noted."

"The envelope is the same color as the bottom of the drawer."

He grunted, but said nothing more.

Once in the living room, she handed him the envelope. He immediately sat down, raised the flap and pulled the whole pile out. He sat quietly, head bent, reading hasty doctor's notations. One by one, he took X-rays from their individual envelopes and held them up to the light, then carefully replaced them. He didn't say a word for more than twenty minutes. Then he gathered everything up, put it all in the envelope and looked at her.

"They both deserve to fry."

She flinched.

His expression became incredulous. "You can't still love them."

"No. Oh, no. I don't remember ever feeling anything like that for them." If she'd ever loved anyone, it had been Maria. She'd grieved so when a strange woman showed up to work in Maria's place. There wasn't even a chance to say goodbye. And then there was Rachel. *I loved Rachel. Of course I did. And...that means I can love.*

Sometimes she'd wondered.

"God," he said explosively. They stared at each other. "This is inappropriate as hell," he told her, "but I think I need to put my arms around you."

She came close to breaking again, then, the yearning was so powerful. They both moved at the same time. He reached for her, she dove for him.

His embrace felt…amazing. His chest was so broad, his arms so strong. Her head tucked below his chin as if it were the most natural resting place she'd ever found. His breath feathered her hair, and she knew the pressure against her head meant he'd laid his cheek against it. A rumbling sound came out of his throat. He held her so tight, she felt the heavy thud of his heartbeat against her breast. She gripped him, too, and tried not to cry.

Why did she want to cry? The sensation was so alien. Until the past few days, she hadn't cried in forever. Not even when she stood at her sister's gravesite.

She was so muddled inside, she didn't know what was happening to her. She wanted to cry because someone was holding her. Trying to comfort her, to give her something no one ever had. The closest she'd come was those times she and Rachel had huddled together, holding each other, whispering. She'd thought she was giving the comfort, but knew now she'd been accepting it, too.

In horror, she realized she *was* crying, that her tears were soaking into his shirt. But he only murmured, "Let it out, Beth. I don't know how you survived. You must be so strong, but that doesn't mean you can't cry."

Yes, it did. The panic returned, and she struggled backward, freeing herself from his arms. This fear wasn't for Sicily; it was for herself. She'd survived because she didn't let herself feel like this. It was dangerous. Too dangerous.

Beth swiped at her wet cheeks and scuttled a cushion away, to her corner of the sofa. She snatched the throw blanket and lifted it over herself as if it would keep her safe. She desperately needed to blow her nose, but she said, "I'm fine," because if she didn't say it, how could she believe it?

It made her mad that she was sure she had seen pity on his face.

"I'm fine," she repeated more strongly.

He stood, went to the kitchen and came back in a minute with a paper towel, which he handed to her. She blew her nose vigorously, then wadded it in her hand and watched him warily.

He stood behind the couch frowning down at her, his blue eyes unsettlingly intense, the lines seeming to have deepened on his face, making it craggier, less handsome, more worn. And yet... *And yet*, she thought, and hadn't the least idea how to define what she felt looking at him.

"I'm going to pour us some fresh coffee," he said abruptly and disappeared again.

Once she was sure she had herself back together, Beth followed. He'd taken over the kitchen as if it were his. He'd gotten her coffeemaker going and was rummaging in the refrigerator. "You going to do something with this chicken?"

"What?"

"I'm not leaving you alone, but I'm starved. I can do a stir-fry." He turned to look at her, caution finally making an appearance. "If that's okay."

Stunned, she finally nodded. He was going to cook for her? Again?

She tried to get up and help, but when he scowled, she sat back down. He did ask where things were. In no time he had rice cooking and was slicing first the vegetables he found in her refrigerator and then the chicken. He located soy sauce, brown sugar and who knew what else. Once the chicken started sizzling in the wok, it smelled so good her stomach growled. She hadn't eaten much of a meal in days.

Cupboard doors opened and closed. "You holding on to those cashews for anything?"

"No."

In less than half an hour, he set serving bowls of rice and the stir-fry on the table, got plates and silverware and said, "Let's eat."

They both dished up. She didn't try to start a conversation, but knew he was watching her as they ate. Beth was almost embarrassed by how much she put away. It was lucky he'd made massive quantities, because she wasn't the only one eating a lot; he was on his third serving.

Not until she pushed her plate away and was cradling her coffee cup in both hands did either of them speak.

Beth knew she had to get this out now. "I'm sorry for what I said this morning."

He frowned at her. "That I was deliberately trying to humiliate you?"

"That, and telling you to get out. Saying not to come back without a warrant."

"You had reason to be upset. I couldn't blame you."

Beth shook her head. "I want you to do anything you can to find Sicily. I know you had to get this out of the way."

He didn't say anything, and she wondered what he was thinking. She supposed a part of her was waiting for him to say, *"You're right, I had to do it, but now I know you didn't have anything to do with Sicily's disappearance."* But he didn't. And she realized he still couldn't be sure.

"I should have handled it with more…grace," she admitted.

"I understood."

Well, that was something. Maybe it was better that she didn't know what he thought of her. Her clients and even her employees considered her to be unshakable, smart, creative, organized beyond belief, with a memory like an elephant. They admired her. Even liked her, though the relationships never quite reached the point of real friendship. She didn't care, because friends got to know each other better than she wanted anyone to know her.

She swallowed an unexpected bubble of laughter. Look at her now—there was an excellent reason she kept to herself. Mike Ryan undoubtedly had her pegged as nuts. He was probably puzzled as to why she wasn't institutionalized. Yeah, he'd been horrified by her childhood, and he undoubtedly *did* understand why she'd had a mental breakdown an hour ago, following the one she'd had yesterday. She cringed to think of the TV lying broken on her living-room floor. Had she really done that?

When you got right down to it, the guy had been incredibly nice to her. The rage her story awakened in him seemed genuine. And this need he had to feed her was downright touching.

But he'd ease out of her life as quick as he could while still being nice, as soon as Sicily was found.

The words *dead or alive* whispered in her head, and she quit feeling sorry for herself and went back to being terrified for the child she'd sworn to protect.

Mike's voice intruded in her brooding. "In the interview, she said you had 'temporary' custody."

Startled, Beth said, "I heard."

"If your sister named you, why would your mother say that?"

Now she could think about it dispassionately. "Because people might wonder why they didn't bring their beloved granddaughter into their own home? And how lucky they are now that someone else looked irresponsible, not them."

"Yeah, I caught that. Hard to miss," he added drily.

She met those blue eyes. "I told you my relationship with my parents—the reason it's so bad—doesn't have anything to do with Sicily disappearing."

"You're probably right, but we can't be positive yet. It sure as hell has everything to do with the mess Sicily's mother made of her life." He'd evidently pulled himself together, too, because the merciless cop voice was back.

"I had something to do with that, too," Beth felt compelled to say.

"No. You're not responsible, Beth. That ball is a hundred percent in your parents' court."

Her heart did a tuck and roll. He could weaken her. The realization kicked the turmoil that seemed to be her new norm up a notch. *I can't be weakened.*

"You don't think this is a setup." He seemed to be thinking it out as he spoke. "A way to get Sicily out of your hands. To make you look so bad, or feel so guilty, so responsible, you won't deploy your armament."

"You mean, did they have her kidnapped so that when she's found they can go rushing to clasp her to their bosoms?" What a horrifying thought. "I can't imagine." But she couldn't be sure, either, Beth realized. She knew her parents, and yet she didn't. They were not quite human, she had understood that long ago. Was there any chance that Rachel's very public death, and the implication that it had been suicide, had damaged Laurence Greenway's reputation? And that he'd decided the damage could be bandaged over by the sight of him and his wife tenderly taking on responsibility for their ten-year-old granddaughter, with her big solemn eyes and her unnatural gravity.

"Oh, God," Beth whispered.

"It's a thought, isn't it?"

"Yes." She'd had to push the word past a lump in her throat.

"A likely one?"

A scheme like that would be twisted, hateful, cold-blooded. All of which her parents could be. "I don't know," she admitted, then winced. One more thing she didn't know.

But there was no hint of irony in his expression. "It's time I go visit your parents again."

On a rush of alarm, she said, "You won't mention...?"

In the act of standing with his plate in one hand and a serving bowl in the other, he raised his eyebrows. "The big guns you haven't yet rolled out? No. But I'll hope to be watching when you use them."

That warmed her. The sensation stayed with her while he helped her clean up, carried her television to the garage, and even after he left. It was as unfamiliar as the way he'd held her. As the kind note she sometimes heard in his voice. She was suspicious of this warmth, as if she were a cat circling a puzzling but irresistible object that had appeared in its territory.

But it feels so good. He might think she was crazy, but he believed her. Maybe even believed *in* her.

SICILY ATE YET ANOTHER cheeseburger and French fries with hunger but no enthusiasm. God, was that all he ever ate? She wondered if this was lunch or dinner or even breakfast. All she knew for sure was that it wasn't the middle of the night, because didn't most Burger Kings close at, like, ten o'clock? And the food was warm. Plus, she thought there must be one nearby. She bet he didn't like leaving her here alone very long. Although what he thought she could do, Sicily couldn't imagine. Claw her way through the wall with her fingernails?

She lay on her side curled in a ball. She was spending most of her time that way. Sometimes she made herself get up and walk around the room, but then she felt like one of the big cats at the zoo, pacing, pacing. She had always felt sorry for them. Now she never wanted to go in the cat house again.

If I ever get out of here.

She felt weird. Lightheaded. She'd really believed she could get away, but she wasn't so sure anymore. He kept surprising her. It was hard to stay alert, when so many hours passed between visits. Sicily was beginning to hope, *a lot,* that he'd called her grandparents and asked for ransom. If they paid, he'd let her go, wouldn't he? He didn't look like a killer.

How would I know what a killer looks like?

If he was her dad, it was less likely he'd hurt her. *Please don't let him be my dad.* But wait. If he *was,* that might mean she was safer.

But oh, she didn't want a father like him.

The thought sneaked in that he wasn't much different from the guys her mom was always bringing home. She used to look at them and think, *I'm glad* he's *not my dad.* For some reason she never thought that, if these were the kind of guys Mom liked, maybe her father was the same. Because *her* dad was a rock star. Well, almost a rock star. He'd been somebody really cool when Mom met him.

Mom, she admitted now, had pretty sucky taste

in men. Mostly she went for guys who liked to party and who knew where to get the drugs she liked. She almost always worked, but at things like waitressing. When she got fired because she overslept too many times, she'd only shrug. There was always someplace else that would hire her.

We got by okay, Sicily thought defensively, as if someone was criticizing her mom to her face. She didn't like knowing *she* was the one thinking bad thoughts about Mom.

Sometime during the night—or day, or whatever it was—she admitted to herself that she liked living with Aunt Beth better than she did with Mom. She didn't exactly feel at home, but she liked that Aunt Beth was neat, too, like Sicily was, and that she planned meals a week in advance and wasn't always looking at Sicily when they got to the store saying, "Do we have any milk?" Sicily had started making grocery lists when she was, like, five. She'd learned a long time ago to count in her head, too, so that she knew whether they could afford that hamburger or not before she or Mom put it in the cart.

And she liked the stuff Aunt Beth had bought her. If she could have Mom back, she thought fiercely, she wouldn't mind that all her clothes came from thrift stores and the collection the school kept for poor kids. But since having Mom back wasn't an option, she did like her new clothes.

Pulling the thin comforter tighter around herself, she wished she hadn't worn shorts to the beach. She'd really, really like it if she had on jeans now, and at least a T-shirt that covered her shoulders. And socks, too.

Except, she had a dim memory of a fairy tale where this man wasted his three wishes because without thinking he kept saying things like, "I wish I'd remembered to grab my coat before I went out the door." And then he'd have his coat on, but he hadn't meant that to be an actual *wish.*

So I *won't be that dumb.* I *won't wish for anything but to get away. To go home to Aunt Beth.*

"AND WHEN DID YOU GET THIS demand for a ransom?" Mike was furious on so many levels, he couldn't count them. Laurence Greenway hadn't been thinking about his granddaughter or his daughter when he'd failed to contact police immediately. He'd been thinking about himself, which was apparently all he knew how to do.

Greenway didn't bother to hide his dislike or disdain. "This afternoon. It came a couple of hours earlier, but I hadn't checked messages. My wife and I had agreed to speak to a television reporter."

It was now eight-thirty in the evening. The message had been left as early as midday. Greenway had heard it as much as six hours ago. Mike didn't even try to hide his disgust. "And, knowing we were searching desperately for Sicily, you kept this news to yourself because…?"

"We were instructed not to involve law enforcement." Beth's father neither sat down nor invited Mike to do so, although he'd led him to the living room. Rowena hadn't put in an appearance. "We had to consider the possibility that we would have more success recovering our granddaughter if we followed instructions."

"Mr. Greenway, as a wealthy businessman you have surely considered the risks of you or your wife being kidnapped and held for ransom."

The other man gave a grudging nod.

"I presume you're also aware, then, that many if not most hostages are not freed once the ransom is paid. They've seen too much, heard too much. They can identify their captors. The moment the money changes hands, the life of the hostage holds no value to the kidnapper."

"That's why we're turning to you now."

"And yet you didn't phone me. You're telling me because I happened to show up on your doorstep?"

The two men exchanged a hard stare. Mike finally shook his head. "It's time we involve the FBI. They're the experts. They've got resources I don't."

Greenway gave a clipped nod.

"First, let me hear this demand."

"Very well." He removed his phone from his

belt, brought up voice mail, listened for a moment then said, "It's on speaker."

A nondescript male voice said, "I have Sicily. You want her back? I figure you owe me some bucks for your precious grandkid. Here, Sicily, talk." There was a small pause. The slightest click? They could hear someone breathing. The man's voice, muffled but edgy, ordered, "Do it."

Mike tensed. Before his mind's eye, he saw the girl's face, too grave, too old for her years, the cheekbones and mouth and poise that promised this duckling would become a swan, given half a chance. He had never in his life despised anyone the way he did the man standing here, pretending he gave a damn about that little girl.

"Grandma and Grandpa, he says he'll do something bad to me if you don't pay him a million dollars." Her voice was not shaky the way Mike might have expected. "I know that's a lot of money...." She gasped, as if... Goddamn it, as if the guy had shaken her or cut her with the razor edge of a knife blade. She finished in a hurry, more rattled this time. "Please will you pay him so I can go home to Aunt Beth."

There was a pause and a shuffling sound. "Get the money together," the scum said. "Cash, not new bills, not sequential. I'll be in touch."

"Play it again," Mike said.

"What?"

"I want to listen to it again. I don't think she was on the phone with him. I think he'd recorded her."

Greenway looked momentarily startled, but was too smart not to grasp the implications. Without a word, he brought it back up again. Neither of them so much as breathed while the message played again.

"All right," Mike said, "I have to make some calls. I'll need to speak to my captain before I contact the Bureau."

"Very well." Did the jackass look chastened? Mike couldn't tell. And why would he? He hadn't rescued his daughters. What would motivate him to save the granddaughter he scarcely knew?

Reputation, that's what. Political power. Beth and Rachel had suffered unseen, unheard. They had therefore been meaningless to this man. Sicily's predicament, in contrast, had become a headliner.

Left alone in the study, Mike made his phone calls. Within an hour, a team of federal agents had arrived at the Greenways' home. Their machinery rolled into action, as they set to work tracing and analyzing the call.

For all practical purposes, Sicily's abduction had been taken out of Mike's hands.

When he excused himself to step outside, one of the four agents gave him a surprised look—*you're still here?*—and then an absent nod. Standing on the portico, he dialed Beth's number, hoping she hadn't gone to bed.

"Mike?" The breathless quality of hope couldn't be hidden. "Have you heard anything?"

Suppressing his stab of pleasure that she'd called him by his first name, he said, "Your parents received a call demanding ransom."

There was a breathless silence. "Oh, God."

"It's better news than hearing nothing."

Her intake of breath told him she got it.

"Beth, Sicily spoke on the message. She said she hoped her grandparents would pay so she could go home to you."

The sound she made was barely audible, but, as if he could see her, he knew she'd clapped a hand to her mouth to silence a sob. It was a moment before she could speak at all, and then it was urgently. "I need to hear it. What if it's not her? Would my parents even recognize her voice?"

"Your father says he's pretty sure it's her." Mike had already made the decision not to tell her that he believed Sicily had been recorded. It could mean nothing—the kidnapper didn't want to take a chance she'd yell out something before he could cut the connection. But there was an uglier possibility: that he'd recorded several messages and then had no more use for his troublesome child hostage.

"Please," Beth begged. "Let me hear it."

He explained about the FBI's Child Abduction Rapid Deployment—CARD—teams, and told her that he would have brought them in by morning even if there'd been no ransom call. "The father is still a possibility, but otherwise we're looking at a stranger abduction. We need them," he said, even though he hadn't been thrilled to make the decision. As lead on an investigation, he'd never had to work with the FBI, but they had a reputation for sweeping in and taking over. Sweeping in so vigorously, Eddie had said once, that he'd felt like some dust whisked out of the way. Like most cops, Mike was enough of a control freak to dislike the idea. But he was damned well going to do what was best for Sicily. He repeated now for Beth what he'd told her father. "I guarantee they'll be wanting to talk to you."

"Does that mean…" She stopped, started again. "Does it mean they'll be taking over and I won't see you again?"

"Yes and no." He gazed at the garden, lit by strategically placed spotlights. "They'll likely be running the show, and for good reason. But they won't expect us to step out of the investigation, either. They may bring in other jurisdictions. If there's reason to suspect Sicily is being held in Seattle or King County, for example, those departments will come on board."

"I suppose my father is demanding the best."

He heard her ambivalence and smiled ruefully. "It never hurts when someone as prominent as your father is involved. In this case, I don't think it matters. The abduction of a child is always taken seriously. And Laurence Greenway may be hot stuff in state politics, but he has no influence on the FBI's funding."

"Okay." She was quiet for a minute. "Thank you for calling. Not knowing is the worst." *No,* he thought. *No, the worst part is when you do know. When you race into the hospital with terror in your heart only to be told your child is dead.*

"Never knowing would be bad," he conceded.

"I can't imagine."

"Now that the guy has made contact, the odds of finding her have improved a whole lot."

"Okay. Um, when they come to talk to me. Will you be with them?"

He rubbed a hand over the back of his neck and felt like a love—or at least lust—sick teenager when he asked, "Do you want me to be?"

"Yes. You've been kind, even when…"

When she didn't finish, he did. "Even when I was pawing through your underwear drawer."

"Yes." Though the reminder had renewed the starch in her voice.

Mike counted his blessings that he hadn't actually poked through her lingerie. He was already holding on to his honor by his fingernails. If he had to picture her in a skimpy black satin bra, he'd be dead.

He closed his eyes and turned his back on the yard. "I'll be there if I can."

"Thank you," she said very politely and with renewed distance. Mike realized she must not have read his gruffness right. And maybe, he thought, that was just as well. This was still, on some level, his investigation, and she still played a significant role in it. He'd be an idiot to forget that.

"I'll be talking to you," he said, and ended the call, feeling like a son of a bitch, but also knowing he had to be careful.

Yeah, he sympathized with her. He even believed, on a gut level, that she was innocent. He kept asking himself how much more he would have suffered if he'd not only had to grieve for Nate, but had also been under suspicion of causing his death. And what if he had been as alone as she was? His marriage had essentially ended that day in the hospital, but through it all he'd had his parents, his sisters. Beth apparently had nobody. She'd probably tell him she didn't want anybody, but he didn't believe it. He remembered the way she'd leaned on him today, clutching him with desperate hands.

He closed his eyes in anguish. The truth was, learning about her abuse had infuriated him, but it had also raised a big red flag he couldn't ignore.

Abused children grew up to be abusers. That was reality. He'd seen her meltdowns and now knew the rigid woman he'd first met sometimes lost control in spectacular ways. He didn't like thinking it—he still didn't believe it—but the possibility existed that she had lost it with Sicily and killed her. That this whole mess really was a cover-up. Maybe she wasn't so alone after all; maybe she had an associate who'd made that phone call. Was that really Sicily's voice at all? Greenway thought so. If Beth insisted that she was sure, she might be lying.

They'd have to get Sicily's teacher to listen to the message, too, he realized. He hoped they could do that without Beth knowing.

He'd been an idiot not to check her finances, too, personal and business. What if this wasn't a cover-up? What if it really was a kidnapping, but Beth was in on it? She had more reason than anyone to hate her parents. Maybe they hadn't been willing to help her out of a bind. Or maybe this was simply a way to hit them where it hurt. He could see her justifying it in her head; Sicily wasn't in any actual danger, and the Greenways *owed* Beth and Sicily, too. He heard again the way the scum had said "your precious grandchild." The bitterness. Reflecting Beth's bitterness?

"Damn," he muttered, dismayed at how sick he felt. At how much he wanted *not* to believe in any of it.

CHAPTER NINE

MIKE WAS THE FIRST TO ARRIVE in the morning, five minutes ahead of the FBI agents. Not until this morning had she gotten a call making an appointment.

Beth felt such a rush of gratitude at the sight of him, her voice cracked when she thanked him for coming.

He looked at her without any emotion whatsoever. "It's still my case."

She automatically drew back into herself. This was not the man who'd cooked dinner for her last night. This was the detective who'd spearheaded the search of her house yesterday. Had everything he'd done and said later been an act? Maybe her suspicion that he was playing good cop/bad cop was truer than she'd known. Playing bad cop hadn't gotten him anywhere, so he'd come back to take another shot at it. Be nice, get her talking.

I exceeded his wildest expectations, Beth realized, shame gripping her. Oh, boy, had she ever opened up to him. She'd been stupid enough to think he did believe her. Believed in her? What a fool she was.

He was back this morning not because she'd asked, or thought she needed support, but because it was his job. Because, even if he wouldn't be the one grilling her this time, he'd still be weighing her every word.

"You've heard everything I have to say," she said coolly, and went to the kitchen without looking to see if he followed.

He didn't. The doorbell rang, followed by the sound of voices. Déjà vu.

Determined to remain utterly composed, Beth went to greet the two agents, a man and a woman, and to offer them coffee. Everyone murmured pleased acceptance. She brought the cups in on a tray along with sugar and cream and let them all doctor their coffee to suit themselves.

Logically she knew there were female FBI agents, but was still surprised to meet one. Middle-aged and pleasant-faced, she introduced herself as Agent Trenor and the younger man as Agent Vandemark. Clearly, they weren't going to be on a first-name basis.

They had all been standing when she brought the coffee. When she sat at one end of the sofa, Mike moved without haste but also without wasting any time to take the other end. The two federal agents, left flat-footed, had no choice but to sit in chairs facing the sofa. Maybe their preference, she reminded herself; they might have even asked him to give them the direct line of sight since he'd had the advantage of earlier interrogations. Or maybe he was intimidated by them… One sidelong glance killed that idea. He was watchful, but at ease. Deferring to their expertise didn't seem to diminish his air of sheer male dominance.

Carefully setting her coffee cup to one side, the woman agent opened a laptop on the table and booted it up. "Let's start with the ransom demand," she said.

Beth tensed.

The message, played from the laptop, was startlingly loud and clear. Her eyes widened at the sound of a click right after the man said, "Here, Sicily, talk." She almost forgot it in a rush of emotion when Sicily's voice came on. She jolted when Sicily gasped. And…was that a smaller click when Sicily finished talking?

"Are my parents prepared to pay?" Staring at the two agents, Beth knew she looked and sounded fierce.

"You haven't been in communication with them?" the woman asked. Her tone was law-enforcement neutral, which failed to disguise her intense interest.

"We don't have a close relationship. I heard about the ransom call from Detective Ryan." She hoped they didn't hear the slight hitch where she'd almost said "Mike." His expression didn't change, while the other two studied her as if she were a bug on a pin. She didn't care; didn't care about anything but the answer to her question.

"We hope it won't come to that," the man said, "although your father has expressed his willingness to follow instructions."

Her sinuses burned. She swallowed, nodded. Of course he would. How would it look if a man as wealthy as Laurence Greenway refused to pay ransom for his granddaughter?

"You believe that's Sicily's voice," Agent Trenor said.

"Yes." Oh, yes. She had never heard Sicily scared before, but for a moment there, she definitely was. "He recorded her earlier, didn't he?"

In her peripheral vision she saw Mike's hand twitch. She wished quite suddenly that it was holding hers. She imagined it warm, strong, possibly callused. *Get over it,* she told herself harshly. The comfort he'd offered her was a tactic, no more. *And don't forget it.*

The two agents glanced at each other before the woman inclined her head. "Yes, we believe so."

"Do you think she's still alive?" Beth heard how calm she sounded, how in control. She'd never been so aware she was pretending.

"The odds are excellent." The woman was

clearly the designated spokesperson. "It's the norm in a ransom negotiation for the person paying— in this case, your father—to insist on proof that the hostage is alive and well. Anyone asking for an amount as substantial as a million dollars will have anticipated that request."

She nodded. *Oh, Sicily.* No. Focus. "Have you learned anything from the message?"

There was the briefest hesitation. They were here to ask *her* questions, not answer hers. But Agent Trenor said matter-of-factly, "It came from a throwaway cell phone, which is what we would expect."

She went on to ask questions, all of which Beth had answered before. Was this new territory to them? How much had Mike briefed them? Were they trying to trip her up? Or merely wanting to gain an impression of Sicily and her family background firsthand? Beth couldn't tell. They didn't seem very interested in family dynamics, but were very focused on Chad Marks. He had an arrest record, Beth heard for the first time, although a glance at Mike told her he wasn't surprised. Mostly petty theft, shoplifting a couple of times—wine in both cases—and he had been identified on a security tape holding up a liquor store but dropped from sight afterward and wasn't arrested.

"You say you went to one of his concerts and

yet you can't identify his voice." They all looked at her. *Explain that.*

"It could be him." Unfortunately, she didn't remember him having an especially distinctive voice, which might be one of the reasons the band hadn't hit it big. "I can't say it isn't." She held up her hands in a gesture of helplessness. "It was only the once, and mostly he was singing. You know what it's like when it's amplified, and the crowd is noisy, and honestly it sounded more like yelling than singing. And a lot of the time there were two of them singing." She had a thought. "Can't you find someone who knew him better? One of his bandmates? And didn't my parents meet him?"

"Yes, but neither of them seemed quite certain of his voice, either. They said the same thing you did. It could be him, but it could just as well not be."

On impulse she asked, "Did you notice the way he said 'your precious grandkid?' Didn't it seem… angry?"

Mike's hand spasmed again, his fingers curling into a fist. Beth pulled her gaze from it to see the two FBI agents studying her. She saw interest in their expressions.

"We did notice." This time it was the younger one who spoke. "Would Chad Marks have any reason to resent your parents?"

"I don't know why he would."

Mike cleared his throat.

Feeling blood heating her cheeks, Beth looked down at her lap. There seemed to be a grease stain on her jeans, she noticed, as if two parts of her brain were operating entirely independently. The silence was absolute; everyone was waiting. For her. Dear God. Had he already told them?

I can do this.

"If he cared about Rachel…" Her throat seemed to thicken. She gave herself a moment so that she could continue unemotionally. "Our mother was abusive, our father indifferent. Rachel likely told Chad about her childhood. At the time, that would have given him reason to dislike my parents. That was a lot of years ago, though, and why would he sound so sharp about Sicily, his own daughter? They have never been interested in her. I can't imagine Rachel ever saying anything to him that would make him believe Sicily was especially precious to them."

Mike spoke up for the first time. "Most of the message sounded by rote, as if he'd written it down for himself. But he slipped there. That was personal. He hates your parents. He blames them for something."

Beth laughed, and saw she'd taken the newcomers by surprise. Perhaps it was the corrosive quality of that laugh. "I suspect there are a great number of people who hate my father."

Agent Trenor's interest sharpened. "Can you name anyone?"

"No, but he's made a lot of money. It's hard not to make enemies along the way. And I'm sure you're aware how deeply he's involved in state politics. Again, I imagine there are people he initially supported then dropped, or went out of his way to see defeated. I can't tell you. I've never been involved in his public life."

"What about your mother?" asked the woman agent.

"I...don't know." Beth tried to think about it objectively. "I guess I'd be surprised. You've met her, haven't you? She's attractive and charming, a perfect hostess for my father. She has a wide circle of friends who aren't close enough to know what she's really like."

"What is she like?"

She supposed they couldn't help their curiosity, even though at this point they had no reason to suspect either of her parents of having anything to do with Sicily's abduction. Unless Mike had shared his conspiracy theory? But she doubted it, because she thought they'd been surprised when she told them she and Rachel were abused. So he hadn't already told them. Small comfort.

"On the outside, very controlled, very conscious of appearances," she said finally. "She's witty, elegant. But I think she feels a great deal of rage. It comes out in...bursts. I've wondered..."

Now she was looking at Mike. His hand, no longer curled in a fist, had somehow moved closer to hers.

"You've wondered?" As if from a distance, Beth realized it was the woman agent who'd prompted her.

"Whether she was abused by her own parents. They lived on the East Coast. Supposedly that's why we never knew them. But she didn't talk about them. They...didn't exist."

The agents left twenty minutes later, thanking her for her cooperation and promising to be in touch. Beth felt less battered than she had expected. Either they hadn't been as aggressive as Mike, or she was becoming inured to being under suspicion. Or it might simply be that they had his notes and didn't need to ask all the same questions.

Mike had risen and walked with them to the door, but he made no move to leave. She closed it. "I suppose you have more questions."

"Not the way you mean."

The way she meant? What way did *he* mean? Anger at the way he blew hot to cold and back again kept her spine straight and her chin high.

"You must want something."

"I do. I want you to talk to me more about Sicily."

She stared at him. "You plan to ask nine million more questions I can only answer by saying 'I don't know'?" No, she hadn't been looking forward to regaining her solitude, but exposing herself to a cruel display of her inadequacies as a guardian sounded way worse.

He had the grace to look uncomfortable. "Nothing like that. The two of you must have talked. Done things together. It's possible she's said things you've forgotten."

"Like?"

"About her mother. Her mother's friends. Boyfriends. Anything that would give me some insight. I spent a good part of yesterday talking to neighbors and the few of Rachel's friends I could find."

"I don't understand." And she wasn't convinced he was admitting to his real agenda.

"I suspect the FBI will be pursuing the possibility that the kidnapper is someone who hates your father. They're better equipped for that than I am. I'm not convinced anyway. How many people that your parents deal with on a business or social level even know they have a granddaughter? They certainly didn't have her on display. And to a lot of those people, a million dollars isn't much. From what I've learned, your sister had some sleazy friends, and to them, a million bucks is a fortune. They knew Sicily. Rachel might have talked about how rich and stingy her parents were. How they didn't even care about their own granddaughter."

"Their 'precious granddaughter'," Beth murmured.

"Exactly. A guy who'd lived with Rachel and Sicily would know about you, maybe made a note of your address. Did you know the last boyfriend stayed on in her apartment until the rent ran out?"

Startled, Beth said, "No. I went to pack and clean, but that was on the last day of the month."

"Nobody remembers his name. That's one of the things I'm hoping Sicily told you. He had plenty of time to hunt through your sister's things. All I do know about him is that he wasn't working and Rachel was about to toss him because he was sponging off her."

"You're saying he might have thought of a way to keep sponging off her."

"You've got it."

"All right," she said, sighing. She wasn't trusting Mike the way she had, but she'd talk to him. She would do anything to get Sicily back.

"Can I have another cup of coffee?" he asked hopefully.

She narrowed her eyes, tempted to tell him not to push his luck, but, damn it, she wanted another cup, too.

BY UNSPOKEN AGREEMENT, THEY sat at the dining room table, facing each other across a width of gleaming maple wood that provided both separation and barrier. It was safer for him this way, Mike thought, and he suspected she had no desire to be close to him right now, either. He hadn't been giving her much reason to like him.

Things were stilted when they started. No, Sicily hadn't had much to say when Beth first brought her home. No, she didn't even cry. She seemed to be in shock.

"She was in school, you know. She didn't know why her mother was on the ferry. Sicily said maybe she'd gone to see a friend."

"She disappeared on the eastbound trip," Mike mused, "so she did cross over that morning and do something. Maybe only drive off and get in line to come back."

At that point Beth seemed to forget she disliked him and became interested in the conversation. She frowned. "Wouldn't somebody have noticed?"

He shook his head. "Too many cars. And remember, there are two ferries covering the route. She could have ridden over on one and come back on a different one."

Beth nodded acknowledgment. "So she might really have had an errand. Or she might have chickened out on the way over."

"If she did commit suicide, your sister might have planned all along to do it on the way back. Suicide," he said, as gently as he could, "is essentially a selfish act." When she didn't protest as he'd expected, Mike continued. "That said, people who have decided to kill themselves sometimes do strangely considerate things. I saw one where the guy spread a tarp so his blood didn't ruin the carpet when he shot himself. What it was going to do to his wife or his fifteen-year-old son when they found him dead apparently didn't cross his mind. Instead, he wanted to make sure the clean-up was easy."

Beth made what was likely an involuntary sound. "Which one found him?"

He focused on her. Damn. He should have edited the story. "The son," he said reluctantly.

She shivered.

"What I'm saying is, your sister might have thought it would be easier if her car ended up on the home side of the Sound. When she planned, a detail like that might have mattered."

He watched her struggle with that for a minute. Then she said, "No one even mentioned the possibility that she might have been pushed. It didn't occur to me then, but now… What if the boyfriend suggested the kidnapping thing and Rachel refused? What if he killed her to get her out of the way?"

"The thought did cross my mind," Mike told her, "but there's no evidence to suggest it. She didn't have a passenger in the car."

"How do you know?"

"The ticket was on the seat when the car was found abandoned."

"Oh."

"A struggle would have been likelier to draw attention, too. If she was caught by surprise, wouldn't you think she'd still have screamed as she went over the railing?"

He saw her swallow before nodding.

"It would be a high-risk place to kill someone anyway, because ferries are loaded with passengers, many of whom spend the ride looking at the view. It's pretty likely someone would see her go over or see her struggling once she was in the water. Then she'd be rescued and name her assailant."

Mike tried to steer her back to talking about Sicily, but the first thing she said was, "We rode over and back on the ferry. Edmonds-Kingston."

"What?"

"Sicily asked if we could." Beth seemed to be looking into the past. "I suppose that sounds macabre, doesn't it? But the funeral didn't seem to have anything to do with Rachel, not really. Riding the ferry was sort of a memorial service."

"Did Sicily talk about her mom?"

"A little bit, but neither of us said much. We walked on—you know, there wasn't any reason to take a car. I thought someday we might go back and have lunch in Kingston, try to take the horror out of crossing over on the ferry, but that day we walked off and walked right back on. Both directions we stood outside, up on the prow, and looked at the water and the seagulls. I tried to imagine how Rachel felt when she went in."

Double damn. He imagined the two of them, this woman who was the loneliest person he'd ever met, and the kid with the solemn eyes who was trying to accept the fact that her mother had chosen to leave her. He wondered if they'd been invisible in the midst of more cheerful riders, or whether they'd generated some kind of force field that kept people away from them.

"Sounds grim," he said.

She shook herself. "I suppose it was, but…" Her head tilted to one side. "It's funny, but that day was also a breakthrough for the two of us. I didn't realize it then, but I think she started to trust me after that. I could tell she thought I'd say no, and when I said, 'If that's what you need to do,' she started to open up. So it didn't turn out to be a bad thing." She smiled, but it wobbled slightly. "We came home and baked. Cheap therapy. We baked bread from scratch, and pummeling dough is satisfying, you know. Then cookies, too. Ginger molasses. She told me she thought about becoming a chef because she really likes to cook."

Mike let her keep talking, only adding a murmured question now and again when she slowed down. Despite how much she didn't know about her niece, it turned out there was a lot she did know. She told him about a reserved, thoughtful girl who had a sly sense of humor and an adult way of looking at people.

"It doesn't sound as if she ever had friends. They moved so much, and it's hard when you're new to start all over. But also..." Beth hesitated. "Mostly I think she was never really a kid. Her main goal was taking care of her mother. I think in her own mind Rachel was the focus, but there had to be an element of fear, too. What would happen to her if her mom overdosed, or if they got evicted, or had no money for groceries?"

Mike nodded with understanding.

"She doesn't like to say anything bad about Rachel, but she didn't understand why her mom kept bringing guys home. 'Things were good when it was just us,' she said once, and then, 'I don't think she even liked them.'"

"That's a pretty mature observation for a ten-year-old."

"Yes. She said..." Beth stopped suddenly, her eyes widening. "Tyler. His name was Tyler."

Mike sat up straighter. "The most recent guy?"

"Yes. Oh, why didn't I remember that? She said most of the guys hardly knew she existed, but she didn't like the way Tyler looked at her."

"Well, now," Mike said softly. "Anything else?"

She shook her head. "I tried to get her to say how he looked at her, but she wouldn't."

"Or couldn't," he suggested. "She might not recognize a sexual appraisal."

"I hope she wouldn't." Beth fastened those big brown eyes on him and said, "I'm scared."

"Yeah, I know."

"YOU SAID SOMETHING TO ME once." Beth tried to remember his wording. "About losing someone important to you. A child."

His withdrawal was visible. Still, after a minute he dipped his head. "Yes."

"Who was it?" She wouldn't blame him if he told her it was none of her business. But at this moment she desperately needed something—a connection to him. He had loomed so huge in her life since Sicily's disappearance. Whether he was enemy or friend or both, she was having trouble imagining him gone from it.

Muscles in his jaw knotted. Finally, he said, "My son. He drowned when he was three years old."

"I'm so sorry." Her voice was drenched with compassion she hadn't known she had in her. The pain in his eyes bounced off the fear and pain in her chest, intensifying them.

He nodded. She wanted to ask how it had happened, but knew she had no right.

"My wife…" He stopped, shoved back his chair and stood, standing with his back to Beth. He continued with obvious difficulty. "She'd taken him to a friend's house. Ellen had put Nate down for a nap. She and the friend got talking, then Ellen took a phone call. It wasn't until the friend looked out her kitchen window and thought she saw…" He sucked in a breath, bent his head and began kneading the back of his neck.

My wife. He was married? But right this second, it didn't seem to matter. Without knowing she was doing it, Beth stood, too, and went to him. She didn't even know where this instinct had come from. *I don't know how to do this.* But he'd held her when she needed it. So, though it felt awkward, she wrapped her arms around him. "I'm sorry," she murmured again, squeezed him hard and then tried to step back.

Clumsily for such a graceful man, he turned and his arms came around her with a kind of desperation.

MIKE WAS ASHAMED OF NEEDING her so much. It had been a long time since he'd felt this hunger to have one particular person in his arms. Since before his marriage had disintegrated, maybe even longer than that. He and Ellen had had a decent marriage.

If someone asked, he'd have said he was happy. After the way he lashed out at her at the hospital, fueled by anger and grief, he had tried not to let her know he blamed her for Nate's death. She was right, accidents happened. No parent could watch their child around the clock. With all the will and love in the world, you couldn't guarantee another person's safety.

But he hadn't been able to shake the blame, and the strain of pretending got to him. It got to them both, he eventually acknowledged. She'd known. Blamed herself, of course. Their only hope would have been him offering her unconditional forgiveness and faith, and he couldn't do that.

It took him time—long after they separated and then divorced—to understand that while he'd believed he loved Ellen, there were things about her he didn't like. She had no ability to be self-sufficient. She hated being by herself. If she wasn't with a friend, she was on the phone. She was desperate for him to get home and miserably unhappy when he didn't make it when she expected him. His job hadn't yet become a big issue between them, but he'd sensed that it would someday. When he did make it home, she wanted to go out, if not with him, with her friends. He knew she loved Nate, but sometimes he thought their child was an accessory for her, not a real person who deserved significant blocks of undivided attention.

Probably, he had come to realize, she'd simply not been ready to become a mother. They'd been so damn young.

She might have been happier if she'd kept working after Nate was born, but the only job experience she had was as a salesclerk, which wouldn't have paid enough to justify child care. Ellen was bright and bubbly and made him laugh in their early days, which kept him from noticing that she was shallow. She liked hearing funny stories from his job, but not the harrowing ones. Most of the time he wouldn't have shared those anyway, so that was fine.

But now, with this woman holding him securely, he realized that once in a while he'd wanted his wife to see on his face that his day had been bad and hold out her arms to him.

He struggled to pull himself together and finally let her go. She did the same and stepped back.

They looked at each other self-consciously.

"I hope you have other children," she said after a minute.

Mike shook his head. "Nate was our only. Ellen and I didn't last another year."

"I'm sorry. You must have been angry at her."

"I was," he admitted. "I knew it was irrational, but I couldn't get past it. She was at a friend's house, she was chattering on the phone, and it turned out the sliding door was open and the screen wasn't latched even though they had a pool in the backyard. Ellen never sat—she tended to bop around while she was talking. I guess her back was turned when Nate pushed open the screen door."

"That's why you were angry at me," Beth said suddenly. "Because I wasn't paying attention, either."

He gripped the back of his neck. "I hoped that wasn't obvious."

"I could feel it." She closed her eyes for a moment. "I don't blame you. I shouldn't have…"

"No." His voice came out too loud. "No, you were right. Sicily is ten, not three." And Ellen was right, too. Could he swear Nate wouldn't have been able to get by him if he and a buddy were watching a ball game on TV, talking? When he'd believed Nate to be fast asleep?

Beth sucked in a breath. "Are you…? Would you like a sandwich?"

Not smart. He should leave. Now.

"Yeah," he said. "Please."

They cleared the cups from the living room, which they hadn't done earlier. Then Beth put together sandwiches with turkey, Havarti and a heap of vegetables on some kind of multigrain bread, and got them sodas.

As they had last night, they ate with very little conversation. She only had half her sandwich, though, before seeming to lose interest. She pushed that shiny brown hair behind her ear and fastened intense eyes on him. "Do you think it's the boyfriend who has her?"

He hesitated, thought about all the scenarios including the ones in which she played a part, then told her the truth. "No. My best guess is still Sicily's father. You're right, there was something really personal in his voice. It's hard to see why an enemy your father earned in business or politics would fasten on his granddaughter that way. Use her, sure. But whoever this is, he is angry at your parents and somehow Sicily is mixed up in that anger. The boyfriend hadn't been around that long. He might have come up with this great scheme, but why would he be angry at your parents? Now Chad, that's different. Could be he's angry that Rachel getting pregnant pushed him into marrying her. Was there pressure from your parents?"

"We weren't talking. But if I had to guess…no. She was only seventeen, remember. They were more likely to want her to fix everything by having an abortion. *Their* daughter getting pregnant at seventeen and marrying a rocker? That would be incomprehensible to them."

"But we don't know what Rachel told Chad," Mike reminded her. "*She* might have put pressure on him by using her parents."

"I suppose that's possible."

She got up and poured them more coffee, which seemed to help his thinking process. "Or maybe he thought the baby was his ticket to serious bucks. In his eyes, your parents were loaded. Why wouldn't they help their precious daughter and granddaughter?" He used the word on purpose, and wasn't surprised at how quickly she caught on.

"He wasn't saying 'your precious granddaughter' bitterly. He was saying it sarcastically."

"That wasn't my first impression, but now... It could be. He was sarcastic, but there was an edge of anger, too."

"Yes," she said slowly. "Oh, God. If it was Chad, how did he find her? How did he know we were at the park?"

"He followed you. Your address is listed. Which is a mistake," he added parenthetically. "Get it out of the next directory." He looked her in the eyes. They were like melted caramel, he thought, warm and soft and rich.

"Did you take Sicily to school, or did she ride the bus?" He should have asked sooner.

"Bus. Right at the corner."

"Was she alone waiting?"

"No, there are two other kids."

"Then, unless by chance she was out there by herself one morning, getting her alone near your house was a no-go. He needs to reduce his chances of being seen. So he waits until the weekend and hopes she'll go somewhere with friends, or the two of you will head somewhere he might have a better chance. Maybe a mall where you let her go get something to eat while you try on shoes. Anyplace that nobody will pay attention to him. The park is perfect. Sicily is by herself briefly, probably because she went up to the restroom alone. He could have been parked right next to the building, which would block him from sight of the parking lot and picnic area. She comes out on her own—did you notice the women's restroom exits that way?—no one visible, he could have her in the trunk of his car in a matter of seconds."

"Yes." Face stricken, she pressed her hand to her stomach.

Oh, hell. He'd been talking to her as if she were another cop, not thinking how vivid this scenario would be to her. "I'm sorry."

"You think I haven't pictured it a million times? And worse things?"

He nodded, accepting. "I know you have."

"At least she's alive." She caught herself. "Probably alive."

"Almost certainly. Who hasn't seen enough movies to know the concept of providing proof of life?"

Her eyes were fastened desperately on his. "Yes, but what about after that?"

"The goal is to find her before the ransom drop

takes place. Or, worst case, follow whoever picks up the money."

"Will you be doing that?"

"Damn straight I plan to be in on it. I'm unlikely to be in charge, though. This is the FBI's show now. What's more, chances are good it'll happen in Everett or Seattle, say. Somewhere more populated. The local P.D. will be brought in."

"Oh." She didn't much like it, he saw, but accepted reality. "Thank you," she said. "For everything you've done."

"For hounding you, you mean?" He offered a crooked smile.

To his astonishment, she returned a genuine one. "Even that. You did it for Sicily. That was what was really important. That you thought about her first. I could tell you cared. That meant a lot to me."

He was reeling from the smile. It lit her face to real beauty. He wondered what she'd look like when she was truly happy, when blue semicircles didn't underlie her eyes, when her mouth wasn't compressed with anguish or tension, when her posture wasn't stiff. He bet she'd been gorgeous three days ago when she'd laid back on her blanket with the sun warm on her face and had closed her eyes, relaxing utterly.

He tuned back in to notice that awareness had flared in her eyes.

"Why are you looking at me like that?" She was almost whispering.

"Your smile…" He cleared his throat. "I was wondering what you look like when you're happy."

Some bleak knowledge stole most expression from her face. "I'm not very often. With Sicily, I've been feeling my way." Even more softly, she added, "I want to be happy."

He held out his hand and surprised himself by a naked truth he hadn't known until this minute. "I want to be, too."

CHAPTER TEN

WITHOUT HESITATION, BETH LAID her hand in his. "How long ago did it happen?" she asked.

"Eight years." He closed his fingers around hers, feeling their delicacy. She was so fine-boned. There wasn't much to her but those bones, smooth skin, vivid eyes and hair of a color so rich he sometimes imagined closing his eyes and inhaling its essence like freshly brewed, dark-roasted coffee.

"You must have been young." Even if he were a few years older than her, he had to be in his early twenties when he had his son.

"We married younger than we should have. Neither of us were ready to start a family that quickly, either, but Nate… When your kid is born, you fall in love like you didn't know was possible." Those memories squeezed his heart. "At least that's how it was for me."

She was holding his hand as much as he was holding hers. Warnings flashed as stridently as the rack of lights on a squad car.

"I should probably get out of here," he said, but didn't let go of her.

Beth nodded acknowledgment. "You must have other cases, too."

It took a little effort to dredge up a memory of the theft reported from J. N. Sullivan Landscaping Services and the half dozen other investigations that had also gone on the back burner the minute he heard the dispatcher report a possible missing child. Sicily still had to be his focus. None of the others were life and death. Now that he had the boyfriend's name, he could go back to the same people he'd already talked to. Tyler could be a first or last name. With that nudge, someone might remember more. Yeah, there were plenty of things he should be doing besides holding hands with a woman who was still a suspect. He didn't know if he *could* let go, though—literally or figuratively.

"Beth." He stood and tugged her to her feet, too, and around the corner of the table. *Stupid,* a voice in his head screamed, but it was drowned out by the little sound she made as she stepped forward and rose on tiptoe. Mike bent his head. Their mouths met urgently, no tentativeness, only hunger and something more powerful yet.

"Hey, kid!"

Sicily pulled the comforter over her head. She didn't want to talk to him. She wasn't hungry. She wasn't…anything.

Worry tugged. *I can't just lie here like a lump.*

Yes, I can.

"Good news. Your grandparents are being smart. They're going to give me my money. That means you'll be out of here before you know it."

She was suddenly so mad she couldn't stand it. Sicily threw back the cover and sat bolt upright. "But you aren't going to let me go, are you?" she yelled. "So quit lying to me!"

"Why would you think…"

"Because I know what you look like!" *I shouldn't have said that, I shouldn't have said it, maybe he was so dumb he hadn't thought about how he shouldn't let me see his face.* But, seeing his expression, she knew—he wasn't that dumb.

"I don't want to hurt you."

"No?" She clutched the comforter up to her neck. "Then why are you doing this?"

"Because they owe me, okay?" He was the one yelling now. A tide of red rose from his neck. "They owe *you,* and you don't even know it."

"I don't want anything from them," she said sullenly. Her heart was pounding hard, but she thought suddenly, *Maybe if we keep arguing he'll come into the room. Maybe I can get by him to the open door.*

But if she did and he caught her, he might not let her use the bathroom anymore.

But I have to try eventually, don't I? Trying not

to be obvious about it, she pulled her feet up close to her body to make it possible to leap up.

"Well, you should care," he said in a really ugly way. "Do you know what they did to your mom?"

"Yes!" she yelled, then whispered, "Yes. That's why I don't want their money."

The color on his face was subsiding and she realized he was getting over being mad. He shrugged. "Your problem. Here's some food." Without looking away from her, he bent and set down the paper bag and drink on the floor right inside the door. The next thing she knew, he'd backed out and closed it.

"Wait!" She threw herself off the mattress and raced over to hammer on the steel door. "I need to go to the bathroom! Come back!"

She kept hitting until her hands hurt so much she couldn't anymore. She kept screaming at the top of her lungs, "Come back, come back, come back."

But he didn't. Maybe he couldn't even hear her. "Please," she croaked, and slid to her knees, her hands balled against her belly. She cried, and that made her so mad she cried even louder and harder.

It was a couple of hours before she discovered the now cold meal he'd left her wasn't a cheese-burger. He'd bought her an egg sandwich with bacon on it and even some pancakes.

MIKE KISSED BETH UNTIL SHE WAS nothing but sensation and need. He lifted her so that she was plastered against him, thighs to breast. She anchored herself with her arms around his neck. Her fingers drove into his thick, unruly hair. Her tongue slid against his, dancing around each thrust. Once he lifted his head, studied her with heated eyes, then tilted his head to change the angle and kissed her with even more intensity, if that were possible.

Her hips pushed against his and the thick ridge of his erection. She wanted—needed—to be closer. Skin-to-skin. To have him inside her.

There were alarms blaring somewhere. She could hear them. This wasn't like her. She didn't dare…

Not until he tore his mouth from hers and swore did Beth realize the beeps were real. His cell phone was ringing and vibrating on his hip.

Growling, he took one hand from her and lifted the phone. Whatever number it displayed made him take a deep breath and step back from her.

"Ryan." His voice was rough.

He listened, his eyes never leaving hers. Shaken, she'd retreated a step of her own and gripped the high back of a chair. Her cheeks burned—his jaw had been rough. The flush on his cheeks told her how aroused he was.

But as she watched, his expression changed. "Tomorrow? What's the plan? Uh-huh." He made a few more sounds and finished with, "Yeah, I'll be there."

When he slid his phone closed, she said, "What?"

"Your father has received instructions for dropping the money." Voice clipped, jaw tight, Mike was making plain that the mood had shifted. "It's happening tomorrow morning. University District." With a hand on her lower back, he nudged her back to a seat and chose the chair across the table from her again. "A sort of command central is being set up at your parents' house. Your father is making the drop, per instructions. The parcel will have GPS on it so we can follow even if we somehow miss the pickup or the guy gets away."

"How can he get away if enough police are watching the drop-off point?"

"Because this is one thing he's being smart about. Your father is supposed to casually put the package behind a trash can right by a corner a short block from the University of Washington campus. You know how many small businesses are along there. The university bookstore is half a block up and it has entrances front and back. Oh, hell—so do the small businesses probably, although they let out in the alley. At that time of day, there'll be shoppers, students arriving for class, bicyclists, heavy street traffic. The sidewalk could be really crowded. He could run a lot of different directions. There's a parking garage for the campus close by. Or if he melts into the crowd successfully enough, he could even hop a bus."

She was wringing her hands. "But you swear you won't lose him."

"Beth…" His voice, at least, had softened. "I can't swear anything. I'm not running this operation. But there's a good chance we'll get him."

She nodded slowly. "Wouldn't it be smartest to let him *take* the money and follow him home?"

"Not necessarily. He might arrange for some hand-offs to a couple of friends who have no idea what they promised to hold on to for their buddy Chad. Or 'home' might not be where he's got Sicily."

What if they arrested the kidnapper and he refused to tell them where Sicily was? "I want to be there," she said.

Mike frowned. "You know you can't…"

"At my parents'."

The laser blue of his eyes locked on her. "You sure?"

"I'm sure," she said steadily.

"All right, that's probably a good idea, in case we pick her up right away."

He left almost immediately after that, his expression completely closed. Classic cop. She felt cold inside. *How could I have hugged him? Kissed him?*

HE HAD JUST COMMITTED THE possibly unforgivable sin of kissing the suspect in a child kidnapping. The knowledge felt like a block of ice lodged in Mike's chest. Sharp-edged, cold and damn uncomfortable. Impossible to ignore. What had he been thinking?

Gripping the steering wheel hard, he gave a grunt that wasn't close to a laugh. Thinking? Right. Sure. That's what he was doing.

He couldn't justify it. There was no way. What really stuck in his craw was the knowledge that he'd be tempted again the next time he saw her. He'd been fighting this attraction since the first day.

Even if she were cleared… Was he really considering getting involved with a woman whose issues made his own look petty?

Brooding, he almost missed his exit and had to flash his lights briefly to get over in time. Damn it, he needed to get his head where it belonged.

But even as he maneuvered city streets, he knew: yeah, he was considering getting involved, all right. He was doing more than that. When she'd told him about her childhood, he had wanted to kill on her behalf. That was new to him.

No, he'd had no business putting his hands on her, not now. But eventually, yeah, he wanted to kiss her again. And more. He had a bad feeling he'd been sunk from the minute he'd seen beneath her utterly controlled facade.

A parking place opened in front of him, and Mike managed to pull himself back into work mode. Finding Sicily was paramount, but clearing Beth of suspicion had become a major motivation.

He spent the next couple of hours chasing down Tyler Whoever. The shocker was that he succeeded. Maya, whom he'd talked to yesterday, was sure Damian would know who'd introduced Rachel and Tyler. Damian was at work, a slightly aging barista who served Mike a caffè Americano along with with a mumbled, "Um, yeah, Jagger, he said Peterson is a good guy. Jagger, see, he's this dude I know."

The sizable barbell through his tongue might have something to do with the way he tripped over words.

"And who is Peterson?" Mike asked, clinging to his patience.

Damian blinked at him. "Tyler. You wanted to know his last name, right?"

Yes, he did. Turned out Damian was surprisingly helpful, even knew that Tyler was currently crashing with someone named Spencer in this apartment down on Sixth Street.

Tyler and half a dozen other people were home. Mike persuaded him to step into the hall where they could talk in semi-privacy. Medium height, hair dyed an improbable shade of yellow, he had a wispy brown goatee and a snake tattoo wrapped around his right arm. The smell of marijuana that permeated the apartment clung to him as well and his eyes were bloodshot.

"Yeah, I heard about Sicily. That sucks, man. She's an okay kid, you know?"

Mike went for blunt. "I hear the way you looked at her made her uncomfortable."

"What?" He looked genuinely astonished and outraged. "That's bull! I never looked at her any way except sometimes I wished she wasn't there so her mom and I could get it on. Having a kid around, it's kind of a nuisance, you know?"

"Where were you last Saturday?"

"I've got this new woman. Alessia." He nodded toward the closed door. "She's here. She can tell you. We slept late and then we went to Pike Place Market. She sells jewelry there. She's really good."

Alessia, hair streaked with purple and green, came out to confirm Tyler's story. Her earrings, Mike had to admit, were eye-catching. Both agreed they'd mostly been together throughout the week. Neither could imagine anyone who would do anything like kidnap Sicily. Looking embarrassed, Tyler said, "I mean, some of Rachel's friends might do some drugs, you know, shit like that, but mostly we all have jobs and are kind of regular."

Alessia gave him a piercing glance that Mike took to mean Tyler was not, in fact, working, but she said he manned her table at the market sometimes so she could make more jewelry.

Mike asked Tyler if Rachel had talked about her sister.

"I didn't even know she had a sister until she died and Sicily said she was supposed to live with her aunt Beth. Rachel was really screwed up about her family."

Tyler had no cell phone, but Alessia gave Mike her number in case he had further questions.

Dead end.

A better way of looking at it was that one thread was now untangled. Pull enough of them, and the knot would fall apart. That's what most detective work was all about.

He glanced at his watch and decided that, by God, he was going home. He might even stop at the grocery store first.

LEFT ALONE FOR WHAT SEEMED like forever, Sicily ate her cold meal and tried not to wonder if the man would come back at all. Her mind kept reverting to the worry, though. If he got the money, why would he want to return to this crappy place? Maybe he was going to leave the country. Her mom hadn't cared if she watched R-rated movies, and she'd seen lots of hostage dramas. That's what kidnappers usually did once they had the money. He could go straight to the airport. If he was paid up on his rent, it might be a long, long time before a landlord even noticed he was gone.

It took Sicily ages to convince herself he wouldn't do that. Except…she hadn't liked the way he'd said, "I don't want to hurt you."

That might mean he would do it anyway, but be sorry. It might also mean that leaving her to starve to death was exactly the kind of chicken thing he'd do. He could lie to himself and figure somebody would find her.

It could also mean he did intend to let her go, couldn't it? Or tell someone where to find her once he'd made his getaway? He *had* been almost nice to her, in a way. And the way he'd talked about Mom meant he knew her well. Really well. It wasn't like Mom met new people and said, "Hi, my mom used to hit me."

My own father wouldn't leave me here to starve to death.

Would he?

IN THE PALE PEARL OF EARLY morning, Mike parked in front of Beth's house, then walked down the street to the only house on the block where he'd yet to find anyone home, the one with the light that might or might not be on a timer. He'd noticed it coming on as he drove down the street. Six a.m.

on the nose. These front blinds were drawn, as they'd been all week, but they were sort of lacy and not light-tight.

Without a lot of optimism, he rang the bell and listened to the far off *ding-dong.*

He was about to give up yet again, when he heard a rustle of sound inside. A moment later, the door opened a foot or two and a woman in a long velour robe zipped to the neck said, "Yes? Can I help you?"

He displayed his badge and gave his usual spiel.

She relaxed and exclaimed, "Oh, I was so upset to read about Beth's niece! She told me about the little girl coming to live with her. I haven't caught up on my newspapers yet, but... Didn't she vanish from that park?"

"We're covering all the bases, ma'am. Have you ever seen Sicily?"

"Well, of course." An attractive woman in, at a guess, her forties, she looked at him as if he were an idiot. "She catches the school bus on the corner right there."

He turned. The corner was indeed clearly visible from the porch and probably her front window.

"I noticed she wasn't there last Friday. I remember hoping she wasn't sick. But if she was, it must have been a twenty-four-hour bug, or she wouldn't have felt well enough to go to the beach Saturday morning, would she?"

"No, ma'am. Is there any chance you saw them leaving the house Saturday?"

She looked surprised at the question. "Yes, I was having a lazy morning and hoping none of the neighbors noticed me sneaking out for my newspaper still in my robe so late. Beth was just backing out of the driveway. Sicily waved. Such a pretty girl. I so hope…" She stopped, not having to verbalize her fears.

First disbelief, then relief punched him. Could it be this easy? He asked, "Do you know approximately what time it was that you saw them?"

"Almost exactly, because I looked at the clock before I slunk out. I like to read my *Times* with breakfast," she explained. "It was almost ten o'clock."

He took out the school photo. "This is the girl you saw?"

"Well, of course it is." Her expression changed. "Surely you don't think…"

"It's our job to consider all possibilities," he said without inflection. "You've eliminated one."

"What a terrible thing to suspect!"

Yes, it was. Walking back to Beth's house, he felt lighter, one burden lifted. He knew his relief was massively out of proportion, given that he was no closer to finding Sicily. While he couldn't one hundred percent eliminate Beth from suspicion of being a partner in the kidnapping—though he'd never really believed that scenario—thanks to this neighbor Mike could at least be pretty damn certain Sicily had indeed arrived at the park. The timing fit, and it was too tight to allow much deviation now that the ten o'clock departure time was confirmed. Mike didn't see any realistic way for Beth to have disposed of her niece within the available time.

The iceberg in his chest seemed to have melted in a steaming rush. The warmth, he discovered as he rang Beth's doorbell, felt something like exhilaration.

She answered the door dressed in black jeans and a camel-colored, V-necked sweater. The fuzzy pink slippers didn't go with the ensemble. Her dark hair was pushed behind her ears, and for the first time he noticed that they stuck out slightly. He felt an odd wrench inside at seeing that small imperfection. He realized in this light he could still see the traces of the scratches she'd gotten crawling through the blackberries Sunday. With circles beneath her eyes dark enough to be bruises, she wasn't beautiful right now. He wanted to put his arms around her and let her lean on him.

With a wary gaze, she said, "You're early."

"Yeah. Sorry. You have one neighbor I haven't been able to catch at home. I thought I might get lucky."

She peered past him, then stood back to let him in. "At least it isn't raining today."

"No." He watched her close the door. "Beth, the neighbor was home. She saw you and Sicily leave Saturday morning."

"What?"

He repeated himself.

"Who?"

He told her.

She blinked. "I didn't see her."

"That's what she said. But Sicily waved at her."

For an achingly long minute, she only stared at him. "Would you have searched my house if you'd talked to her sooner?"

"No." He heard the roughness in his voice. "I know it's inadequate, but I am sorry."

She stood there taking it in, looking so damn fragile it was all he could do to keep his hands to himself.

Who says I have to?

Coming on to her was still inappropriate and he knew it. She was central to the investigation; she was scared. She was grieving. He'd be taking advantage of her vulnerability, and that's not what he wanted.

She gave an odd laugh. "I suppose I should say it's fine."

Fine? Oh. That he'd turned her house inside out. Brought a cadaver-sniffing dog in. Ensured the whole world knew she was under suspicion in Sicily's disappearance. Destroyed her reputation, she'd said.

He braced himself. She *had* hugged him, and he was sure she'd kissed him as intensely as he'd kissed her, but from the moment Sicily disappeared Beth's emotions had to have been as unsteady as a boat caught out in high seas. He'd been arrogant enough to assume it was up to him whether or not he got involved with her, and the truth was she might not forgive him for the humiliation he'd heaped on her.

She shook herself. "I'd better get ready. I set out a couple of travel mugs if you want to pour us both some coffee."

He probably should consider himself lucky she hadn't said, "Well, guess what? It isn't fine."

And maybe she'd have been right. Maybe there was no way to get past the fact that he'd suspected her of something as terrible as killing a child. "Oh, oops, turns out you're a good person after all" probably wouldn't cut it.

He went to the kitchen and poured the coffee as instructed, wishing he'd met her under different circumstances. But something told him he wouldn't have gotten to first base if she hadn't been traumatized. Even if she did much dating—and he seriously doubted she did—why would she have looked twice at a man like him? A cop?

Rough-looking, with nothing that could be called style, probably possessing lousy manners compared to what she was used to. Given what she did for a living, she'd meet plenty of smooth men with slick social skills who made a hell of a lot more money than Mike did. Men who'd fit her better. She had that air of class he'd never match.

He might not have been interested, either, he told himself in what was probably self-defense. Yeah, he liked her looks even if she was too skinny—those melting brown eyes, the high, defined cheekbones that made her face unforgettable, those long legs and subtle curves. But his initial interest was no more than any man felt now and again for an attractive woman. The real pull had come later, when she started to fall apart and he saw beneath her chilly facade.

God. What if she didn't forgive him?

And then it hit him: forgiveness wasn't even a distant possibility if he didn't return Sicily to her alive and well. Something that might not be in his power to do.

SHE HATED THIS HOUSE. EXCEPT for the memorial service for Rachel, Beth hadn't stepped foot in it since a couple of years after college graduation, when she'd returned for a few keepsakes still in her old bedroom. She had to drive by from time to time; she'd put on parties at other mansions nearby. A high brick wall kept glimpses of the house and garden limited to peeks snatched through the iron gates. She couldn't always keep herself from turning her head at the right minute to see her childhood home. Sometimes memories would rush over her. Sometimes the sight was more surreal, as if life inside those walls had happened to someone else.

The gates stood open today and half a dozen vehicles filled the space in front of the detached triple-car garage and blocked the circular brick driveway. They were all unmarked, all dark sedans or SUVs. Mike parked behind them, right at home among the cortege.

He turned off the engine and neither of them moved for a moment. "You okay?" he finally asked, and she stirred herself.

"Yes," she said, then got out and started for the portico.

Within a few strides Mike had caught up with her. The front door stood open, as well, a cluster of men just inside. Mike's hand on her elbow gave her courage as they walked in. Beth saw her father almost immediately.

His eyebrows rose. "Elizabeth. We didn't expect you."

"Father." She inclined her head slightly, grateful that Mike had stuck to her side rather than stopping to talk to the other cops. "I wanted to be here if the police are able to rescue Sicily."

"I see." As always, his expression was pleasant but gave the impression something more important to him waited for his attention. "Your mother is in the living room."

She nodded and moved in that direction with no intention of seeking out her mother. Mike muttered something under his breath that Beth didn't catch.

"What?"

"I hate to leave you with them."

"I've dealt with them before."

His jaw relaxed. "Yeah, I guess you have."

"Thank you." She smiled at him.

A stir of activity shortly thereafter led to the departure of about half the vehicles. Some rearranging was required for her father to get his Mercedes out of the garage. All concerned agreed that he should drive his own car in case the kidnapper would know it.

Beth had a picture in her mind of all those unmarked cop cars lingering not-so-inconspicuously within a block of the drop-off point, but assumed the experts on kidnapping knew better.

The remaining agents and someone introduced to her as a Seattle P.D. lieutenant moved into the living room and she went with them. Her mother was smiling graciously at the men when she saw Beth.

"Elizabeth! What on earth…" She checked herself and presented an artificial smile nowhere near as warm as the ones for the men in the room. "Darling, come sit down. Let me pour you a cup of coffee."

Beth accepted the coffee in a fine china cup and sat in a wing chair well away from her mother. She concentrated on the conversation around her rather than the setting. But out of the corner of her eye she could see the tiled fireplace where she'd once broken an arm when her mother threw her against it.

No! I won't think about it.

From the conversation she gathered that a surveillance van would be parked within visual line of the trash can. Many of the law enforcement personnel would be packed into it, watching events on a monitor, listening to the undercover officers on the street who would be wired. How on earth, she wondered, did anyone ever get away with the money in a crime like this? She hadn't asked if dye had been inserted like she'd read it was in a bank robbery. Maybe not, as they wouldn't want to panic the kidnapper before they caught him or he led them to Sicily.

Dear God, please. She imagined floating outside her body looking down. She was very good at appearing serene when she was anything but. Here she sat, back straight, ankles crossed, sipping coffee. There her mother was, engaging in conversation with the agents and the lieutenant as though they were her invited guests. All so civilized. Some tension was palpable in the room, but for the men, this was part of their job. Some of them probably had children and she didn't doubt they cared. Her mother—oh, yes, Beth very much doubted that her mother cared at all.

A woman who had always been solitary, Beth had never felt so alone as she did now, understanding that she was the only one for whom the wait would be truly agonizing.

CHAPTER ELEVEN

WHY DID THIS FEEL LIKE A goddamn disaster waiting to happen?

Mike couldn't blame it on the CARD team. They weren't the ones who'd set up the location or timing of the drop-off. But he could see right away that the numbers of civilians around was a problem. They introduced too many variables that could go the kidnapper's way—or not.

Given that this was out of his jurisdiction, he'd been situated a block away, where he was perusing headlines in a little storefront. His clothing had been deemed casual enough for him to pass unnoticed, but he wasn't close enough to the scene to affect the outcome unless the guy grabbing the money bolted his way.

Surreptitiously, he checked his watch. One minute. As if on cue, the silver Mercedes turned the corner, waited politely and then backed into a parking spot vacated with impeccable timing by a Seattle P.D. officer driving his daughter's red Jetta. Beth's father got out, looked both ways and crossed the street midblock, the money carried in a worn canvas messenger bag.

He stood out among the more casually dressed students and shoppers. Not necessarily a bad thing, except the drop should, ideally, go unnoticed by anyone but the kidnapper.

Greenway paused by the garbage can, which was battered, dirty and damn close to overflowing. It had the kind of flat-topped lid that would be lifted off to allow the sanitation worker to pluck out the trash bag. All they needed was for the garbage truck to roll up in the middle of the operation.

From this distance, Greenway looked a little flustered to Mike. He pretended he was tossing away a piece of trash, a pretty obvious fake for anyone looking closely. His head turned; right, left. He waited as a group of laughing women carrying Starbucks cups passed, paying no attention to him. Then he slid the messenger bag off his shoulder and hastily stuffed it behind the battered brown trash can. He was in such a hurry to get away, he stepped into the street without checking for traffic and causing someone to put on their brakes and lean on the horn. Waving an apology, he hurried across and got in his car.

Mike didn't care if he drove away or not. His attention was all on the can and the sidewalk to each side. He'd quit even pretending to look at headlines.

A couple of people passed by, oblivious. But a minute later a figure sidled toward the trash can. He looked like a homeless guy wearing army camouflage and carrying a black plastic trash bag that Mike guessed held aluminum cans. The guy's head turned as furtively as Greenway's had and he began to pick through the garbage. He seemed invisible to passersby, who were used to the homeless in this part of town. He shuffled to one side to get out of way of a group of students, seemed to notice the messenger bag and again darted a look each way. Mike saw long, stringy dark hair and a beard. With a quick movement he snatched up the bag, slung it over his shoulder and took off.

Movement erupted, cops coming out of the woodwork. Running himself, Mike heard the yelled commands.

"Police! Freeze!"

Everyone stopped for a block in each direction and stared. The fool kept running but he didn't get half a block before someone brought him crashing to the sidewalk. The plastic trash bag exploded, aluminum cans flying every which way. A couple of students across the street cupped their hands and yelled something about police brutality. Within seconds, the guy was dragged to his feet, cuffed and pushed against a wall, his cheek ground into the concrete block.

"It was garbage," he whined. "Somebody threw it away! Why are you arresting me?"

Oh, crap. What if he *was* a homeless guy?

Mike stopped and rotated in place, taking in everything around him. Some people were still staring. Others were dissipating. People walking away in every direction. *Click, click, click*, he took mental snapshots. *Remember faces. Expressions. Vehicles.* A man was heading into the depths of the parking garage not far away. Another turning into the alley. Cars came and went out of the book-store parking lot. A battered small blue sedan— American, he thought, maybe a Ford?—pulled out of a slot at the curb up the block. The driver had long blond hair, was all he could tell. Mike took a couple of steps after it—*get the license number*, his gut told him—but too late. *L*... Was that a *U?* Shit, shit, he couldn't even be sure of the second letter. Lucky to hit the light green, the car made a left turn and accelerated out of sight.

The handcuffed dude was four-deep in cops yelling questions at him. One of them had something in his hand—a driver's license with a hole punched in it, which made it no good—and he was on the phone.

Mike tipped his head back, looked up at the sky and said a few, very profane words.

"YOU DON'T THINK HE'S THE kidnapper," Beth said, dazed.

She stood now beside her parents, the three of them facing half a dozen law enforcement officials led by Agent Trenor of the FBI.

"We can't be positive yet, but it's looking like he may be someone who was in the wrong place at the worst possible time." To her credit, Agent Trenor sounded apologetic. "We couldn't do anything *but* grab him," she said, "but if our guy was watching he now knows your father didn't come alone per instructions."

She was paralyzed with fear. "What will he do?"

There was an uncomfortable silence. Mike walked into the room as if he'd only now arrived, his gaze going straight to Beth. He circled the group but stayed back.

"All we can do at this point is wait for the kidnapper to once again contact you, Mr. Greenway."

"Will he do that?" her father asked.

"He wants his money. The only way to get it is to give you another chance."

"What if he cuts his losses?" Beth said harshly.

The agent tipped her head regretfully. "That is a possibility, of course. I can only say again that we had no options today. Our goal was to grab whoever picked up the money. It's unfortunate that it appears the wrong person took it."

Unfortunate.

"We recommend that you insist on proof of life," she said, looking at Beth's father. "Tell him you won't pay if he doesn't provide irrefutable verification that Sicily is alive."

In case he'd disposed of her today, before he left to collect his money. Not *disposed of*—murdered.

Beth realized she was breathing hard.

A discussion began. Would the kidnapper punish them in some way for today's fiasco? How? What kind of situation would he demand next time? How would Greenway convince him that he'd made a mistake, that he regretted involving the police and was willing to do anything to get his granddaughter back?

Mike nodded as if agreeing with this point, frowning slightly to refute that one. Beth watched, incredulous, yet knowing that from long practice she was expressionless. She felt like a statue, frozen in place, the fear trapped in her like waves boiling in a lava cave. Rising, falling, tumultuous with the pressure. Everyone was ignoring her now. She didn't look toward Mike again, to see what he was doing, whether he was participating in this ludicrous, all too serious dialogue based on fiction.

What if the man doesn't *call?* she wanted to say, even as she knew there was no answer. If he didn't call...someday, somebody would find Sicily's body. And there would never *be* an answer, only another funeral. And guilt, so much guilt.

Movement toward the door suggested at least some of the people were leaving. The excitement was over. A phone rang, everyone turned to look at her father, but no, it was someone else's, and the momentary heightened interest diminished.

"We'll keep someone here 24/7," she heard Agent Trenor say. "You won't be alone."

She no longer listened, until she heard the tail end of a question. "Watching the house?"

"It's highly unlikely," one of the unnamed agents—or was he Seattle P.D.?—assured her parents. "Maybe in a different neighborhood, but not here."

Suddenly her mother was in front of her, face rigid. "I don't know how you had the nerve to come here today," she said coldly, "when Rachel's daughter was taken because *you* were irresponsible."

For a moment Beth stared in shock. Guilt—oh, yes, she felt it. But rage was stronger, so powerful she said, "Only for Sicily's sake would I have stepped foot in this house."

Silence fell around them; she knew it and didn't care.

Her father turned, alarm on his face. "Rowena, my dear, please, not now...."

Her mother didn't pay him any more attention than Beth did. "If we're fortunate enough to get Sicily back, she won't be going home with you. I'm giving you notice right now. If you have any common decency, you'll leave her here where she'll be safe."

"No." She heard herself; it was an echo of what she'd told Mike. "I will never leave Sicily alone with you. And I promise you, you don't want to take this to court."

"If you think Rachel's ridiculous request that our granddaughter go to you will have any weight if we take this to court…"

Rachel's daughter. Our granddaughter. Only once had her mother brought herself to say Sicily's name. Sicily, Sicily, Sicily.

Beth became aware that one person in the room had moved. Mike. He had stepped so close to her, she felt his warmth at her back. His unspoken support made tears prickle in her eyes, but she refused to cry. A part of her wanted him to stay near, a part of her wished he'd back off. The less she felt, the stronger she was.

"I will not allow you to abuse Sicily the way you did Rachel and me."

Fury made her mother's face momentarily ugly. "How dare you make such an absurd allegation!"

"Not absurd. Do you know how many broken bones I had, Mom?" She looked pointedly at the fireplace. "Do you remember the way my arm cracked when you threw me against the tile there?"

"So that's your game," her mother whispered.

"Turn your clumsiness into accusations against your own parents to counteract your clear negligence."

She had never expected to feel so calm when this confrontation came. Had never really believed it *would* come.

She was calm, she realized, because she'd already told Mike. Because instead of the expected pity and disbelief, he'd offered her anger and belief. He had helped her erase vestiges of the childhood fear that it was somehow her fault.

"Proof of life." The term popped into her head and she suddenly laughed out loud. Then she looked around the circle of staring faces. "Isn't that funny. I have proof of *my* life. Not Rachel's, I'm sorry to say, but I suppose she could be exhumed."

Nobody else was laughing. She saw shock on every face except her father's, where horror superseded anything else. *What are you doing to me?* his expression said. It was always about him.

"This isn't the time or place for us to talk about family issues," he said, grasping his wife's arm. "I know you and Elizabeth have some bitter feelings between you...."

"Oh, I think it's a perfect time," Beth told them all. "When better? In court?" She pretended to think. "Well, I might enjoy that. But if you expect

I'm going to let Sicily spend a single night under your roof in the meantime, you're wrong."

"It's ridiculous to claim you have proof of anything," her mother sputtered.

Mike laid a big hand on Beth's shoulder and gently squeezed. *Okay, now he'll butt in, Detective Domineering.* But no, he stayed silent. She remembered what he'd said about hoping he'd be watching when she deployed her armament. That's what he was doing: watching. And keeping that warm, reassuring hand on her.

"I have copies of doctors' notes. X-rays." It was *her* voice that filled the room. Confident, determined. "A dozen or more." She told them all how many bones she'd had broken. About being burned. About the broken wine bottle raking her side and back, her blood mixing with the red wine on the floor to make slippery crimson pools studded with lethal shards of glass. A part of her saw that shock had begun to show on her father's face, that his gaze shifted from her to his wife and back.

"You bitch!" her mother screamed. "How dare you…?" Beth's father gripped her when it seemed she might leap forward.

"Is any of this true?" Laurence Greenway asked, staring at his daughter. "Or are you attempting to destroy your mother and me out of some twisted motivation I don't understand?"

"You know it's true, don't you, Dad? Because I

told you. I cried. You saw the medical bills, didn't you?"

"You were clumsy…" he began.

"Nobody is that clumsy." Mike's hand tightened on her shoulder. "I saw Ms. Greenway's medical files. If it wasn't fifteen years too late, I would have taken great pleasure in placing you and your wife under arrest, Mr. Greenway. I can assure you, and everyone here—" his glance took in their audience "—that your daughter suffered unspeakable abuse from the time she was barely a toddler until she left home. I think it's safe to assume your younger daughter did, as well. *I* would not permit Sicily to stay under your care."

Beth consciously stored the memory of this moment in her mental files for later retrieval. The way her mother's true self was displayed for everyone to see in twisted rage and fiery color, in the quivering tension of her body. The humiliation on her father's face, his utter disbelief that this could be happening. His…doubt? Could it be that he *hadn't* believed her as a child and then teenager when she tried to talk to him? Eight—count 'em, eight—law enforcement officers witnessing the first salvo of Beth's big guns.

I did it, she thought, astounded and…something. Not proud. What was there to be proud about? And she didn't feel the satisfaction she'd expected she would, if it ever came to this. Instead, she realized her legs wobbled as if they were *al dente* and her hands had acquired a tremor.

Mike may have felt a quiver all the way up her shoulder, because he said abruptly, "Excuse us." He turned Beth and started her toward the foyer and front door, but paused long enough to fix Agent Trenor with a hard look. "You'll keep me informed?"

Her eyebrows flickered, but she nodded. "Of course."

SOMEWHERE NEAR NUMB, BETH allowed herself to be propelled out to Mike's black Tahoe and boosted into the passenger seat. The earlier departures made it possible for him to drive right out of her parents' estate with no lengthy maneuvering. Beth sat quiet beside him, a new fear appearing as the tiniest of seeds that swelled until it filled her.

"Oh, God," she whispered. "What if Dad won't pay now?"

MIKE WATCHED BETH PRETENDING she was absolutely fine. He'd spent the entire drive to her house working to convince her that there was no way her father could back out of ransoming Sicily now.

"What's he going to say? 'My daughter is right. My wife and I are scum of the earth, and I've only been pretending to give a damn whether my granddaughter lives or dies'?" She winced, but he didn't let that stop him. "Hell, no. He's back there shaking his head and saying you've always had mental problems, and Carol is patting his hand and saying, 'Don't worry, this kind of stress always gets people to saying things they don't mean. Now here's what we're going to do next.'"

"Carol?"

"Carol Trenor. The agent in charge."

"Does she believe what she's telling him? That I've gone a little crazy?"

"Nope," he assured her. "Didn't you see her expression? No, she looked as disgusted as everyone else there felt, but she's going to do her job, which is to keep your father cooperating."

Beth had mumbled something he'd interpreted as "Please, God, see he does." So he'd kept talking, and eventually she seemed to believe him. That she hadn't blown Sicily's possible rescue sky-high by taking on her parents then and there, at a moment when her father could decide to withhold his million dollars.

Or two million. Nobody had said it, but Mike's best guess was that the kidnapper would punish Greenway by upping the ante.

Once he'd delivered Beth home, he ignored her polite "thanks and so long," stepped past her into her house and said, "I can make phone calls from here as well as I can from the station," and then added, "Would you mind if I order a pizza?"

Of course, that set her to bustling in the kitchen

making pizzas mostly from scratch—turned out she had some crusts frozen. All, he diagnosed, in the interests of proving to him that she was fine and dandy.

He was locked on the memory of that blue maybe-Ford, rusting left back fender, dent in the trunk, watching it turn the corner. He had glimpsed dishwater-blond hair, long and pulled into a ponytail. *LU.* What else could that second letter have been? A *V,* maybe, or half of a *W* although he didn't think so. He wanted to find that car.

While she was cooking, he asked to use her computer and she turned it on for him. He started browsing car models—1970s? 1980s?—starting with Ford. He couldn't remember seeing the insignia of the maker, but maybe he had. Taurus? No, even the early ones were too sleek. Tempo? Still not right. The car had been real boxy. Not twenty minutes into his hunt, he saw it. The Ford Fairmont. Yeah, yeah. He knew why he'd identified it, if only subliminally, right away. Wide receiver and class clown Curt Osborne had driven one all through high school. Kind of a gas guzzler, but not as bad as the Oldsmobile Robby Relnick drove.

Now it was time to start a search. How many Ford Fairmonts with Washington State license plates starting with LU—or possible LV or LW—

would still be on the road, given that they hadn't been made after the early eighties?

And he was betting he could find some other models shaped similar enough to also be possibilities.

His mouth lifted in a wry grin. He was going to be popular somewhere when he asked for this list.

The pizza was damn good. All veggie with at least a couple of different cheeses on it including feta. Beth had made two, both bigger than personal-size. He ate his and finished off hers when she claimed to be done.

"Whole-wheat crust?" he asked, examining it at one point.

She looked surprised that he'd even asked. "Better for you."

"Yeah, I guess so." He didn't think of pizza as a health food, but, come to think of it, this one could qualify.

"I eat out a lot. Lately I seem to have trouble even getting to the grocery store," he explained.

She gave him a strange look. "Me, too. Lately."

Uh-oh. "I suppose you haven't felt like shopping this week, have you?"

"There was always the possibility of a reporter materializing in the canned food aisle." After pausing long enough for him to wince, she added, "I'd loaded up Friday evening. I usually shop on

Saturday, but since we were planning to go to the beach…"

He reached across the table and covered her hand with his. "I'm sorry to remind you."

"I hadn't forgotten," she said with dignity.

He took his hand back. "I haven't seen any reporters hanging around."

"No, they stayed for a few hours that first day, then gave up. They haven't been able to get my cell phone number, but they're driving my assistant at work crazy."

"I'm sorry," he said again.

Beth shook her head. "Why did I hear you talking about a Ford? Is it a different investigation of yours?"

He hesitated. He didn't want to give her false hope—his first instinct said that would be cruel. But maybe hope of any kind would be better than none. She might be claiming to be "fine," but she wasn't. For all that she wasn't falling apart, he thought she was as close to complete despair as he'd seen her.

Making up his mind, he said, "No. This morning, right after fifty cops descended on that poor su   r who grabbed the money, a car that was park d conveniently close to the corner pulled out and drove away. There was something about it."

She stared at him. "But…weren't there lots of cars around?"

"Yes, of course. It was where this one was situated—close to the corner for a quick getaway. Good visual on the drop-off. And it was heap of junk—late seventies, early eighties, I think, rusting."

"The kind of car Chad would be driving," she said slowly.

"Exactly. The driver could have been female, but I don't think so." He'd give anything to have seen the face. "Dirty blond hair, ponytail."

"You must have checked to see if Chad is registered as owner of any kind of vehicle, haven't you?"

"Sure, and he's not, but he's bound to have friends. Maybe the tags on this one have even expired, although that would be stupid if you're carrying a kidnap victim around or extorting a million dollars."

"Haven't I read that criminals most often get arrested because they do something stupid, like getting pulled over for expired tags?"

"Yeah." He smiled at her. "Thank providence, it's true. And from what we've learned, Chad hasn't run his life like he's any genius."

"No." Was there a spark of renewed life in her eyes? "Why are you and not the FBI looking into it?"

"Right now, it's nothing but a hunch. I can find out where it leads as well as anyone."

"And you feel like you're doing something."

"Yeah." He cleared his throat. "I guess you've nailed me."

She was quiet for a long time, her eyes searching his in a way that was unexpectedly disconcerting. "I wish," she said finally, her voice low and bleak, "there was anything at all I could do."

"Waiting is hard," he said gently.

Her lashes swept down, veiling her eyes, and then she surged to her feet and said, "I'll clean up and let you get to whatever it is you need to do."

He took over her office for the rest of the afternoon, following up on DMV records. For now he ignored Fairmonts registered to owners not in the immediate Puget Sound area, although he couldn't rule out Tacoma, hell, down to Olympia and north to Bellingham, even Bremerton although it was a ferry ride across the Sound. He kept doubting himself and going back to browsing other makes, other models, then looking again at the Fairmont online and thinking, *Damn it, I know that's it.*

Late afternoon, Carol Trenor called. "He's pissed," she said.

"Greenway?"

"No. Well, yeah, he is, too. But I mean our kidnapper."

"So he got in touch," Mike said, his mood lightening.

"Hopping mad. Said he's going to have to think

about whether he'll let Greenway have another shot at it."

"Which means he is."

She made a sound of agreement. "To his credit, when he got the phone call Greenway stayed cool and did his part."

"Demanded proof of life."

"Quite a scene this morning," she observed.

"Long overdue," Mike said.

"I had that impression. Ms. Greenway had told us she was abused, but this sounds like KGB torture techniques."

Tension rode him even thinking about it. "I'd say her mother is crazy, except the way Beth describes it she was careful most of the time to make sure the damage stayed hidden. Sometimes she totally lost it, but more often she was calculating what she could get away with even while she was walloping her four-year-old kid." He found he was squeezing the back of his neck, keeping an eye on the open doorway to be sure Beth didn't approach and hear him talking about her. "I think it's the father that gets me most."

"Maybe I shouldn't have said that it was to his credit that he stayed cool."

"Maybe you shouldn't have," Mike agreed.

They signed off a minute later and he went looking for Beth to tell her the good news.

In her sphinx mode, she listened. She'd expended whatever emotional leakage she dared allow this morning. "What if he thinks about it and decides *not* to give my father another shot?"

"If he wasn't going to, he wouldn't have called at all."

After a minute, she nodded. "Are you, um, going to be here for dinner, too?"

Mike took that for an invitation. "If it's okay with you. You don't have to cook, though. I can go out and get us something."

"Cooking gives me something to do."

It was a little bit of a letdown to suspect that was the only reason she'd decided he could stay. Probably she wouldn't have bothered to cook at all—or eat, for that matter—if she'd had only herself to think about.

So hanging around is my good deed, he thought virtuously.

Back to work. He ended up with more possibilities than he'd expected. In theory, licenses beginning with *LU*—or any combination, for that matter—should have registered owners clustered geographically, but in the long run it didn't end up that way what with people moving so often. Especially people who drove a thirty-year-old car that hadn't been restored. They tended to be drifters. Addresses and phone numbers out of date.

Beth made a really excellent veggie lasagna for dinner complete with crusty garlic bread she claimed she'd had in the freezer. Conversation while they ate was sporadic. Her tension was climbing, as was his. It had now been five days and counting since Sicily had been snatched. Time was not on that little girl's side.

HE BROUGHT HER PIZZA THAT night, although he was in a *really* bad mood. He said, "Your grandfather must not give a shit about you."

Sicily knew it was night, because he had let her out to use the bathroom and she could see it was dark outside.

"What do you mean?" she asked as she crossed the room.

"He screwed me over today. I guess he thinks I'm stupid or something. He dropped off the money, but there were cops all over the place."

"How did you know?"

"I saw them, what do you think?" he snarled.

"Oh." That made her feel breathless. "Then… then you didn't get your money?"

He said a lot of bad words that meant "no."

"So, um, what are you going to do?" she asked apprehensively.

"He's going to pay for not keeping his promise. I'm going to ask for two million this time or he doesn't get you back. Tomorrow you're going to talk to him on the phone, and you're not going to try anything if you know what's good for you."

She slid into the bathroom and closed and locked the door, her heart pounding hard.

Would her grandfather be willing to pay that much? Did he even have that much? Why would he?

She stood there shaking, until she thought, *Tomorrow. I've got to get away tomorrow.*

She dawdled in the bathroom just to see what would happen. It didn't surprise her that he pounded on the bathroom door and yelled, "Hurry up in there!"

"I have to...you know," she called back. "You're making me nervous."

He growled something and paced back and forth in the hall. She could hear his footsteps. She strained to track him by sound. Toward the door at the end of the hall, then back, and he kept going. He must be down to the kitchen, maybe the living room.... Would he go sit down, or start doing something else? No. His footsteps came back, heavier. He sounded even more impatient this time when he slammed a hand against the door and told her to get her ass out of there or he was coming in.

"All right, all right." When she came out, she said, "Do you have anything I can read? I'm getting really bored."

He looked at her like she was crazy. "Why would I have kid books?"

"I'm a good reader. I don't need a book for kids. Don't you have anything?" She was practically begging.

"I picked up a *Stranger* the other day. You can have that." He snatched it off the couch as they passed and thrust the fat magazine-style newspaper in her arms as he hustled her into her room.

Sicily clutched it gratefully, even though she'd have rather had practically anything else. Her mother used to pick up *The Stranger* sometimes, since it was free out of newspaper bins on lots of corners. It was a weekly, and sort of counterculture or something. Mom said it was cool. Sicily didn't actually get most of what she read in it. But right now she was excited to read anything, even the personal ads for escort services, which she thought might be prostitutes, although she wasn't sure. Did they advertise in a newspaper? It seemed like there *were* ads for phone sex, which she'd heard Mom tell a friend she'd do to make money except she didn't have a very sexy voice. The friend had giggled and said, "Yeah, do you know Sandra? She's, like, two hundred and fifty pounds and she's got chin hair, but she has this voice that makes guys stand up and notice, and she makes big bucks working for... Oh, I don't remember. One of those phone-sex lines. But wow, sorry, Rach, I don't think you have what it takes."

Sicily didn't want to know exactly what phone

sex involved. She was sure she didn't want her mother doing it, just as she didn't want her mother behind her closed bedroom door with whatever guy was hanging around. Sometimes the bed banged into the wall, or someone screamed or yelled or… Sicily got good at packing her pillow around her head.

"Mom didn't know I could hear," she said out loud. She could have told her, but she never did.

Aunt Beth hadn't had a single man spend the night since Sicily had gone to live with her. In fact, the only guy that came by at all was a meter reader and all he did was wave when he saw them in the window as he raced around the house. Oh, and once the UPS driver delivered something, but he practically threw the package at Aunt Beth and ran back to his truck before tearing out of the driveway. Neither of *them* seemed to want to stay. Sicily wondered if Aunt Beth ever would have a boyfriend.

She sat on her bed and ate pizza—which was *not* her favorite kind, she had to pick off the pepperoni, ew, greasy, and the mushrooms, too, and she didn't know why anyone wanted pizza with so much on it—but it wasn't a cheeseburger, yay, so she ate really slowly, enjoying every bite, and read *The Stranger* slowly, too, even stuff about the Seattle mayor's quarrel with the city council about light rail, and reviews of movies she'd never see. She even studied the ads carefully. She bet *he* brought it home to look at the ads of naked women.

The Stranger was a really *fat* newspaper, which made her happy. Maybe if she ever got out of here she'd write them a dear editor letter and say, "Your newspaper was the best thing I ever read. Oh, by the way, I'm ten years old. Do you think I'm your youngest reader?"

I'll get out of here. I've got to get out of here.

CHAPTER TWELVE

"I'VE GOT TWO BEST possibilities," Mike finally announced, pushing back from her computer desk and stretching. "Then a second tier, but I might get lucky with one of these two."

"They're the right color?"

"Yeah, and this car hasn't been repainted, I can tell you that." He hesitated. "I may be chasing my tail, you know."

"You said you had a feeling." She wanted to believe in this hunch. It was all she had to believe in. Maybe the FBI was pursuing significant leads, but if so they weren't telling her. And she didn't think so. She thought they were waiting for another ransom call.

He shrugged. "As you pointed out, there were a lot of cars in the vicinity."

She nodded to tell him she understood, although she believed he'd focused on this one car for good reason. "Would you, um, like a cup of coffee before you go?" Beth asked.

He glanced at his watch and seemed surprised. "No, not if I want to get any sleep. Thanks, though."

He looked so relaxed and at home here in *her* desk chair. She couldn't believe the way he'd moved in on her today. Or that she'd let him. This was the man who—was it only the day before yesterday? Was that possible?—had led the team that ransacked her house, assaulting her privacy and dignity. She thought then that she could never forgive him, and now she'd cooked lunch and dinner for him and was, if she were truthful with herself, wishing he weren't leaving.

His hair, a sort of gold-streaked bronze, was ruffled, as if he'd run his fingers through it a dozen times. She knew the texture now—thick, heavy, cool—and that made her palms tingle. He was growing stubble on his jaw that glinted bronze like his hair. As she watched, he rasped a hand over it. He'd long since rolled up his sleeves, exposing tanned, strong forearms lightly dusted with hair. A few healing scratches decorated them, from their Sunday search. Beth remembered staring at the droplets of blood strung along one scratch when it was fresh. He'd carelessly wiped them off on his T-shirt and she'd thought in automatic protest, *but blood stains,* as if at that moment in time she'd have cared if *her* entire wardrobe had been ruined, never mind his.

"Thank you," she felt compelled to say, "for what you did this morning."

His head turned sharply and she felt pinned by his pale, clear eyes. "This morning?"

"When you...stood beside me. Let me know you were supporting me."

"I told you I hoped I'd have the chance. Didn't you believe me?"

"I expected you'd take over and you didn't."

"I didn't keep my mouth entirely shut."

"No, but what you did was serve as a witness."

One corner of his mouth lifted in a crooked smile that made her heart flip-flop in her chest. "Surprised you, huh. So you thought you knew me?"

She had to smile, too. "Apparently, not that well. Those first few hours at the park, I remember thinking that nobody would question who was in charge. You were that kind of guy. And I was sure you didn't take orders well."

His laugh came out rusty. "You were right. I don't."

"But you seem comfortable handing over the case to the FBI. Not resentful at all." That had perplexed her, she had to admit.

"Comfortable?" He seemed to mull it over. "I wouldn't put it that strongly. But I believe in letting experts do what they do well. I don't have a lot of experience with kidnapping." He lifted his arms over his head and stretched again, producing a few pops and a throaty groan. "You notice I'm looking over their shoulders, don't you?"

"Yes." She smiled again, even though she hadn't had much reason to smile in a long time. "I did."

His head tipped to one side and she realized how unnervingly thorough his scrutiny was. "You okay?"

"Of course I am." It wasn't exactly a lie. She'd pushed all her emotions down deep. But maybe they were leaking out like poisonous fumes from a toxic dump? Oh, heavens, what did he see that she hadn't meant him to? She shouldn't ask, but... "Don't I look okay?" It came out sounding anxious.

"Truthfully..." He grimaced. "No. I think you've lost weight this week, Beth. I can tell you're not sleeping well. You've got to be scared to death, and that scene this morning with your parents had to be harrowing."

"It wasn't," she said truthfully. "I'm actually a little surprised. It was harder telling you. Once I'd done that... Well, I guess I was ready. And really, it didn't achieve anything. For a minute I felt strong, and then...deflated."

He rose to his feet, the chair rolling back. He was smiling again, so tenderly she'd have cried if she had been more susceptible. "You were strong, Beth. I was proud of you. And you're wrong. You did achieve something. There's no way in hell your parents will ever threaten to take Sicily from you again."

She had to close her eyes, both to protect herself from him and because once again the tide of fear had risen in her. "But Sicily isn't here," she said softly. "She's not safe at all. So what difference does it make?"

She knew the moment he stepped closer, even before his arms came around her.

"We have a good chance of getting her back. With luck, tomorrow we'll hear her telling us herself that she's okay."

"Proof of life," Beth murmured, and let her forehead rest against his broad, strong chest.

"Yeah." He sounded a little hoarse.

"Tomorrow, will you track down the owners of those cars?"

"Yeah, first thing." His cheek was resting on top of her head.

She sniffed a little, then made herself step back. His arms fell to his sides. "You live north, don't you? I'm sorry you have to go home so late. If you'd brought a change of clothes, I'd suggest you sleep in Sicily's bed."

He was quiet. She didn't quite meet his eyes, but had a feeling she wouldn't have been able to tell what he was thinking anyway. Still in that same husky voice, he said, "I wouldn't mind staying if you're okay with it, Beth. I don't like leaving you alone right now."

She lifted her head in surprise. "Why not? I told you, I'm used to being alone."

"That doesn't mean you have to be."

Those commonplace words jolted her enough to make her mouth drop open. *I don't,* she thought in amazement. *I've done all right with Sicily. I like having her. I like having* him *here. Part of my life.*

Beth knew herself to be reserved, but was rarely shy. This was an exception, though. Her cheeks were hot. She didn't know if he was even hinting at what she was thinking, and…oh, heavens. She wasn't an impulsive person. She wasn't about to say, "*Will you spend the night with me?*"

Even so, she hoped he didn't leave. Having him across the hall would be…a comfort.

"I can let you have a toothbrush," she heard herself say. "And a disposable razor, too."

He smiled again, with that same tenderness she had trouble believing in but wanted, oh, so much. "Sold," he said. "Who cares if I look a little rumpled tomorrow?"

Beth couldn't help letting her eyebrows lift as she scanned him, and this time he laughed.

"You noticed I don't like to iron, huh?"

"If everything you have on is washable, I can put a load in. I could even set up the ironing board in the morning." She was definitely flushed now. "Well, I guess I can't take all your clothes."

"Probably not." Amusement sounded in his voice. "I'll keep on my boxer shorts. I can do without tomorrow."

He was getting aroused. She was shocked and aroused herself to see it. Cowardice had her backing toward the door. "Um…the hall bathroom is all yours. I'll make sure there are clean towels. And let me get my hamper."

He turned off her monitor and then the office light and followed her. Beth got him fresh towels from the linen closet and a new toothbrush—Sicily's toothpaste was in the bathroom, as were soap and shampoo, and she hovered until he handed out his chinos, socks and button-down shirt for her to put in the washing machine.

By the time she'd done that and turned out the other lights, he was in Sicily's room, only the bedside lamp on. "I borrowed a book from your office," he called.

"Good night," she told him, and went to her bedroom, where she discovered she felt shaky and she didn't even understand why.

MIKE HAD TROUBLE SLEEPING FOR a lot of reasons, not least that the twin bed was too small for him. He'd had to untuck the sheet so his feet could hang over at the bottom, and when he flung out an arm it didn't come down on the mattress. Then there was the fact that this was Sicily's bed. He felt like an intruder. He kept thinking about her—wondering where she was, whether she was sleeping, how she'd feel if she knew there were an interloper in her room.

Mostly, there was Beth.

He'd wanted to make a move on her like he'd never wanted anything in his life. He'd told her the truth earlier, when he said she didn't look good. Yeah, he could see the strain on her face, the exhaustion; the bones were even more prominent now. None of which seemed to stop him from reacting to her like a randy teenager. And there'd been a moment there, when her cheeks turned pink, when he'd again become aware that, despite everything, she was breathtakingly beautiful—if only to him.

He lay sprawled on his back, hands clasped under his head, and tried to concentrate on today's events and what he had to do tomorrow, not on the fact that his body still hummed with desire. Eventually he began to relax. *Yeah, good*, he thought, on the edge of sleep.

He must have fallen over that edge, because when he snapped awake he knew he'd been roused from sleep.

He reached for his weapon even as he otherwise lay still, waiting to hear a repeat of whatever it was that had woken him quicker than any alarm could. And there it was…a whimper. It sounded eerily like a child. A hurt child.

Oh, damn. He was on his feet and crossing the hall before he knew he intended to move. It came again, the most pitiful noise he'd ever heard. It raised the hair on his nape.

He paused long enough to snap on the hall light so that he could make his way to her bed by its illumination. And see her. He needed to see her.

For an instant he thought it *was* a child in her bed, and then knew why. She was curled into the smallest ball he'd ever seen a person get into. Only the top of her head showed. When he sat down beside her and gently touched her, he discovered she lay facedown with her knees drawn up beneath her, her elbows pinned to her sides and her hands balled beneath her. She shook all over but was quiet, so quiet. Until another betraying moan, stifled against the pillow, escaped.

"Beth. Sweetheart." He moved his hand up and down her back. When that produced no reaction at all, he thought, *What the hell,* lifted the covers and got into bed with her. He gathered her against him, turning her so that her knees dug into his belly and his body was spooned around her.

She stiffened more. He hadn't thought it was possible.

"Sweetheart. Wake up. You're okay. You're dreaming, that's all. You're okay. Come on, love."

She gave a little gasp.

He kept repeating those words over and over. There was never a moment when he knew she'd awakened and was listening to him. It was more that her muscles gradually eased, the tight clench of her body opening up. He had to shift to let her straighten her legs, then regathered her so that her head rested on his shoulder. That was when he discovered her face was wet. God. She'd been crying in her sleep. He wiped her cheek and let his shoulder soak up the rest of the tears.

"That's it," he murmured. "I won't let anybody hurt you. I promise. You're safe. It was only a dream."

He could make out the contours of her face, even though the pale path of light didn't touch the bed. Her lips were slightly parted, her eyes closed. Her breath, which he realized had been too shallow and fast, had become deep and slow. Did she even know he was here?

Mike gave brief thought to her reaction in the morning at waking to find a nearly naked man in her bed, but he didn't seriously consider letting her go. He liked having her in his arms. Her breath on his chest, the scent of her hair sweetening the air he breathed. He'd stayed tonight because he was worried about her, and he'd sleep better himself with her close. Especially now that he'd seen her regress, in the throes of her nightmare, to the child who'd had to squeeze herself into a tight, dark space to hide, who'd learned to cry silently but who must, sometimes, have been betrayed by those smallest of whimpers.

He could feel all her bones, but also the soft press of a breast against him. She wriggled briefly, and her hand found its way onto his chest, where it momentarily flexed as if surprised by this unknown surface, made a tiny circular, rubbing motion, then relaxed in contentment.

I'm a goner, he realized with resignation and something else that could be happiness, if she were willing to let it be.

BETH RARELY SET AN ALARM CLOCK. She didn't sleep well enough or long enough to need one. She'd wanted to get up early to move the wet clothes to the dryer so Mike could shower and get dressed rather than padding around her house in his shorts.

She didn't wake suddenly. A vague knowledge of how comfortable she was, how warm, floated into her awareness. Maybe she could go back to sleep. She was so cozy, felt so *good.* She had a brief fantasy that she was a puppy, sleeping with a heap of litter-mates piled against their mommy, whose heartbeat was strong and steady in her ear. She was smiling, a silly smile that froze on her face. She would swear…there *was* a heartbeat beneath her ear.

Abruptly and completely awake, Beth discovered that she was snuggled up to a very large, solid and *male* body. Her head was pillowed on him, his arm wrapped securely around her, and her arm lay across his belly, with her hand nestled in his chest hair.

She lay there trying to figure out what had happened. They hadn't had sex. Had they? She'd remember that. Of course she would. She *knew* he'd gone to bed in Sicily's room. So…what happened?

She could ask…but that would mean waking him up. And that would be…exposing herself to too much temptation.

Beth was surprised at the thought. She'd never spent the night in a man's arms, never woken cuddled up to one. She'd tried sex, of course, but had never been very good at it. Self-conscious about her visible scars, she'd been too protective of her invisible ones to ever lay herself bare, which she suspected truly great sex—certainly real lovemaking—required.

Why am I so calm?

Because he'd held her other times, too? Because this was what she'd really wanted last night, when she hoped that he would stay. Because…she trusted him?

Oh, really smart, she told herself sharply. She'd

known the man for less than a week, and in that time he'd been enemy as much as friend. Hot and cold, remember?

And yet, she thought, bemused, *I do. I do trust him.*

She let herself stay where she was long enough to savor this unfamiliar feeling of security and warmth and something more. The sense of being cherished, illusory though it was. *I can dream,* she thought almost angrily, closed her eyes, breathed him in…and finally, finally, made herself ease, inch by inch, away.

His chest continued to rise and fall in the same slow rhythm. Reassured, she slipped from bed, found her slippers and robe, and went to deal with the laundry.

If he'd woken up first, would he have kissed her? What would she have done?

The ache of hope went cold and died when she thought, *What am I doing? How can I be feeling any of this when I don't know what's happened to Sicily? When she could already be dead?*

Guilt was an emotion she knew well, one that came naturally to her. It made an excellent protective garment, she discovered as she moved wet clothes to the dryer and then went to the kitchen to start the coffee.

HE BROUGHT A CELL PHONE IN with him for the first time, along with her breakfast. Sicily thought it was breakfast, that this must be morning. When she asked, he said she could use the bathroom before eating.

Her eyes went right to the window, seeking a glimpse of green plants and daylight. But something glistened blue and purple, like stained glass, and she stopped in place. "What's that?"

Behind her, he said, "What's what…? Oh, the guy upstairs is a loony. That's a… Nothing that matters to you." His voice had sharpened. "Go on."

She hurried, because she could tell he wasn't relaxed enough to wander away while she was in the bathroom. When she came out, he herded her back to her room. Sicily took one last look over her shoulder at the shimmery something outside the window, but she still couldn't see it well enough to be sure what it was.

Once she sat down on the mattress again, he told her, "Here's what you're going to say. 'Grandma and Granddad, it's Thursday and I'm okay. Please do what he says so I can come home.' That's it, got it?"

Sicily nodded. She *could* blurt something out really fast…but what? She didn't know where she was. Telling them he was holding her in a basement apartment wouldn't help. Seattle was full of older houses with basements, many of them probably rented out as apartments. And they might not be in Seattle at all. She wished she knew what she was seeing outside, what made the guy upstairs— probably the landlord—loony. But...she didn't. This meant there was nothing she could say that would do any good.

Besides, if she cooperated he'd be pleased with her. He might relax. The door was unlocked right now. If there were some way she could, she didn't know, trip him or something, this might be a good time to run.

Excitement rose in her. If she could get out of the bedroom far enough ahead of him to shut the door, she could lock it. Lock him *in*.

She realized he'd said something and she didn't know what. She couldn't let him see what she was thinking! *I have to look crushed,* she decided. *Like it would never occur to me to try to escape on my own.*

She mumbled, "I'm sorry, I was trying to re- member what I'm supposed to say." She made her- self sag a little.

"I told you what to say. I'm going to call now. You keep your mouth shut until I tell you to talk, okay?"

She bobbed her head. There was a nasty edge to his voice that scared her.

He'd squatted beside the bed, close enough to hand her the phone. He was *way* bigger than her. She could push and he'd fall on his butt...but he could probably grab her before she could get out of reach.

He pushed a button and she heard ringing. So he'd already dialed. It only rang twice before a man answered.

"Laurence Greenway."

"Mr. Greenway. Today's your lucky day. You get that second chance. It's going to cost you, though. Another million. You have today to get the extra money together."

The voice said something.

"Here's your proof," her captor said, and thrust the phone at her. His eyes narrowed to slits. "Don't blow it, kid."

Sicily drew a deep breath. "Granddad? Um, this is Sicily." She tried frantically to remember exactly what she was supposed to say. "I'm okay." Something else. On a rush of relief she remembered. "This is Thursday. If you do what he says I can go home. So…will you, please?"

"Sicily!" her grandfather exclaimed, but *he* snatched the phone back. Before she could make any move, he stood and walked out. She heard him say, "Here's the deal." And then he was gone, leaving her breakfast sitting where he'd left it.

But he had, she discovered on investigating the contents of the bag, brought her an egg-and-bacon sandwich again, this time with little blueberry biscuits.

THE MINUTE HE SAW THE CAR sitting in its designated spot at the Mountlake Terrace apartment complex, Mike knew it was the wrong one. No rusty fender, no dent in the trunk. The paint had been decently protected and still had some shine. He kept going, easing over a speed bump and following the circle around the half dozen identical buildings to reach the exit.

The address for registered owner number two was in Ballard, a historic Seattle neighborhood. He got back on the freeway and headed south, his thoughts reverting to this morning.

He'd awakened to find himself alone in Beth's bed. He wondered if she'd set a Guinness World Record for getting out of bed once she discovered he was also in it. His clean clothes were nowhere to be seen, so he made his appearance in the kitchen in his shorts. Beth had been there, to his disappointment enveloped in a thick, fuzzy robe that was belted snugly around her waist, not revealing the gown of some thin fabric he knew she wore under it.

She had given him one startled, shy look. "The load should be done any minute," she said really fast. "You'll hear the beep. If you think anything needs ironing, I'm glad to do it. I'll take a shower now. Oh, and the coffee is ready." And she fled the kitchen.

He was dressed by the time she reappeared,

also dressed. "I never think my clothes need iron-ing," he reminded her, and for a moment she al-most smiled.

She had bustled unnecessarily around the kitchen to produce pancakes, really good ones with some kind of whole grain. He was almost done, reaching for his cup to take a last swallow of coffee when she said suddenly, "You slept with me."

"I did."

"Why?"

"You had a nightmare. You don't remember?"

Her lips compressed. Her "no" was doubtful enough he suspected she did—or that some un-easy memory was forming.

"When I held you, you relaxed. I guess I fell asleep."

She gave one brief, sharp nod.

"Sorry," he said, not bothering to sound as if he meant it.

"I…" She was choking on whatever she was trying to get out, but at last she managed. "Thank you."

That was all either of them said about last night. Mike found he was feeling pretty good about it, relieved she hadn't been mad or seemed horrified. He'd set a precedent now. Getting back in her bed would be a little easier next time.

You wish, he thought, amused at himself.

Before he'd left her house, Carol Trenor had called to let him know Greenway had gotten another call. He put his phone on speaker so Beth, too, could hear the message as it played. Her breath caught when Sicily spoke, sounding flustered, less sure of herself than she had the other day. Scared?

Beth had confirmed that yes, that was definitely Sicily, and Carol let the rest of the message roll. Their guy had gotten smarter. Tomorrow morning, Greenway was to set out by himself, if he ever wanted to see his granddaughter alive again, and take his cell phone with him. He'd be given instructions on the go.

"That'll be a bitch for you," Mike said, and he and Carol threw around ideas while Beth withdrew before his very eyes.

"Just remember, she's okay," he reminded her after he'd ended the call, and she nodded, but he could tell this message had hit her hard. He'd hated to leave her.

He took the Forty-fourth Street exit in Seattle and drove east toward the Sound. The hilly neighborhood consisted of small houses dating to the 1940s or '50s, many painted white. Some had nice gardens, while other yards had been abandoned to yellowing grass and overgrown junipers. Home owners versus renters, he suspected. To his surprise, the home that was his target had a front yard brimming with flowers, including roses covered with red blooms growing over an iron arbor. The street was steep, the narrow driveway had been carved out of the hillside. A single-car garage made up the basement. He parked at the curb and had to climb a set of concrete steps to reach the level of the yard. Heck, the house actually had an over-the-rooftop glimpse of the Sound.

A woman came to the door, looking suspicious. He showed his badge and explained that a 1982 Ford Fairmont had been seen at the scene of a crime. He asked if the Fairmont registered to her was still in her possession.

"No, I sold it. But…oh, no." She pressed her fingers to her mouth, eyes dismayed. "I never turned in that form to the driver's licensing place. The man who bought it said he'd register it right away so I didn't think it was important. He didn't?"

"No, ma'am."

She'd sold it—well, let's see, maybe a month ago? For hardly anything, which was why she hadn't thought much about the registration. She thought the transmission was failing, and the brakes had been making noises, and really she'd thought she was lucky to get anything for the car. Had she known the purchaser? No, she'd never met him before. Well, no, she hadn't advertised, she'd told friends she was getting rid of it and put up a notice at the grocery store where she worked.

She remembered that the man had been a friend of a friend—or at least an acquaintance of another checker at the store where she worked. She gave Mike his name and number.

His last question was, "Can you describe the individual who purchased your car?"

Her nose wrinkled slightly. "Tall, skinny, long-haired, beard. He kind of made me nervous, to tell you the truth. I'm not sure I'd have let him take a test drive if Chris hadn't sent him over here."

"Brown-haired, black…?"

"Blond," she said without hesitation. "His eyes were…well, not brown. Gray or hazel."

Mike took out the driver's license photo of Chad Marks. "Does this man look familiar to you?"

Her mouth formed a circle as she looked from the photo to Mike's face. "Why…that's him!"

He smiled at her. "You've been a great help. Thank you."

At last, he had something to go on.

Back in his Tahoe, he reluctantly decided he had to tell Carol Trenor what he'd learned.

Her initial reaction was to be irritated that he'd pursued a lead without keeping her informed. When he told her that a woman had identified Chad Marks as the purchaser of the car Mike had seen less than a block from the drop, though, she got over her pique.

"You're on your way to talk to the friend who supposedly knows Marks?"

"I'm ten minutes away from the grocery store where he works."

"Good. If you get an address—" her voice had become steel "—you won't go near it without talking to me first, you understand?"

Pissed, he said tightly, "I understand. I'll call as soon as I talk to him."

"All right." He thought she was going to hang up on him, but instead she said, "You've got sharp eyes. No one else noticed the car."

"I was hanging back a little."

"Good thing," she said, and left him with dead air.

Forty-five minutes later, his optimism had taken a dive. The manager informed Mike that Chris Adler had the day off. He wasn't scheduled to be on again until Saturday, but the man asked if there was anything they could do to help.

Yeah, they could help him by giving him Chris's home address. Mike had one, courtesy of DMV records, but it wouldn't hurt to be sure he hadn't recently moved.

There was some discussion, because of course personal information was kept confidential. Chris wasn't in trouble, was he? Once the manager was reassured that Mike needed only to ask him some questions about an acquaintance of his, the address was grudgingly handed over. Good thing, because it was different from the one Mike already had.

It was a basement apartment maybe half a mile from the lady who had previously owned the Fairmont. No one answered the knock. Mike walked around the house to check upstairs, where he got a home owner who said, "I didn't hear him come in last night. He's got a girlfriend. He stays there sometimes."

Unfortunately, the landlord didn't remember the girlfriend's name, much less where she lived. "He's got a cat, though," the guy added. "He doesn't leave it for a more than a couple of days."

Mike explained the urgency. The man kept shaking his head. He really didn't know.

Back to the store. Nobody working today had met Chris's latest. "Becca? Becky? Something like that?" one of them said. Nobody could think of the full name of *any* of Chris's friends. Nobody thought he was especially good friends with any coworkers.

Mike returned to his SUV, simmering with frustration and ridden by the knowledge that he didn't have time to wait for the grocery checker to decide to come home from his girlfriend's. But he couldn't think of anything better to do than stake out the apartment.

Wending through streets made narrow by cars parked on each side, he called first Carol and then Beth.

"Somebody he works with must know him," she said, taut voice telling him she shared his feeling that time was running out. "People talk at work. You know how it is. You chat even when you aren't friends. Maybe none of the ones there today are on regular shifts with him. *Somebody* might remember a name. Can't you get the names of other employees that aren't working today and ask them yourself?"

"I should have done that. You're right," he told her. "Okay. I'll check out the apartment again and then go back to the store." He signaled to turn into the alley that led behind Chris Adler's apartment.

Goddamn. Mike's usual patience had deserted him. He was so close. He could taste it. So close to finding Sicily. But the chill he felt inside told him close wasn't good enough. The kidnapper needed her to give proof of life, but she'd already done that this morning.

That little girl's time had run out.

CHAPTER THIRTEEN

THIS WASN'T EXACTLY A STAKEOUT, since Mike wasn't trying to be surreptitious. Sitting and waiting was close enough. Usually staying alert was the challenge. The monotony was there, but not the boredom. In one way the minutes crawled, in another way time passed with the roar of a freight train bearing down on a stalled car.

Sitting still so long, Mike developed nervous tics he'd never had before. He thought he might have gone nuts if he'd had to stay unobtrusive in his car, but at least he could get out and stretch, walk around a little since the home owner knew he was there.

Other people were trying to locate Adler. Every Adler in the phone directory was getting a call, in case one of them was related. The FBI had taken on the task of tracking down the grocery store employees that Mike hadn't managed to contact. So far, no cigar.

It was killing him. To be lucky enough to get this kind of break and then be stuck was almost worse than having nothing at all to go on.

After calling Beth again this morning to let her know where they were at, he hadn't phoned again. He didn't want seeing his number to get her hopes up. And *that* was killing him, too. He wanted to talk to her. He wanted it for himself, and he hated to think about her alone, waiting.

Midafternoon, on impulse, he called his parents. His mother answered.

"Michael?" she said in alarm. "Aren't you working? You're not hurt, aren't you?"

"I'm all right. Sorry. Didn't mean to scare you." He'd gotten out of his Tahoe and leaned against the front bumper. The day was gray but not cold. He was being scrutinized by two cats, a brown tabby with tomcat jowls that sat on a fence post across the alley, and the dainty tortoiseshell looking out the window of the basement apartment. Chris Adler's cat.

"What's up?" his mother asked.

"Bored," he said, although that wasn't quite it. "Thinking about you."

There was a long silence that made him realize he'd given something away.

"Something *is* wrong."

"I'm working the kidnapping of that ten-year-old girl. Sicily Marks. Have you followed it?"

"Of course I have! I wondered if you were involved."

"It's been a hell of a week," he told her.

"You don't like the ones involving children, do you?" his mother said gently.

He rubbed the back of his neck. That's what you got, talking to people who knew you too well. "No," he admitted. "Do you know Nate would have been about the same age?"

"Yes. There's something about her, too...."

"She's got that real pale blond hair like he had."

"His probably would have darkened. Yours did."

"Yeah, I suppose so." They didn't talk about Nate much anymore, although Mom kept photos of her grandson on the mantel and in the collage on the family room wall along with the ones of her other grandkids. She mentioned him more naturally than Mike did.

"I'm sorry you didn't have other children." She sounded sad, and he knew this time it was for him, not Nate.

He grunted, not telling her he was glad he and Ellen hadn't had others. He wouldn't have wanted to be a divorced father, but staying in a broken marriage wouldn't have been good for them, either.

"I've met someone," he heard himself tell his mother, and knew this was really why he'd called.

A car started up the alley and he straightened away from the fender, then watched as a small red pickup passed without the gray-haired driver even turning his head. "What?" Mike said, realizing his mother had been talking.

"Who?" she repeated. "Why haven't you brought her for us to meet?"

"Uh…this is new. She's Sicily Marks's aunt."

"The one whose house was searched?" His mother sounded shocked.

"That was routine. We had to do it."

"You must have had some reason to suspect her."

"Nobody at the park remembered seeing Sicily. We were at a dead end. We had to consider the possibility that she never had been there."

"Oh, dear."

"I don't know if Beth is going to forgive me for doing that. She, ah, she's an event planner. Not weddings—more like auctions, parties, sales pitches, that kind of thing. She thinks the publicity won't be good for business."

Mom was quiet again for long enough to have him twitching. "Why her?" she finally said, surprising him.

"I don't know," he told her, then grimaced. "She's…been wounded, Mom. Abused as a kid. Her parents are unbelievable. Her sister is dead. Sicily is all she has. She's scared to death and I keep thinking of her alone, waiting for news."

And *that*, he realized, was really why he'd been

thinking about his parents. He wished he could share his family with her, but knew it was too soon.

"Do you want me to go to her?" his mother asked with no hesitation at all, her voice warm.

"No. She and I, we aren't to that point. But I wish we were, for her sake. And…it got me to thinking about how lucky I was to have you and Dad and Jen and the rest. I don't know if I ever said that."

"We're family," she said simply, and he thought about the Greenways. In one way he'd always known he was lucky, but it had never hit him *how* lucky.

"I won't keep you," he finally said. "I'm, uh, waiting to talk to someone, killing time—" four hours and counting "—and felt like hearing your voice, that's all. Say hi to Dad."

"You'll come to dinner when this is over?"

"Sure."

"And bring this…Elizabeth, isn't it?"

"Beth. That'll depend."

"And Sicily, of course," his mother said sturdily. "We want to get to know her, too."

"I'll be in touch," he told her, and ended the call. He shouldn't have told his mother about Beth, gotten her hopes up for something that might not happen.

What if we're too late? he asked himself. What

if Sicily were already dead? Would that completely destroy Beth, fragile as she already was? He would give anything to be able to take back those first hours—no, the first days of the search, to have said at the beginning, "It is not your fault. Shit happens. Kids are careless. Your niece is ten years old, you shouldn't *have* to watch her the way you would a toddler." He wished Beth had never seen the way some of the search-and-rescue people had looked at her. He was afraid that nothing he could say now would ever convince her that she wasn't to blame for what happened to Sicily.

He could have convinced Ellen, if he'd believed it himself. Convincing Beth would be harder. But he had a chance to get it right this time.

Mike groaned. He turned to look at the poor cat, still sitting on the windowsill, waiting.

Chris Adler, where are you?

BETH STARED AT THE WALL WHERE she should have had a television. It occurred to her that she could have run over to one of the big-box stores and picked out a new one. If she carried her phone, it wouldn't matter if she was here or there.

She didn't move.

And I thought Saturday was awful. Sunday.

But at least both those days she'd been occupied—Saturday by Mike's endless questions, Sunday by the search. And by *more* questions. But today there was not one single thing she could do that would in any way help find Sicily.

When he left that morning, she'd resolved to stay busy. Cleaning house was the obvious solution.

Fine. She stripped and changed the beds, putting the sheets in to wash. She dusted, vacuumed, scrubbed toilets and sinks, mopped bathroom and kitchen floors—and never once succeeded in distracting herself from the terrifying wait. She couldn't concentrate enough to pay bills. She tried to focus on possible themes for an upcoming fundraiser, and found herself gazing into space while she bargained with God. She got everything out to bake cookies, and couldn't…not without Sicily. So she put it all away again.

And she waited. Pulling out the phone at least every fifteen minutes didn't help. No, there were no missed calls, no texts, no messages. Mike would call if he had news, she knew he would, so…what was he *doing?* What were any of them doing?

At least her father was willing to pay. It might be to save face, but right now Beth didn't care. The money was atonement of a sort. *I will forgive him,* she decided, *if his two million dollars brings Sicily home safely.*

But she wasn't dumb enough to think it would be that easy. Chad had had Sicily—his daughter, a thought that brought fresh horror—for almost a week now. He didn't know that he had been traced through the car, but he must have shown himself to Sicily, or how else had he gotten her to record the one message and talk on the phone for the second one?

How could he let her go and expect to get away with this?

He couldn't. And that knowledge left Beth hollow and breathless with fear.

Eventually, she was reduced to sitting on the living-room sofa, doing nothing *but* waiting, the phone held cupped in one hand.

At nearly six o'clock, it finally leaped in her hand and rang. She saw Mike's number, and fumbled to answer.

"Adler came home at last," he reported, his voice flat. "He has no idea where Marks lives these days. He happened to run into him at a party, and when Chad mentioned he was looking for a cheap used car, Adler told him about the one a coworker was selling. Says Chad stopped by the store the next day to get the phone number. Adler has no current contact info for Chad."

So stunned she could hardly speak, Beth managed an almost-numb response. "But…he was our only hope."

"No, he's calling friends. He thinks he can find someone who knows someone who knows…" She could hear the depth of Mike's discouragement. "I'm heading north. I can't do anything else to-night, not unless he comes up with an address."

"I'll bet you've forgotten what it feels like to go home." *Don't,* she pleaded silently. *Come here. Please come here.*

He didn't say anything at all for a minute. Then, "Tell me you weren't alone all day, Beth."

"Having to make conversation wouldn't have helped."

"No." He sounded wry. "Maybe not. I feel like I owe you a meal. Can I take you out to dinner? I might have to drop you back home quick if some-thing comes up, but…"

"You know you'd be welcome to come here again," she said simply. "Cooking would give me something to do. But please don't feel I need my hand held if you're hankering for home. It was… nice of you to stay last night. But I'm okay," she lied. "Really."

"Good," he said, "but if you're willing, I'd be glad to eat another home-cooked meal. And, truth is, I don't plan to go home no matter what. Too long a drive back to Seattle."

Beth was so grateful her eyes stung, but she strove to sound casual. "I'll see you in a little while, then." Only after she hung up did it occur to her to wonder that he was already driving north when he called; had he been counting on her? Or had he intended to go home but felt sorry for her?

Twenty minutes later, the doorbell rang and she hurried to let him in. Halfway across the doorstep, he took her hand, tugged her forward and kissed her lightly, releasing her before she could tug free. Lips tingling, stunned anew, she stepped aside to let him pass. Then she took a second look and stared at him in shock. He seemed to have aged ten years today. Every line on his face had deepened.

"Did something happen…?"

He shook his head. "No."

Leading the way to the kitchen, Beth asked tentatively, "Do you dare have a glass of wine?"

Mike shook his head. "Something could break any minute. I'd have grabbed dinner in Seattle and hunkered down with the CARD team if we were sure Chad lives in Seattle. But what if he's in Everett? Lynnwood? Hell, even the east side, I'd be damn near as close from here." Even his shrug seemed weary. "Toss of the dice. And I'd rather be here with you."

He said it so simply, so absolutely, Beth couldn't doubt he meant it. *Not pity, then. Or not only pity.* "Sit down," she invited. "Dinner will be another half hour." She looked at him closely. "Do you need coffee?"

He shuddered. "Maybe later. As good as yours

is, I've been living on it all day. Skipped lunch. Milk or juice would be good."

Conversation over dinner was sporadic. They'd start on a subject and one of them would drift off. The case had to be pulling at him, as well as tiredness. It was only for fleeting moments that Beth could forget Sicily and the looming likelihood that they wouldn't find her before tomorrow's ransom drop.

Mike was telling her about Chris Adler's cat, which he'd sworn had stared at him without blinking for hours on end when she interrupted. "What time is Dad supposed to set out tomorrow?" Then she flushed. "I'm sorry. That was rude."

He shook his head. "I was trying to distract you. No surprise it didn't work. Ten o'clock."

"Chad will want to keep Sicily until…until he has his money, won't he? In case it gets fouled up again this time?"

"I don't know, Beth." His eyes were slightly bloodshot. As tired as the rest of him clearly was. "It went bad the first time because your dad lied to him. I think he may see this as all or nothing."

She felt as if fingers had tiptoed up her spine. A ghost walking by? Please not Sicily's. Beth nodded, saying nothing.

"Today felt interminable." He spoke with sudden anger, even violence. "I can hear the damn clock ticking. Hell." He closed his eyes and bent his head. "I'm sorry, Beth. This isn't what you need."

"Yes, it is." She'd surprised herself, and him, too, she saw when he lifted his head. "I need you to be honest with me. You've given me hope, but I don't want false hope. If Sicily is dead, she's dead." It sounded so blunt, so bleak, and she felt so angry. Her throat wanted to close. "Maybe... maybe I need to start preparing myself."

"No!" He surged to his feet. "No, damn it! I will not give up on that little girl."

Beth found herself standing, too, without quite knowing how she'd gotten up. "She's not Nate, Mike."

He scowled at her. "I know that. It's her... I keep seeing her picture. Wishing she'd smiled when it was taken. Wondering how many chances she had to smile."

Her vision blurred. "Not enough," she whispered. "After she came to stay with me, the first time I heard her giggle, she looked so surprised. I kept telling myself it was because her mother had died so recently, that...that I shouldn't assume she was always so serious, but I'm afraid she was. That last week, I thought..." Her tears fell unashamedly now. She couldn't finish.

Mike had her in his arms, and she cried against his chest. He rocked slightly on his feet, as if instinct drove him, and she had a sudden image of this man doing the exact same thing with his baby against his shoulder. He'd have been endlessly patient, she knew. He should have had other children. He was so generous with everything he had to give. He'd been generous with her even when he suspected her of hurting Sicily.

I'm in love with him, she realized in shock. Almost immediately she wiped her wet cheeks on his shirt and withdrew. *Ridiculous. I'm grateful. I'm...*

In love. It hurt to think about. He was being so nice, but she knew it had to be the shared intensity of their worry about Sicily. Yes, he'd kissed her, but she shouldn't assume anything.

She didn't even know if she wanted anything more. Up until five weeks ago, it had never occurred to her that she would ever share her life with anyone. She couldn't forget how hard it was adjusting to the addition of a ten-year-old girl. In her desperation to have Sicily back, she was blocking out how much Sicily's presence had disrupted a life Beth was comfortable with. A man would change everything all over again. And Sicily deserved her full attention. When she came home.

Beth couldn't make herself think about the possibility that she wouldn't. Not yet. No matter what she'd said about preparing herself.

"Sorry," she muttered. "I guess it's getting to me."

"You think?" His rumble might have been a laugh. "Here, let me help you clear the table."

His phone rang and he answered immediately, his eyes never leaving Beth's. She waited, stricken.

His side of the conversation consisted mostly of uh-huhs. At the end he said, "You understand how important this is. Every minute counts."

He restored his phone to his belt and told Beth, "That was Adler. He's getting a lot of 'who knows?' Seems Chad moves often. Sleeps on friend's couches until they get tired of him. One of Adler's friends says he heard Chad rented a place a month or two ago, but he has no idea where. He says his roommate would know, but the roommate let him know earlier he'd hooked up with someone and wouldn't be home tonight. It's like a curse," he added, the frustration further gouging lines on his face. "Anyway, we're fresh out of luck until the guy shows up for work in the morning. Early," Mike said, seemingly to read Beth's instinctive protest. "Flower market, where florists go pick out their blooms. Crack of dawn."

She didn't move. "I keep thinking this is a nightmare."

"Maybe it is. Maybe we'll both wake up."

Beth turned blindly and picked up dishes from the table. A moment later, Mike did the same.

THE MAN LET SICILY OUT TO USE the bathroom that evening. She was so hungry, she thought it might be later than usual. She'd even wondered if it might already be morning until she saw the dark outside the window. A faint blue haze hung over the living room and she could smell marijuana. His eyes were red and kind of puffy. That would make him slower, sleepier, she thought on a burst of hope, but he stuck really close as he walked her to the bathroom, and once she shut herself in, she couldn't hear any footsteps at all. He had to be standing there on the other side of the door. She gave up finally and came out. There he was, leaning against the wall, blocking her way to the exit.

"Do you, um, have any juice or anything?" she asked, pausing by the kitchen.

His laugh went on too long, like she'd said something really funny. "Beer. You want a beer?"

"No, thank you," Sicily said politely. She also thanked him for dinner when she passed him to go back into her room. She even closed the door behind herself, thinking he might forget to lock it, but he didn't.

Cheeseburger and French fries.

She *thought* he was feeding her twice a day, and she'd been keeping track, but all of a sudden she couldn't remember how many days had passed. Her heart raced, making it harder to think clearly. Forgetting like that was scary.

He'd been weird tonight. Weirder than usual. He was supposed to get the money tomorrow. Maybe he was nervous.

She looked at the bag of food. The food he'd brought way later than usual. Maybe he didn't need her anymore.

OF COURSE MIKE WOULD BE leaving now. The dishwasher was loaded, the counter wiped clean. He'd have no reason to borrow her computer. She wondered where the FBI team was gathered—*hunkered down,* was the term he'd used. Her parents' house? Beth bet Mom would welcome *him* when he walked in the door. But when she asked whether a permanent headquarters had been set up at the house in Magnolia, he shook his head.

"No, they're operating out of FBI offices. Carol's got someone staying there, though, keeping an eye on your dad. Offering a shoulder if either of your parents need it."

She huffed.

A faint smile, the first of the evening, flickered on his mouth. "No, I guess not. Mostly—" his voice hardened "—the agent's role is to be sure your father doesn't get another phone call and decide he doesn't need us."

She had to say this. "It might be better for Sicily if he did."

Mike shook his head. He made sure she was meeting his eyes and then said, "If I thought so, I'd be arguing for it. No, I don't think it makes any difference at this point. What does count is us being able to follow him."

She swallowed and turned away. He thought Sicily was already dead. Earlier, he'd come close to saying so. *Please no.*

"Would you like a cup of coffee before you go?" she asked.

"Truthfully…" He hesitated, his blue eyes watchful. "I'd hoped you would let me stay the night again."

The leap of…not hope, something else, shook her. Was he asking for his own sake or hers? She almost opened her mouth to say again, "I'm fine alone," but didn't. Because she wasn't. She remembered the modest epiphany when she'd understood that she didn't have to be alone, that she was okay with caring about other people. So instead she said, "Of course you're welcome if you'd really like to stay."

"Didn't bring that warrant."

Despite everything, Beth gave a small laugh. "Next time."

"Do I have to wait until you have a nightmare before I get into your bed?"

She stared at him in shock. "You know I can't…" She stuttered, fumbled for words. "Sicily…"

Mike shook his head, the already weary lines on his forehead deepening. "I didn't mean that, Beth. I wouldn't ask. God! I may have the sensitivity of a bull moose, but even I know better than to hit on a woman so scared for your child."

"She's not mine."

"Sure she is, and you know it."

She couldn't be more startled if he'd conjured flame on the palm of his hand. *Mine? Is she?* The notion settled in her stomach. Of course Sicily was hers. That's what had been happening the last week. They hadn't only been getting comfortable with each other, they'd been…accepting. Sicily believing that Beth wanted her, would keep her. Beth accepting that she could love this too-serious child her troubled sister had trusted her with.

"I…didn't exactly think of her that way," she admitted.

"You've been grieving as if you did."

"Yes. I have." Grieving more than she had for Rachel, which was a sobering realization.

Mike nodded, as if he'd settled something, and said, "I'd sleep better holding you. And I bet you will, too."

"Isn't that a little out of the job description?"

He smiled wryly. "You and my job description have been going head-to-head since I first set eyes on you. Haven't you noticed?"

With a blink, she thought, *Hot and cold.* That's what she'd been seeing and not understood.

"Um…no. I guess I didn't."

"I'm not trying to push." His expression had

closed down. "In fact, I should have kept my mouth shut. Sicily's bed is fine."

Her heart was drumming hard, but she found the courage to say, "If you aren't, um, hitting on me, what *are* you trying to say?"

He looked at her for a long time without answering. Finally, he rolled his shoulders as if to ease tension and said, "That I want to be here. That I'm hoping I'll never need a warrant, that you'll keep opening the door for me when this is all over. I guess I'm serving you a notice." He paused. "I liked sleeping with you. I'm thinking I'd like to do it every night."

Oh, boy. Straightforward, intense and completely unexpected.

"You spent the night in my bed and we haven't even been on a date."

He grimaced. "We've spent a lot of time together this week, Beth. Adds up to more than a few dates."

A hysterical laugh bubbled in her chest. "While I was smashing my television set? Showing you the X-rays of my broken bones? And let's not forget about you searching my house. Interrogating me."

That induced some wariness. He cleared his throat. "You have to admit, we got to know each other well."

Beth sank onto a chair and finally did laugh.

She probably didn't sound quite sane, but then when had she ever when he was around?

He squatted beside the chair so that they were close to eye level. One hand squeezed her shoulder. "You okay, honey?"

A hazy memory surfaced. His voice during the night, deep and kind. There'd been a few endearments in there. *It was only a dream. I won't let anyone hurt you.* The dream had been trying all day to surface, too. Little niggles. Curled up tight. Dark, so dark, but she kept her mind shut, too, because she was afraid to look.

You're safe. Wake up.

She gave a long, shaky exhalation. "Yes. I'm fine." Once more she sought for courage, and found it. "I've spent a lot of years trying not to feel much of anything. You noticed."

He nodded.

"Five weeks ago, my sister died. Sicily came to live with me."

He only waited, watchful.

"I felt more the month with Sicily than I knew I could. And that was nothing compared to this week. This week has been like getting tossed in a blender. Or maybe a bread machine—I've been mixed, kneaded, stretched, I've risen and flattened again. I started as flour and I don't know what I am anymore."

The hand that had been kneading her arm went

still. "You telling me you can't deal with anything else, including me?" he asked.

"I'm telling you I'm scared," she said honestly. "Scared for Sicily, scared for me. A little scared of you."

"Because I've been such a jackass." He rose to his feet and let go of her.

Beth shook her head, then offered a wobbly attempt at a smile. "Because you've been nicer to me than anyone ever has. Because… Okay, I haven't known whether I could trust that, because you can also turn icy faster than the street on a sub-zero night. Because…you make me feel things, all right?" That burst out without her knowing she was going to say it.

It brought emotion storming into his eyes, darkening them. He stared down at her. "Good," he said, in a voice that was rougher than usual. "We're on the same page, then."

Were they?

"I'm a patient man," he began, but she interrupted him with another laugh. A little more sane, she hoped.

"You're so patient, you somehow managed to spend the night in my bed despite not having an invitation. You're doing your best to spend the night there again, even though we've barely kissed. Once."

His grin was sheepish. "I *can* be patient," he corrected himself.

"You're welcome to Sicily's bed," she told him. "I'm…" Her voice cracked, surprising her. She tried again. "I'm not ready for anything else, Mike. I'm sorry."

"That's okay," he murmured, then bent and kissed her. It was gentle, sweet, coaxing—and lasted long enough to stir heat in her. When he ended the kiss, he nuzzled her cheek before straightening. "Two kisses."

"What?"

"Actually, three. I kissed you when I walked in the door. Not to mention the top of your head during the night."

The heat in her belly was warming her cheeks, too. "Sneaky," she accused.

"Yeah." He grinned. "And maybe not as patient as I pretend to be."

They gazed at each other. Beth acknowledged something she'd been able to push out of sight for the past few minutes: fear for Sicily.

"I wish there was something we could do," she whispered. "I'd go spend all night at the park with my flashlight if that would do any good."

"I'd be right beside you." He held out a big hand to her and boosted her to her feet. "Maybe it's too early for you, sweetheart, but I need to get some sleep. I'm beat, and I have to be on my way by five."

"You're going to talk to the man at the flower market yourself?" she said with relief.

"Of course I am."

She swallowed. "Thank you."

"Sure you won't change your mind?"

She started to ask what he was talking about, then knew. "I'm sure," she lied. "Shall I wash your clothes again?"

He looked down at them in distaste. "I hate to ask, but…yeah, if you don't mind. Give me a minute. I stopped and bought a package of shorts this morning. Let me grab some clean ones."

He disappeared outside and returned quickly. He locked her front door and went to the bathroom, shortly handing over everything he'd been wearing including his socks. No matter what else was going on inside her she couldn't help noticing that he had a truly beautiful chest—broad, muscular but not bulging, enough hair to be interesting without having a heavy pelt. The view was even better than it had been when she'd awakened to find her head on his shoulder.

She averted her eyes, wished him good-night and went to start the load of laundry. After trying to read for half an hour, she moved the load to the dryer and decided to give up and go to bed herself. She couldn't imagine that she'd sleep—but if she were going to worry she could do it in the dark in bed as well as anywhere else. And she wanted to get up in the morning with Mike.

Sometime during the night, the familiar nightmare began. This time, she was behind the armoire in her parents' bedroom. Her mother had never even looked behind it because the crack that allowed Beth to squeeze in was so narrow. It was her least favorite hidey-hole, but sometimes it was the only one she could reach. *Scared, so scared. Have to make myself so small, like a mouse. And quiet, not even a squeak. But, oh, it was hard not to let a terrified moan escape.*

Only, suddenly she wasn't alone. Strong arms held her, and a deep, tender voice told her he would keep her safe, she didn't have to be afraid. The voice called her "love," and she frowned in puzzlement but was astonished to find she did feel safe, and so warm, and she wasn't hiding and couldn't remember why she had been.

CHAPTER FOURTEEN

"THINGS WERE MOVING, AND there was this weird music all around me. And yeah, I was drunk, but I'm telling you, it was a creepy place."

The words played over and over again in his ears, and Mike wondered what in the hell he was looking for.

Maybe this was useless, but he was too stubborn to believe it. The roommate had been surprised to be cornered by a cop, but he'd talked readily enough. Sure, he'd been to Chad Marks's apartment a couple weeks ago. He hadn't paid that much attention to where it was because Chad was driving. And they were drunk. It was a basement apartment between Aurora and Greenwood Avenue, the guy was sure of that. Pretty sure. Eventually Chad had passed out, and the guy—Luis Hernandez—had decided to catch a bus. He'd walked uphill to Greenwood instead of down to Aurora, which suggested the house was closer to Greenwood.

"Somewhere between Sixty-fifth and Eighty-fifth," he said. "Uh, I think it was Greenwood before it turns into Phinney."

Carol Trenor was less than optimistic about their chances of finding Chad Marks's apartment in the next two and a half hours, based on a vague description that placed it in the basement of a house somewhere within a square that was twenty city blocks by four—and that was if Hernandez's drunken memory wasn't off. Their best hope was spotting the car—assuming it wasn't garaged, parked behind another one, or that Marks hadn't already taken off in preparation for his planned morning pickup.

No, Luis Hernandez had no idea what color the house was. He knew the basement apartment was entered from a back alley that ran uphill and downhill. His face had brightened at that, and Mike had to admit this particular memory did suggest the house was on an east-west street, not one of the north-south ones. Good. Great.

The only other thing Hernandez remembered was that he'd stumbled around toward the front of the house thinking he'd walk up the sidewalk of the street instead of the alley in back. But he'd gotten freaked because something bumped into him and when he whirled around things were moving all around him and there was this weird music that sounded extraterrestrial. He swore it was coming from the ground or the trees or something, not from one of the nearby houses. Spooked, he'd broken and run, back to the alley.

Carol had asked if Mike thought he could drive those blocks himself and he had agreed. With the clock ticking, he wanted to request bodies to help, but without more to go on… Hell, he couldn't blame her for the skepticism. There was time, he told himself. Nothing else useful he could do. He'd drive slowly, looking for possible basement apartments. For anything weird. For a rusting, blue Ford Fairmont.

He had asked if the music could have been wind chimes, and Hernandez said doubtfully, "It was kind of like that, but times a hundred. Like, cranked up. You know?"

Wind chimes on steroids.

Likely someone had been playing some kind of music. Gregorian chants, Peruvian flutes or who the hell knew. Weird music didn't rise from the soil.

But Mike kept thinking it might mean something. And he was afraid if any other cops joined him, they'd concentrate on spotting the car and discount anything "weird."

He'd been to Taproot Theatre on Northwest Eighty-fifth once, eaten at restaurants on Greenwood Avenue maybe a couple of times, but this neighborhood just west of Green Lake certainly wasn't familiar to him. He quickly discovered that the houses had been built in the same era, and many of them, if not most, appeared to have basements. The streets were typical for residential Seattle neighborhoods, narrow and clogged with parked cars that allowed only one lane traffic in many stretches.

By seven-thirty he was driving a grid pattern, sometimes having to tuck the Tahoe to the curb to let another car pass as residents left for work.

Sicily, he thought, *are you here?*

"YOU'VE GOT A BUCKET," HE snapped. "What's the big deal?"

Sicily's heart banged against her rib cage. If he was going to collect the money from her grand-father today, this might be her last chance. And… she might not have a chance at all, but she *knew* she wouldn't if she couldn't talk him into letting her out of the bedroom.

"Please?" she begged. "I have to go. You know. Number two. And it'll be really gross and smell all day."

Last chance.

She fixed a pleading expression on her face, all big eyes. It had worked with Mom sometimes.

He glared at her. "Damn it, will you hurry?"

Sicily nodded vigorously.

He swore and then said, "Okay, you win. Come on."

She had to do *something*. But what? she wondered frantically.

Nothing had changed in the apartment. He hadn't left a gun lying out, or a big knife, or a baseball bat or... *Could* she stab someone—him— if she had the chance? Sicily didn't know.

Her eyes fastened longingly on the big door at the end of the hall that led out of here.

Last chance.

But he walked so close behind her he was practically bumping her. "Hurry it up," he growled, and she nodded.

"I'm sorry."

She had to go into the bathroom. What else could she do? Really she only had to pee, but she'd stay in here as long as she could get away with. If she could block the door so he couldn't get in, he'd have to leave eventually, wouldn't he? But that was a dumb thing to think, because there was no way to do it. Nothing in here could be wedged against the door to keep it from swinging in. And it was kind of flimsy anyway. He could probably crash through it if he wanted.

She didn't flush but instead stood with her ear practically pressed to the door, listening. He was pacing. She could feel his tension in here. Or maybe it was hers.

The lid from the tank of the toilet. It was heavy. She could swing it at him. If she could hit him in the head… But he was way bigger than she was. He'd probably be able to grab it out of her hands, and then…

Sicily shuddered.

Last chance.

MIKE HAD STARTED THE GRID BY driving west on Eighty-fifth, then turning south on Greenwood when nothing caught his eye. They were screwed if Hernandez's memory was off—if the apartment were a block or two on the *other* side of Green-wood Ave.

Sicily was screwed.

Go with the odds, he told himself.

Up and down, his gaze raking the parked cars, the yards, the hint of a window here and there that suggested a basement. When an alley ran east-west, he drove that, too. Some of the houses had six-foot-high fences around their backyards, a few with gates and detached garages. Buildings *designed* to hide a car.

He saw some weird stuff, but nothing that jibed. One place had a fountain that looked like an old-fashioned well: water leaped up into the bucket, which tipped when it was full spilling the water

out to start over. He rolled down his window and
heard the water, but it was more a pleasant splish-
splash than wind chimes on steroids. Another yard
was shiny white gravel decorated with plastic garden gnomes. Not a single living thing.

His tension rose. He had to drive very slowly
to be sure he didn't miss anything. The minutes
were racing by. Every so often he got out to check
a car tucked behind others, to peek into a garage
when he could. He reached Eightieth, went slowly
east on it, downhill. Right on quiet Linden Avenue instead of going all the way to busy Aurora.
Right on an alley, left on Greenwood, left down
Seventy-ninth. Damn, damn, damn.

"WHAT ARE YOU DOING IN THERE?" the man yelled.

"What do you think I'm doing?" Sicily yelled
back.

He was wired this morning. His eyes had had
a wild look. What if her grandparents didn't give
him the money? What if they did?

Was he still standing there on the other side
of the door? *Please,* she thought. *Please, please,
please, please.*

"Yeah, well, hurry it up," he grumbled, but his
voice came from farther away. Back toward the
kitchen or living room.

Sicily strained to hear the slightest sound. Then

it came—a thump. Her heart sank. He'd bumped into the wall or something, not that far away.

How long could she get away with staying in here?

If she went back into the bedroom and let him lock the door, she had this really awful feeling she'd never get out again.

WHEN MIKE SAW THE YARD, HE could hardly believe his eyes. His first thought was, *Now there's weird.* The owner gardened, sure, but it wasn't the flowers that caught his eye. It was the ornaments. At first sight, the trees seemed to be decorated for Christmas, only not with Christmas colors. Then he realized that what he was looking at was glass balls—big ones. Probably hand-blown glass. Witch's balls. He didn't remember where he'd heard that term, or even whether it was accurate, but it seemed to fit. There were balls as small as a few inches in diameter, some as big as eight or ten inches. Every color in the rainbow swirled together. They hung from the branches of trees, the leggy arms of big old rhododendrons, the thorny canes of rambler roses—even the eaves of the house and the railing of the porch.

He'd come to a stop in the middle of the street, staring. Not giving a damn that he was blocking the road, he set the emergency brake and got out, crossed the street and climbed the few concrete steps to yard level.

The witch's balls weren't the only thing hanging from branches and eaves. There were long, thin shards of blown glass, too, in myriad colors. Some hung alone, like icicles. Others were suspended in clusters from pieces of driftwood. Wind chimes. So many of them he stared in awe.

Dazed, he stepped into the yard and almost whacked his head on a big mother of a glass ball. Only a quick shuffle saved him.

Hernandez said something had bumped into him. Hell, yeah. Imagine if the wind blew. Even a mild breeze.

Things were moving, and there was this weird music all around me. And yeah, I was drunk, but I'm telling you, it was a creepy place.

Mike's gaze dropped to the well that protected a basement window. He reached for his cell phone.

HE SUDDENLY EXCLAIMED, "WHAT the…? There's somebody in the goddamn yard!" There was a clatter in the living room, and Sicily knew it had to be now.

She reached for the knob, turning it as quietly as she could. As she opened the door a crack then widened it, she heard him say, "It's a cop! It's gotta be a cop," and then a bunch of obscenities. His voice was shaking. She'd be glad if she weren't so scared.

The hall was empty.

Sicily left her flip-flops behind, slipped out of the bathroom and hurried toward that extra big door that must lead to the outside. She'd left the bathroom door closed, hoping it might give her a minute as he waited for her to come out.

She was fumbling with the dead bolt when she heard, "Kid, what're you…?" and then a roar.

Her hands were shaking. He was coming. She flung the door open, leaped through and slammed it behind her. She found herself in an unfinished part of the basement where there was a washer and dryer and a bunch of junk. A bike. She grabbed the bike and threw it where he'd trip over it, then tore up the wooden steps to yet another door.

He was bellowing with rage that turned into screamed obscenities when he fell over the bike. Sicily got the other door open and threw herself out, running even before she looked around her.

Gravel crunched under her bare feet and it hurt so much she half fell against a car, but she pushed herself up and kept going. Beyond them was an alley. There was nobody around although she could hear traffic. She wanted to scream but didn't dare waste the air. His pounding footsteps weren't far behind. He was yelling at her.

"MIKE, THAT YOU?" CAROL Trenor said in his ear.

"Yeah. I've found it. Haven't gone around back yet to see if the car's here...."

He heard the bang of a door, a crash, a bellow of rage. A sob? He started to move, but on this side of the house a six-foot fence blocked him from the backyard. Around to the other side... No. He could drive around to the alley as quickly and block it.

Bounding down the stairs to his SUV, he told Carol the address, slammed the door, tossed the phone aside and accelerated hard enough to burn rubber.

A SOLID FENCE LINED THE ALLEY on the other side. Downhill? She could go faster, but so could he. Up? She didn't even know why or how she decided, just ran with everything she had. Sicily was only distantly aware her feet were in agony. She tore behind a panel truck parked at a neighbor's a little way up the alley. A gate was open; she dodged into the yard. Which way? A brick path led around the house, there was a shed she could try to hide in... But her desperate gaze fastened on some two-by-fours nailed to the side of the shed in a stair-step arrangement. For a cat? They gave enough footholds and handholds for her to clamber up. She was almost on top of the shed when a hand closed around her ankle and yanked.

Sicily kicked out with her other foot and felt it

connect with a crunch that had him screaming in fury. But then he grabbed that ankle, too. Sobbing, she scrabbled for a handhold, any kind of handhold, but her fingers were trying to dig into a gritty, flat roof. She slid backward, leaving skin behind. Her hips momentarily lodged against the edge of the roof. Now she was screaming, too. Why, oh, why wasn't someone coming out of the house? Didn't anybody *hear* her?

And then came the roar of a truck coming down the alley. The driver wouldn't be able to see them. Whoever it was would keep going and miss them, and *he* would drag her back down into that horrible apartment and he'd kill her.

But the truck skidded to a stop, a door opened, there were running footsteps and the next thing she knew, her ankles were free.

Wounded, terrified, Sicily pulled herself back onto the roof, far enough from the edge so that nobody could grab her, and waited.

Somebody heard. Somebody came.

MIKE SLAMMED THE SON OF A BITCH onto his face on the ground in seconds, cuffed him, said in a guttural voice, "Police. You piece of scum, you're under arrest."

He didn't bother reading him his rights. The real arrest would be in someone else's hands. This wasn't his jurisdiction, and truth was that he'd never wanted to kill somebody more.

The creep lay there sobbing, not resisting. His face was bloodied. Mike was betting his nose was broken, something he hadn't done. *Good for you, Sicily.*

Satisfied the bastard wasn't moving, Mike hitched himself up on one of the boards nailed to the side of the shed. He only got high enough to see over the edge of the roof. Sicily huddled there, shaking, like a wild animal waiting to die. A little girl in red shorts, a white tank top and nothing else. Big, haunting eyes stared at him.

"Sicily?" he said quietly. "I'm a police officer. I've been looking for you." When she kept quaking, he gentled his voice further. "Honey, your aunt Beth can hardly wait for you to come home. Will you let me help you down?"

Only the relief kept a cap on the rage that filled him. Now she'd carry scars to equal Beth's. Would either of them ever feel safe again?

Yeah. If he had his way, they would. Without hesitation, without a second thought, Mike dedicated his life to protecting and loving this girl and the woman he'd coaxed from another nightmare last night.

She's not Nate.

Answering was easy. *I know.*

He heard movement below and turned his head to glare at Marks. "I told you not to move."

"She broke my nose!"

"Good," he said heartlessly, and smiled at Sicily. "You are one gutsy girl, Sicily Marks. I can't tell you how happy I am to meet you at last."

A shuddery sigh rattled her thin body. She sniffed and, with difficulty, sat up. Mike winced at the sight of her knees, thighs and arms rubbed raw. And her feet. It was all he could do not to swear. They were soaked with blood.

"You know my aunt Beth?" she asked in a small voice.

"Yeah." He managed another smile. "Maybe this is the time to tell you I've slept in your bed the past two nights."

Already big eyes widened. They were an amazing color, green and gold, like the swirled blown glass balls.

"That's okay," she said. "Will you take me home?"

He became conscious of approaching sirens. A police car turned down the top of the alley. Lights flashing, an aide car passed up above, on the cross street.

"Eventually," Mike assured her. "But first you're going to the hospital. You, kiddo, are going to have really sore feet for a while. You need to get cleaned up and bandaged."

She sniffed, nodded and inched forward. Mike

waited until she'd almost reached him, then stepped to the ground.

The police car had stopped behind his vehicle. An unmarked car raced up the alley from the other direction. Chad Marks lay cuffed, crying, blood bubbling out of his nose. And the brave little girl he'd kidnapped scooted to the edge of the roof, looked down at Mike and said hesitantly, "Maybe I should climb down."

"No." He held up his arms. "A little bit farther forward, tip and and let yourself fall. I'll catch you."

She eyed him with the tiniest bit of suspicion. "Promise?"

Man. Sicily was definitely Beth's kid. He was smiling when he waggled his fingers. "Promise."

"Okay," she said, and launched herself.

He caught her.

BETH PACED, THE PHONE CLUTCHED in one hand. Mike had called earlier to tell her what he'd learned—which wasn't much. What hope was there he could find a house with no more description than that it had a basement apartment, and things that *moved* in the yard and played creepy music?

Eight o'clock came, went. Eight-thirty. The clock crept toward nine. Dad had been instructed to leave at ten on the nose, to drive a winding route through city streets to prove nobody was trailing him. Soon he would be getting into his Mercedes, backing out of the garage, following the circular drive to the gates.

Oh, God, Sicily.

Mike hadn't been in her bed when she'd awakened that morning, which had left her momentarily confused. She would have sworn she remembered him holding her during the night. But she heard Sicily's bathroom door close, and a few minutes later the sound of the shower. When she cocked her head, she realized the dryer was running to shake the wrinkles out of his clothes.

She showered, got dressed and came out to find him in the kitchen buttoning his shirt. He'd given her a lazy grin that only looked a little tired, held out his arms and said, "See, ma? No need for ironing."

Gripping her phone, Beth held on to the memory of that smile as if it were one of those rice- or bean-filled socks that could be heated in the microwave to relax sore muscles. It felt good. Thinking about Mike was the only thing that did feel good right now.

Eight fifty-six. Only three minutes since she'd last checked the time on her cell phone. Mike hadn't found the house. Hadn't found Sicily. Soon Chad Marks would be on his way to collect two million dollars bought with his own daughter's blood. They would catch him eventually. Surely they would. If he hurt Sicily, she wanted him to get the death penalty.

Her cell phone rang and Beth jumped six inches. Mike's number. Breathless, she answered.

"I've got her, Beth. Sicily is safe. She's right here, and wants to talk to you."

Beth stumbled to her sofa and collapsed on it. "Sicily? Oh, God, Sicily, are you all right?"

"Aunt Beth?" She was crying. "I got away, only then that man caught me, but Detective Ryan— Mike—rescued me and he's taking me to the hospital 'cuz I cut my feet and will you please, please come?"

"Yes. Oh, honey, yes. Let me talk to Mike again."

The phone was passed. He said, "We're going to Harborview."

Tears ran down her face, but she was smiling, too. Maybe laughing. "I wish I could fly."

"Drive carefully," he ordered her. "Promise."

Past a lump in her throat, Beth said, "Cross my heart."

DETECTIVE RYAN HAD TOLD HER TO call him Mike, but Sicily wasn't sure. Mom's boyfriends always told her to call them by their first names, but it felt funny because she was a kid and they weren't and they weren't *her* friends. But he was awfully nice, so she resolved to remember.

He pulled up in front of the emergency entrance

at the hospital, and a couple of people wearing green scrubs came out with a wheelchair. But Sicily didn't open her door, and when he reached for his handle she said, "Detective Ryan? I mean, Mike?"

He looked at her. "Yes? What is it, Sicily?"

She took a deep breath. "Is *he* my father?"

Mike took her hand. She saw the answer on his face before he said kindly, "I'm afraid so, Sicily. Biologically. He isn't your father in any other way."

She sighed—she'd already known.

Mike glanced past her and shook his head. Nobody opened the door on her side. He didn't look impatient at all. "You have questions," he said.

"Will I see you again?" she blurted.

He smiled. "Sweetheart, you will see plenty of me. So much, you may wish I'd go away."

"No." Sicily shook her head. "Will you stay until Aunt Beth gets here?"

"You bet."

"Okay." She made a face. "This is going to hurt, isn't it?"

"Don't you already hurt?"

"Um…yeah."

He let go of her hand and tucked her hair behind her ear. "Washing the grit out of those scrapes *is* going to hurt. I can't lie to you."

"That's okay," she decided. Then said very politely, "Thank you for coming when you did."

"You're very welcome." His smile was all for her. It was like no one else was waiting. "You ready, kiddo?"

"I guess so."

"Then let's do it."

They'd opened the door by the time he came around, but he was the one to lift her down and set her carefully onto the wheelchair. And he walked right beside her into the hospital.

"HE'S MY DAD," SICILY SAID sadly. She had been nestled deep in Beth's arms, but pulled back. "Did they tell you?"

"Yes. We were already pretty sure," Beth said. She, the woman who had never been a hugger, wanted only to drag this skinny girl back into a never-ending hug. Before, they hadn't done much touching. Maybe it was Mike, she thought, bemused. Being held when she needed it had taught her something. She didn't look away from Sicily's worried face. "I'm sorry. I wish he wasn't your father."

"Me, too." Sicily squared thin shoulders, sniffed and said, "I didn't wait for you to find me. Except…Detective Ryan—Mike—did find me."

Beth laughed, although it broke in the middle.

"Oh, honey! That was the best phone call I've gotten in my entire life. You are so brave."

"He lived in this horrible, messy *pit*. Did they tell you that?"

Beth found herself laughing again. "No. They didn't say that. To tell you the truth, I don't know anything yet."

The emergency room curtain was open and a cluster of law enforcement people hovered in the hall. The curtain rings rattled and Mike walked in. His smile was huge. "Beth."

Nothing could have stopped her from stepping into his embrace and burying her wet face against his shoulder. His arms closed around her and he stroked a hand gently up and down her back. After a moment she sniffled, wiped her cheeks with the back of her hand and moved back. "I'm sorry."

"You're entitled," he said gently. He smiled at Sicily. "Your aunt has been really scared."

"Oh." She studied them both with her usual serious air. "I was afraid she'd think I'd...well, just gotten lost or something."

"We did think that at first."

"The sun was so warm, I fell asleep." Guilt twisted in Beth's stomach. "I'm so sorry, Sicily. If I'd been awake…"

"I know you were asleep. I didn't think you'd care if I went up to the bathroom. Mom wouldn't have."

"No." Mike squeezed Beth's shoulder, a brief, casual gesture. "You're ten. Why would she?"

It touched her that he was so determined to make up for his original harshness. The astonishing thing was, she thought maybe she could believe him. Doing so was easier, of course, now that Sicily was safe, but even so… *Maybe I really* didn't *do anything so wrong.*

"Can we go home now?" Sicily asked.

"I don't know." Beth looked around. Agent Trenor was among the group desperate to interview Sicily. Beth didn't recognize any of the rest. "Mike?"

"I don't see why not," he said. "They can talk to her later. But let's make sure she's been cleared to go by the doctor."

A passing nurse went to get the doctor, who swept the cops with a scathing look, saying, "Move them out into the waiting area." He whipped the curtain closed in their faces. Fortunately, Mike was on the inside of it. "You're the aunt?" the doctor asked. "And who are you?"

"Detective Ryan, Sauk County Sheriff's Department." He smiled. "Also Beth and Sicily's chauffeur."

Not strictly true, as she had her own car here, but Beth wasn't about to get him evicted. She wanted him here.

"Ah." Brisk and graying, the doctor told them

that Sicily had withstood her ordeal well. The cuts and bruises on her feet were her worst injuries. She was mildly dehydrated. He told them how to watch for infection, but didn't believe there was any need to hospitalize her. He saw no indication of a blow to her head and suspected she might have inhaled ether or another gas to knock her out when she was grabbed. "She doesn't remember anything from leaving the restroom until she woke up in the trunk of the car. We've drawn blood, but after so many days…" He shrugged.

Beth put her arm around Sicily's shoulders. "She wasn't…"

Thank God, he understood without making her finish the question. "No. Nothing like that."

"Like what?" Sicily asked.

"I wanted to be sure he didn't hurt you."

"He stared at me a lot." Sicily shuddered. "It was creepy."

"He was probably curious," Mike said mildly.

"I didn't like it. I didn't like *him*."

Beth was torn between tears and laughter. The laughter won. "He didn't give you much reason to like him, did he?"

"It's fine for you to go home," the doctor concluded, "assuming you can get by the mob out there." He smiled at Sicily. "Take care, young lady." His eyes met Beth's. "You might take her to her pediatrician for a follow-up in a few days."

"Yes." At least they had a pediatrician. Beth had to find one first thing when Sicily came to live with her, since the school insisted on vaccines for which no records existed. "I'll do that."

Sicily rode out in a wheelchair, Mike and Beth a protective step behind her. Beth had to stop to provide her insurance information, and then asked Mike, "Will you stay with her while I go get my car?"

"I'd rather drive you home." He held out a hand. "Give me your keys, and I'll have someone drive your car." He nodded toward the conglomeration of cops. "They might as well make themselves useful."

Feeling giddy, Beth laughed, hesitating only a moment before peeling the car key off her ring, dropping it in his hand and telling him where she was parked.

Then, with a few hard stares and fewer words, he cleared the way and only the three of them exited the emergency room door into the parking lot and a misty, gray day.

They were going home.

Beth was overwhelmed by a huge swell of emotion she couldn't identify. As Mike and Sicily told her about everything she'd missed, she kept watching their faces. They must have been halfway home before she knew.

It was hope.

Choked by astonishment, she caught Mike smiling at Sicily in the rearview mirror, then he turned the smile onto her. The skin beside those blue eyes crinkled and her heart did a peculiar hop, skip and jump. She'd never felt anything quite like that before, either.

It had to be hope, she thought. A belief that good things could happen. That she could trust someone and have him live up to it, and that maybe Sicily could trust her, Beth, and that she wouldn't let her niece down.

At the very least…she *wanted* to believe, and that was something, wasn't it?

CHAPTER FIFTEEN

BETH SAT DOWN ON THE EDGE OF Sicily's bed. She'd never tucked anyone in before. That's what she was doing, wasn't it? Before, she'd hovered awkwardly in the doorway to wish Sicily good-night. But that and a whole lot of other things were going to change. They were going to become a family. A real one, the kind other people had.

Took for granted.

She'd never made this kind of resolution before but when she set an objective, she was determined.

"Hey," she said. "We haven't known each other that long."

Sicily had gotten into bed but sat cross-legged, the covers only pulled over her lap. Loose bandages covered the worst scrapes on her arms and legs. Beth noticed how ratty her pajamas were. *That's another thing we need to buy her.*

"No," Sicily said, looking wary. "I bet you missed work because of me, huh?"

Beth's laugh was choked. "Gee, and that's the worst thing that ever happened to me."

"I missed school, too." Sicily sounded worried. "I bet I've gotten behind."

"Unless we send you in a wheelchair, you need to be able to walk before you go back to school," Beth said firmly. "I'll leave a message for your teacher Monday. She can email your assignments so you can start catching up. Anyway, I hate to tell you this, but we have something more immediate coming up. All those police officers and FBI agents insist on talking to you again."

"Oh." She thought about it. "I guess that's okay." Sicily picked at the covers. "When I go back to school, will all the kids know what happened?"

"I'm afraid so."

"Oh." She pondered that, then shrugged. "They'll get over it."

Beth found herself laughing again. Laughing felt easier than it ever had. She was giddy with relief.

"You're right," she said. "They will. Hey, you'll be a heroine."

Sicily's usually solemn expression lightened. "I guess I kind of am, aren't I?"

Driven by sudden impulse, Beth leaned forward and hugged her. "Yeah, you are."

Sicily didn't melt into her, and Beth straightened pretty quickly, but still it had felt good.

"Do you feel really bad about him being your father?"

"Mike—Detective Ryan—said he isn't really. That's what Mom said, too." She scrunched up her nose. "Because he didn't actually want me. Until he figured somebody would pay for me, I guess." She was trying to sound as if it didn't matter, but Beth could tell it did.

"My father wasn't much of a dad, either."

Sicily's eyes fastened on Beth's face. "Mom said that, too. Sometimes. And then she'd get drunk and say she was Daddy's little girl only it was really hard for him because a divorce would look bad and he couldn't put his family first."

Beth couldn't quite suppress her snort.

Sicily frowned. "She said your mom was mean."

"Yes. She was abusive. She hurt us both and our father wouldn't do anything about it."

"Did he see?"

"She never hit us or burned us or anything in front of him. But I told him. I tried to tell him," she corrected herself. "He refused to hear it, even though he knew how often Mom had to take one of us to the emergency room with broken bones or infected burns or whatever. He didn't care." It felt cleansing to say that out loud: *my father didn't care.* She had never told anyone about the abuse until Mike. Now she'd lost track of how many people knew. *Why did I keep it a secret so long?* she wondered.

The scrutiny of those big eyes was almost unnerving, but Sicily finally nodded. "So how come you and Mom aren't more alike?" A ripple of emotion puckered her forehead. "I mean, why *weren't* you more alike?"

"I don't know. Maybe we wouldn't have been no matter what. Siblings often have different personalities. I might have been born—" Stronger. Startled, Beth examined the thought. She rarely considered herself in a positive light. Her life had been shaped by too much shame, but now she let herself believe. No, she hadn't been strong enough to save Rachel, but ultimately she had made something of herself. She hadn't let their parents utterly destroy her the way her sister had.

"Born what?" Sicily asked.

"I was trying to think of the right word," Beth lied. "Maybe there isn't one. Only that we reacted differently to what happened. I was determined never to let anyone hurt me again. I wanted to be financially successful so I didn't need anyone else. Your mom still needed other people."

"She called my grandparents a lot. She still needed them."

"I didn't know that," Beth said. She shook off the sadness.

"Other people, too. Guys." The ten-year-old's expression said *yuck*.

"Yeah." Beth's smile felt a little shaky. "You, too."

"She did need me." Sicily looked satisfied, but also…something.

Maybe, Beth thought, Sicily knew in her heart that her mother had needed her and used her in ways that weren't right.

"The biggest difference between us," Beth said, reasoning out something else she'd never put into words before, "is that she could still love other people, and believe they might love her."

Those amazing, all-too-knowing eyes widened. "You don't?"

"I…didn't." Oh, boy. A marble had lodged in her throat, and even if she got it down it was going to be indigestible. Somehow she managed another smile. "I guess I'm ready to give it a shot."

"Because of me."

She nodded, although Mike was in her head, too. Had he meant what he'd said? He'd seen deeper into her than she'd ever let anyone see before. Seen her at her worst, she guessed, but she also suspected real emotions didn't spring from seeing people only at their best.

"I thought maybe you didn't really want me," Sicily admitted.

"You were wrong." Although it was hard, Beth took her hand and squeezed. "I'm not very good at showing how I feel sometimes. Losing you…" She couldn't help the shudder. "It made me realize I needed to tell you how much I do want you."

Sicily's eyes filled with tears and she abruptly launched herself at Beth, whose arms opened as if by instinct and then closed about the sobbing girl.

"I miss Mom…but in the basement I kept thinking…she wouldn't even know how to *do* anything…and maybe she wouldn't…but I knew you would," she finished on a wail.

"Oh, sweetie." Beth found herself rocking the distraught girl. Her own eyes burned. "I think your mom might have surprised you." She wanted to believe that, and it wouldn't hurt if Sicily did would it? "But you and I… We're going to do okay, aren't we? Better than okay."

Sicily nodded hard, her blond hair tickling Beth's nose. She didn't cry long; Beth suspected she hardly ever did. Her mother had been dramatic enough for both of them. No, this practical, take-charge kid would have begun refusing to indulge in displays of emotion before she started kindergarten.

Eventually, settling back, she said, "At least I know what my dad's like now. I won't keep wondering."

Beth nodded. The matter-of-fact statement made her think about Mike, about how she had told him that the worst was not knowing. The expression on his face had been pained. Wondering was bad, but knowing wasn't so great, either, not when the reality wasn't what you'd yearned for.

She wished she was the kind of person who could have easily said, "I love you," before kissing Sicily good-night. But then she realized that, in a way, she'd already said it. And…it would get easier, wouldn't it?

So she settled for patting Sicily's leg through the covers and saying, "Once your feet are healed, we're going shopping. You need new clothes. And I am not taking my eyes off you for a second, so be ready for me to come into the dressing room with you."

Sicily giggled, so maybe that was the right thing to say. Beth's chest felt lighter when she stood, said good-night and turned out the light.

MIKE THOUGHT ALL AFTERNOON about Beth and Sicily, but he had to give them time. Didn't mean he couldn't call, though. And he'd see them tomorrow for questioning. Nothing would have kept him away even if he wasn't the lead on this kidnapping anymore. If Sicily or Beth got too stressed, he'd cut the interview off with no hesitation.

He waited until almost nine, figuring Sicily would be in bed. Beth answered on the third ring, sounding slightly breathless as if she'd hurried for the phone.

"Did I get you at a bad time?" he asked.

"No, I was saying good-night to Sicily."

Was that bemusement in her voice? Intrigued, he asked, "Everything okay?"

"Yes. Really okay. I think I'm floating two feet off the floor."

"Too bad Sicily can't. It'd save wear and tear on her feet."

Her laugh took a painful bite out of his heart muscle.

"That would be nice, wouldn't it?" After a moment, she asked, "Did you finally get to go home?"

"I decided to work the rest of the day. I'm due some time off, but I'll save it." *Until I can spend it with you.* "I took on a new investigation right before Sicily went missing. It's been eating at me a little. So I went back to it today."

She made an interested sound, so he told her about J. N. Sullivan Landscaping and the alleged theft of $200,000 worth of landscaping equipment. Ruliczkowski had confirmed that Mike's suspicions about the financial stability of the landscaping service were right on.

"I did a door-to-door today," he said.

That caused a little pool of silence. "Like you did in my neighborhood."

"Uh…yeah." Sometimes he forgot the landmines waiting to trip him up.

"Did you learn anything?"

"Plenty." What he found wasn't unexpected; many of the neighbors said, "Who?" when he asked about the Sullivans. With houses on acre-age like that and no shared driveways, folks had no reason to know each other. A lot of those peo-ple who chose to live where they didn't have to see their neighbors didn't *want* to know them.

The sign at the head of the driveway, though, that said J. N. Sullivan Landscaping Services helped. It helped a lot. Pretty much everyone nodded when Mike mentioned it—oh, yeah, older guy? And they'd seen the wife coming and going.

Mike hit pay dirt at the tenth house, a good half mile down the road. Turned out that by chance the woman had chatted with Sullivan's wife while both were getting gas at the tiny, old-fashioned grocery and gas station that served this rural area. Therefore she knew they'd be in Ocean Shores for a couple of weeks. But she distinctly remembered seeing John the week before last, coming out of his driveway pulling one of his trailers with the big tractor on it.

"So I was surprised to see him," she said. And yes, she knew it was that week, because it was right before she saw on the news that a little girl disappeared at the county park down the road.

Mike told Beth, "Once I had a witness, the guy crumbled. He had the attitude that defrauding the big bad insurance company was okay. He's in deep trouble now."

They talked for a long time. About the case,

about ethics, about his job and hers. He was surprised when he glanced at the clock and realized it was nearly ten.

As if realizing the same, Beth said, "This thing in the morning? Please tell me you don't think it'll go on for hours."

"I won't let it." He made sure she heard the steel in his voice.

"I'm so glad you'll be here. Sicily is, too. She seems to have…taken to you."

"Good," he said, softly but with clear intent. "I'll see you in the morning, Beth."

"Yes."

Mike frowned. "Forgot to ask. Did you talk to your parents?"

"My father. Very briefly. Agent Trenor had called him, which was nice of her. He wanted to know how his granddaughter was."

"Did he say anything about the scene the other day?"

"No, and I don't suppose he ever will." She paused. "Sicily said Rachel called home a lot. She wanted them to love her."

"Where our parents are concerned, I'm not sure we ever grow up."

"No. Are yours alive?"

"Yeah. My mom and dad are good people." He didn't have to wonder whether they'd accept Beth. Mom would see immediately beneath her defenses. She would chatter and next thing Beth would know they'd be working side by side in the kitchen. Beth would be telling her life story and feeling like she'd been hit by a bus. Mom, he thought, would see her wounds and love her.

Mom hadn't been crazy about Ellen. He'd been young and dumb enough to feel resentful instead of thinking, *huh, wonder why?*

Mom hadn't been able to understand why he wouldn't fall in love again and get married and produce grandkids. She'd grieved for him and for Nate, but wanted him to be happy.

Mom would love Sicily, too.

He and Beth said good-night, but she was all he could think about while he got ready for bed. *I want to take her home to Mom and Dad.* He shook his head over the last thought. *Am I off my rocker?*

No.

He dreamed about Nate. Even in the dream, as he plunged in the water he didn't know for sure if he were searching for Nate or Sicily. But this time an errant ray of sunlight seemed to penetrate the depths and he saw Nate's face. Empty, dead. He was sinking, farther and farther away, and Mike was so frantic for air he knew he wouldn't be able to get his hands on his son. He woke sitting up in bed gasping for air. Groaning, he wrenched at his hair. What the hell did *that* mean? Did he need constant reminders that he hadn't been able to save his own child? *God.*

Why couldn't he dream about Nate when he had been alive? Good dreams, like pushing him on the swing set Mike had built from a kit. Watching his laughing face as he went down the blue plastic slide, shooting into his daddy's hands. Why couldn't he dream about nights of walking baby Nate to his crib, or the first smiles? His face covered with green chocolate-mint ice cream, his chortle every time they saw Mrs. Llewlyn's dachshund in one of those sweaters?

His chest ached. Those memories were painful, too. As bad. Maybe this version of the nightmare had been meant to tell him Nate was finally leaving him.

For the first time ever, he thought he was ready to accept that. It was time. Trust and love would be hard for Beth—he didn't want to think impossible. He needed to be strong and steady for her. Healed.

Yeah. He was ready.

DETECTIVE RYAN ARRIVED THE next morning before anyone else. Aunt Beth seemed glad to see him, which relaxed Sicily. He strolled into the kitchen as if he felt practically as at home as she did and said hopefully, "Coffee on?"

Aunt Beth reached into the cupboard for a mug. "Somebody didn't get enough sleep?"

"It wasn't a great night." He turned really blue eyes on Sicily. "How about you, Sicily? You hanging in there?"

She nodded. "Aunt Beth and I talked."

"Did you." It wasn't a question. His gaze flicked to Aunt Beth, and Sicily wondered what that was about.

"We talked about her dad and my parents. Nothing I said surprised her." Beth smiled at Sicily, differently than she had before. Sicily tried to figure out *what* was different and wasn't sure.

The detective took his coffee and said, "Sicily, why don't you sit down. Let's talk about what's going to happen today."

He was really nice. He went through the kind of questions she'd be asked, without expecting her to answer any of them for him. He told her why the FBI agents were involved *and* Seattle *and* Sauk County police departments. "A surfeit of cops," he said, laughing, and told her what *surfeit* meant although she could have guessed.

He seemed to be done about the same time the doorbell rang, but his eyes stayed on her face and he didn't move, leaving Aunt Beth to go answer it. "What's on your mind?" he asked.

Sicily looked down at the flowered place mat. "Well, I was kind of wondering. I mean, what'll happen to *him?*"

"That depends. He'll definitely be charged with first-degree kidnapping."

"What's the *first-degree* mean?" she asked, thinking maybe it wasn't the really bad kind.

But he explained that if her dad had taken her only because he wanted her to live with him and didn't think it was fair Aunt Beth had custody, then he would have been charged with second-degree kidnapping. "But he asked for ransom, and that makes the crime first-degree." He went quiet for a minute, watching her. They could both hear voices in the living room, but Detective Ryan acted like they had all the time in the world to talk. "There may not be a trial if he pleads guilty. But if this *does* go to trial, you'll probably have to testify, Sicily."

"You mean, sit there in that box like on TV and lawyers will ask me questions?"

"Yes, and the defense attorney—the lawyer taking your dad's side—will try to confuse you or make you say he didn't do things he really did do."

"Will he go to jail for a long time?"

"Yes. Kidnapping is considered almost as bad as murder. It's punished severely. Sicily…" He took her hand. His was big and warm. "Are you feeling bad about what may happen to him?"

She gulped and nodded. "It's really dumb, isn't it? Because it was awful. But…well, he didn't hurt me or anything and I don't know if he would have." She said that in a rush and wished she knew.

"Maybe not." Detective Ryan was still holding her hand, and his voice was really quiet and nice. "But we don't know. When he left a message like that, he was making an implicit threat. 'Give me the money or else.'"

She nodded. The doorbell rang again, and there were more voices. She straightened and squared her shoulders. "So it doesn't make any difference what I say today?"

"Unless you lie and say you went with him of your own volition—because that's what you wanted to do—then no." His voice and expression got harder. "Because he didn't want to get to know you, Sicily. He thought he could use you to soak your grandparents for money. Whether you got hurt or scared, that didn't matter to him. I know it's complicated for you because he's your father, but he doesn't deserve for you to care."

She nodded again, because she knew he was right, but she still felt funny inside about it. "When I told him I was tired of cheeseburgers, he brought me an egg sandwich the next time."

The detective's face softened again. "That's the kind of thing that may influence the judge when he sentences your father. It may suggest he's not all bad, that he really wouldn't have hurt you. There's a recommended range for sentencing. What you say could mean he won't get as many years as he otherwise would have."

"Okay." Sicily took a deep breath. "I'll say exactly what happened then."

He smiled at her. "Good girl. Are you ready?"

She straightened her shoulders and nodded. "Yes."

THE THREE OF THEM WENT shopping that afternoon. When Mike heard the idea, he volunteered his services as bodyguard and wheelchair-pusher. Beth made a call and determined that the mall had loaners available. Sicily, it appeared, sort of liked the idea that everyone might stare at her.

"You don't have to work?" Beth asked.

He grinned at her. "Remember that time I'm due?"

"Yes, but…"

"This is how I want to spend it."

She blushed, which made his smile widen. "You'll probably be really bored."

"Somehow I doubt it," he said, feeling satisfied.

On the short drive to Everett Mall, he kept sneaking glances at her, often looking over her shoulder to talk to Sicily in the backseat.

The huge ease of tension made Beth a different woman. She still sat primly and she didn't laugh outright, but he kept feeling a clutch in his belly when he remembered thinking that her face was too bony for real beauty. He'd wondered why his body had responded so powerfully to her. Now he thought, *Damn, she's gorgeous.*

Was this what she'd looked like before, or had the events of the past week opened her somehow? He was hungry to know, but mostly hungry to be near her, to listen to her talk about anything at all, to watch her interact with the unexpectedly cheerful girl whose photo had caught at his heart. Had Sicily ever been as solemn and…fragile as he'd imagined, either? Had the photographer caught her at a bad moment? Or was she, too, finding some peace?

Mike's role, as he'd anticipated, was to do a whole lot of standing around, guarding the entrances to dressing rooms and to occasionally give a thumbs-up.

Sicily was not a greedy shopper. She pondered each possibility, agonized over this or that, even when Beth said, "Let's get both." Sicily worried about price tags and what was on sale and what wasn't, making Mike suspect she'd been the one to figure out how to stretch her mother's limited income. Beth stayed patient. She also slipped a few purchases through that Sicily hadn't okayed— socks, underwear, a cute sweater, a second pair of pajamas, a pair of dressy sandals Sicily had rejected even while watching wistfully as the shoe clerk packed them away in their box. Mike left them a couple of times to ferry purchases out to his SUV.

They ate lunch at the food court, which took an astonishing length of time because Sicily wanted to inspect the menu board at every single vendor, go back twice, and finally a third time before she made up her mind.

"She'd better learn a gear faster than first before she has to sit down and take the SATs," he muttered to Beth.

She giggled. "Don't see that happening."

He stared at her in amazement. The sad, withdrawn, wounded woman he knew had *giggled* like a carefree girl? Was it possible?

The sound elated him. Made him feel young, too. Hopeful. He had an overpowering desire to kiss her, but the middle of a crowded mall food court didn't seem the place, especially since Sicily had finished maneuvering the wheelchair and was gazing across the table at them with interest.

Over lunch he kept having a feeling of unreality. *Mom, dad, kid,* he thought bemusedly, *except I'd never heard of either woman or girl until a week ago.*

Man, I want this. A bubble of humor rose. Go figure. His mother was right. She always said she was, and damned if it didn't usually turn out that way. He looked forward to admitting it.

Falling in love didn't happen to order, though.

Maybe he hadn't been ready until now, but he thought it was more likely that he hadn't met the right woman. He wasn't the man he'd been before his son's death. Every time he'd dated a nice, uncomplicated woman, he had found himself fidgeting and scrambling for conversation.

Apparently he'd needed a woman who was scarred inside and out. A complex woman whose emotional repertoire often made him feel as if he was standing on shifting ground. A woman who was somehow also fierce in protecting this girl she hadn't known until a month ago. And he had been surprised at her sexual response when Mike touched her. Almost…virginal.

Mike studied her speculatively. How experienced *was* she sexually? Given her history and the wall she kept around herself, he had to guess she hadn't had a wild and crazy sex life. Man, his body was hardening at the thought of her peeling that T-shirt over her head. At wondering whether she'd touch him boldly or timidly.

It was a good douse of ice water when he thought, *Or whether she's ready.* Could she open herself to the risk of allowing anyone's hands all over her, or the bigger risk of letting herself care about someone else?

Sicily might be the biggest risk Beth was able or willing to take right now.

Then he'd wait. Mike's jaw firmed. It had taken

him eight years to get here. He was the right man for her. He'd give her the time she needed, even if it killed him.

"Sicily going to stay holed up in her bedroom?" It was after dinner. Mike had helped clear the table. Now, one hip propped against the kitchen cupboard, he watched her fill the dishwasher.

Her mouth curved. "There's a certain ceremony to putting away new clothes. She didn't have a chance earlier."

"You rip off the tags and shove whatever it is in a drawer."

She laughed. "Women do it differently. And Sicily... Well, I told you she hasn't had much that's new."

"You weren't kidding about how seriously she takes shopping."

Turning off the faucet, Beth made a face. "She takes almost everything that seriously. Send her to pick out a cantaloupe with instructions on how to tell whether they're ripe, and ten minutes later you find her carefully handling every single one. It's like..." She hesitated.

"She can't let herself make a mistake."

Surprised, she looked at him. "I suppose that is it."

Those laser-sharp eyes watched her all too intently. "Do you let yourself make mistakes?"

She snapped her attention back to what she was doing. "I made a big one last week."

"Aren't we past that?"

"Sometimes, you can keep bad things from happening."

"And sometimes you can't. We both know that, Beth." His voice was so gentle, she could hardly bear it. Didn't know whether she could trust what that tone suggested.

"I do know that."

"She's resilient."

Beth took a deep breath and closed the dishwasher. "She astonishes me."

"You astonish me." A notch deeper, his tone was intimate and warm. "You and Sicily have a lot in common."

She felt extraordinarily vulnerable when she looked at him. "Do you think so?"

"I'm getting the feeling she's a lot more like you than her mother. I wonder if that's occurred to her."

"I hope it doesn't. It might seem disloyal."

"Maybe." He was quiet for a moment. "Those nightmares you have. Are they about your mother?"

Beth stiffened but hoped he couldn't tell. "No. It's weird maybe, but what I remember best is hiding. Squeezed into this tiny, dark space, trying desperately not to make a sound. That's when I felt safest, so why does it haunt me now?"

"Maybe—" his voice was a soft growl "—because you knew you weren't safe."

"Maybe," she whispered.

"You know I want to be here every night to hold you when you have a nightmare." His mouth quirked. "The rest of the time, too."

She squeezed her hands together. "You don't know me."

"I do." He'd been keeping his distance, but now he took a step closer and ran his knuckles up the side of her neck, ending up with them tucked beneath her chin. "Maybe we have something to discover about what we're like in happier times. But don't tell me we don't know each other. You know better."

Stunned that the moment had escalated so fast, before she'd had time to think it all through with her usual meticulous care, she searched his face. "I suppose I do," she admitted. "But I have to think of Sicily, too."

"She likes me. I like her."

The big bubble of emotion that had so shocked her yesterday swelled in her chest again, as if she'd been pumped full of helium. It was astonishing to discover that despite it, she could feel humor. Narrowing her eyes, she said, "You sound smug."

Just like that, he was grinning. "I feel smug. Because she does like me. And because you didn't say, 'I'm sorry, I don't know how I feel about you.'"

You implied the only hang-up is her. Which means *you* like me."

"I let you sleep with me, didn't I?"

"Not exactly." His grin became wicked, then died. Suddenly, she could see his uncertainty, even…vulnerability? "I'm pushing you. Everything has happened fast, I recognize that. But within a few days of meeting you, I knew. I haven't wanted to go home to my own bed all week, Beth. I'll do it for now. Maybe Sicily does need some time. Or you do, too. But I want you to know I'm serious. I'm in love with you."

She gaped.

"Probably I'm not the kind of guy you'd normally fall for. You're class. I keep picturing you with a man who has money, sharp looks, dresses well."

"A businessman. An attorney."

"Yeah. I guess that's it."

"A man like my father," she said flatly.

Mike took that in. "Or maybe not," he said slowly.

This was scary, in a different way than anything she'd felt before. *No. Really?* Beth came close to laughing. How funny. It turned out the woman who feels nothing had been kidding herself all these years.

"I think I do need time." She let herself look into Mike's eyes, and believe what she saw. *I'm braver and stronger than I knew,* she reminded herself, and took a frightening leap. "But…I'm in love with you, too."

He groaned, and took her into his arms. "I want you two to be my family," he told her, in a near echo of her earlier thoughts.

"I want that, too," Beth admitted, shaken but… happy. Yes, happy. The real deal.

He bent and nuzzled her cheek. "Beth…"

"Hmm?" Instinctively, she turned to seek his mouth.

He brushed his lips across hers. "I won't ask you to marry me yet."

There it was again, a laugh rising up in her, part of that happiness. "How patient of you."

He nipped her earlobe. "It's my middle name."

And then she was laughing, and somehow crying, too, and holding on tight to him. He watched her, worried.

"I never thought…" she gasped.

"Thought what?" He brushed away the tears so tenderly.

"That I might ever have everything. That I'd ever *want* it. Poor Rachel did, so much, and now here I am, the lucky one."

"You deserved it as much as she did." His voice had deepened. "You know what I live for?"

She shook her head.

"The day when you'll laugh without being surprised. When you'll throw yourself into my arms without a second thought. When you'll do something Sicily already has—you'll trust me. Absolutely and completely."

Maybe her mouth wobbled a bit, but she answered with a smile. "I've come so far in a week, I feel safe to say you're going to be amazed."

"I already am," he whispered, and kissed her.

* * * * *